Baby Basilisk

Baby Basilisk

Aimee Danroth

Trigger Warning

Trigger warning- Torture, gun violence, violence, underage drinking, abuse, manipulation

Dedication

For Carling, who needed more of the Basilisks.
You inspired me to write another book in the series.
Without you, this book wouldn't have been written.
Cameron

Cameron

My professor will not stop talking. I love history and now, I'm a history student. I thought it would be great because I'm obsessed with America's history. I've always wanted to work in a museum, or in an old building that gives tours every hour. I want to educate people on what fantasizes me. This is New York, the history here never ends. Gangs in the 1800's, pandemics, bombings, fires, the roaring 1920's. The stock market crash in the 30's, the story behind the architecture of old buildings. Not even to mention the organized crime that's swept over this city. I'd never want to live anywhere else. New York has everything a history nerd needs to be happy. This city is where I thrive.

I have everything I need here. There's just one issue. I'm bored. My life's always been perfect, and it's fucking boring. I have an overly large family, and parents who tolerate each other. My life has never been tragic. It's always been predictable.

Is it bad that I hope something will happen to stir up the pot? I wake up every single morning at the crack of dawn to work out, I eat breakfast, shower, get ready for school, learn, eat lunch, learn some more, study, bed, repeat. Every single day. On the weekends I let myself spend time with my friend, Monday to Thursday though, that's game over. I've always had my grades higher than a B+, once they hit a B+ it's time for me to cancel my plans and open my books. There has to be more to life. So no, I don't think it's bad to need something to stir the pot, but this weekend something good needs to happen. I need a tragic event; I need someone to break my heart.

My phone shivers on the table, my best friend's picture lights up on my phone.

Your fake ID is here

We can go to Willie's, or the speakeasy.

I repeat. Your fake ID is here.

We're going somewhere that your family can't spy on us.

I exhale a deep breath of air. I never had a sip of alcohol, not until Lucia became my best friend in junior year. We drank a lot when she came into my life, and my family just let it happen. To say the least, she made high school interesting for me. She gave me memories of parties that I wouldn't have been invited to otherwise.

Weekends my daily schedule is a tiny bit more interesting than school nights, but it's still boring. Friday nights I see my family and do laundry while I visit. On Saturdays I work out, eat, study, get ready to go out, and consume alcohol in large amounts. Sunday, I don't move from my bed. I just enjoy watching movies on my laptop, alone without a single soul lingering around me. My hangovers are usually gone an hour after I wake up, Sundays are my day to recharge my mental battery.

If there was a serial killer trying to plan around my schedule to kill me, it would be very easy.

My stomach is turning thinking about having to use my ID. I don't get in trouble. I'm a good girl, the only bad thing I do is underage drinking. I'm nineteen, so to be fair, I'm not *that* young.

I hope to hell this fake ID thing works. Breaking the law is not what I mean about stirring the pot.

I step inside uncle Adam, and Aunt Charlie's new house. They just sold their last place, apparently Adam used it to propose to her? My uncle Spencer did the same thing to Aunt Brittney, it was more like an early birthday present, but the events happened so close together.

Like excuse me sir, what the *fuck* did you do for work to just casually buy an entire damn house? The worst part is, they are only in their forties, so this all happened when they were twentyish. Can I find someone who can just buy me a house? Please?

The entry way is huge, and full of boxes. The only time I've ever moved was when I went from my dad's house to my dorm in college. I hated every second of moving. I couldn't imagine moving while having two children under the age of five running around, at least the older two can sort of help them with smaller boxes. Looking straight ahead I see the same picture that is in every other house. Spencer, Adam, Charlie, Liam, Dillon, William, and Josh are all in matching snowman pajamas.

I'd like to mention that we still wear matching pajamas. Every single year on Christmas eve. We are all way too close. It's great and all, but in the end, it completely screwed up my immediate family.

"Cameron." Spencer walks by me stealing my laundry basket from my hands walking downstairs to the washer and dryer.

If I had to pick a favorite aunt and uncle, it would be Spencer and Brittney. Every single one of these adults took me in, loved me, helped raise me, I just connected better with Spencer. Maybe it's because he's closest with my dad, I really don't know. But at the end of it all, he's my second dad, and Brittney is the only mother figure I ever really knew.

"Offspring." Dad wraps his arm around me hugging me from the side.

This man has always been my number one supporter. He's always had my back. The only downside of the Watson gene, I've inherited his anger. Not once has he ever jumped down my throat about it. When I got in fights from school, when I got suspended or expelled, he was down there ready to throw fists with me. Of course, when he brought me home, he would let me cool down, then he would speak to me like I was human. My mom on the other hand, would yell at me, and it would only make me see red for longer.

My mom's been okay for the short time she's been around; she's never understood me. Dad understands me.

"Erik. Go help those fucktards upstairs. I can't deal with their level of stupid right now." Charlie steps downstairs, her hands raised to her head, her fingertips gripping her skull just above her temples.

Charlie has scars that wrap around her shoulders, going all the way down her back. I can see one poking out from her V-neck above her collar bone. I've never asked, and I want too so bad. Every summer I'm tempted when I see her in a bikini. I've tried to ask my parents, and they just said "I don't know. It happened before I met her." It's always such a fast response. It makes it hard to believe them.

Dad let's go running upstairs. He used to be a police officer; I've seen pictures of him around the house. You can tell because he moves so swiftly, even though it was before I was born.

"So, dad's here." I walk into the kitchen, walking directly towards a brown moving box crushing it between my palms, watching the cardboard cave into itself. It was taped together, sometimes my own strength surprises me. "I'm assuming mom won't be." She's never around, but once every few months I like to ask.

Charlie puckers her lips together. "Are you okay?"

"I'd rather have Dad around." My words aren't even a lie. "If dads around, I have all these morons."

Josh sucks in a breath of air, "I never."

William comes up behind me, hovering over my shoulder. "Been more insulted in my life."

Josh sits beside me kneeing my knee with his, I know his eyes are locked on the hefty box I just destroyed. "How's school going?" He asks nervously, his eyes are going back between the box in my hands, and my face.

"I didn't give into my intrusive thoughts and jump off the fourth floor today to plunge to my death, so I'd say it's going good." I shrug, with a dead serious expression.

Josh looks at me with his lips in a straight line, "Yeah. You need a girlfriend."

Last time I ever dated someone was when I was sixteen, and she was scared of me. She never told me. She didn't have to tell me for me to know she feared me. I knew she was. I never once touched her in any harmful way. She was fine until she saw me in a fight. The fight turned out to be so minor and unimportant, I don't even remember what it was about, ever since she saw that, she would flinch when I moved too fast. I dumped her ass. Like, I get it. But I don't go around beating people for fun. It's not fun for anyone involved, including me.

I just never dated anymore after that. I let people believe that I'm only into girls, because if I date again, it'll probably be a woman. I do find guys attractive; I've had feelings for boys before. I just would rather share a house with a girl, not a disgusting guy. My dad would rather that too. Then he doesn't need to worry about me accidentally getting pregnant at nineteen and screwing up my life.

I've always been lacking in the friend department too. Girls are absolutely terrified of me. I keep to myself now, I'm super introverted until someone comes along pulling me out of it. Guys have the same reaction as girls do, I just learnt it's easier if I keep my distance. Gender doesn't stop someone's fear.

"I need a girlfriend? Says you." I laugh responding to Josh, he's been single for years. Both him and my dad have zero interest in ever dating again.

"Is it time to bully Josh for being single?" Spencer leans on the counter watching Josh shift on the seat under him. "There's a teacher at the university. She has kids."

"Yeah, fuck you. I'm out. There are enough unhinged children running around already." Josh stands to leave.

I turn around with my mouth open trying to not look offended, "I'm not unhinged."

"You're the worst." Max drops a bottle of whiskey on the counter, with Theo and Liam in tow.

"Where's mom?" I ask, waiting for one of the three to speak up.

Her husband Liam is the first to talk. "At home with the kids."

I surprisingly feel bad for Liam. My dad left my mom years ago, he's been single ever since, my mom on the other hand. She jumped on the first guy she saw. The first guy she saw, happened to be one of my dad's best friends.

My dad and my mom got pregnant with me way too soon in their relationship, he tried to make things work, but after I was born things turned for the worst, she got extremely depressed. Everyone tried to get her the help she needed, she refused. I overheard dad talking to my aunt April the same week she left, I was hardly a preteen, he was saying that Mom has sucked the life out of him for years, he tried to make things last because of me, he was just so unhappy. Of course, me being me, that made me angry, and I broke into the room with tears running down my face mad at him for putting me first and not thinking about himself. I'm okay that he was putting me first, but I think it's because he was putting me first for what, eleven years? That set me off. He was so miserable, and I never knew. It used to put me in rage, now it just breaks my heart.

I wish I could say my emotions leveled out since she left. They didn't. I'm still happy for one minute, then crying because someone offered me the last bite of ice cream, but I told them to eat it, and they did, so I cried.

I really wish I was making that up. I put my uncle Dillon through that last weekend.

My mom was single for maybe a month before her and Liam started dating. This threw curve balls into the family thinking that they were sneaking behind my dad's back while they were together. Apparently, Liam has a shitty past with girlfriends? Whatever happened in Liam's past made everyone believe that Mom and Liam were together long before. It turns out neither of them stopped to even think that people were going to assume the worst. They just assumed everyone would know the truth. Max, Theo, Liam, and Mom are like a package deal. Liam and Mom spent so much time together that they naturally happened when dad left her. Everyone made sure I wasn't in the room when they talked, I was always close, listening to every word. I was always in tune with what was happening around us.

It's been eight years, I have three siblings, and mom still won't show up when everyone is here. She will only show up when they have a girl's night, and that girl's night cannot involve Brittney, or mom will refuse to go. The only other rare time she will show her face is at Christmas time. Almost every single person here has forgiven her, but she still won't show up on the weekends. She doesn't even show up for me. Brittney was shook that everything went down this way because mom's always been a motherly human. From that day on Brittney refused to look in her direction and completely took me under her wing. I don't see how anyone could say my mother is a motherly human. Hopefully, her other kids can see it, because I don't.

I forgive her for it. Getting pregnant randomly after a month of dating someone? I don't even think they were together that long, neither of them knew exactly who they were marrying. If she decides she wants a relationship, then excellent. Some of that is my fault. I don't put an effort in, I don't care too. She has other kids, it's probably stressful. And as bad as this is, I'm not bothered because I have way too much family to even try to keep track of. It sucks not having a mom, but at the same time, I'm not at a loss.

I look at Liam after a long silence fills the room. "Liam. Can you tell her that if she wants, she can call me?" I hold the crushed cardboard box tight.

"Yes." He spits the words out with a hard nod.

I don't even want to know how uncomfortable it is for him to have a relationship with me.

***

"I hate you." I curse out Lucia. She has her long brown hair in loose curls, against her olive skin, she looks like a porcelain doll. She's wearing a short black dress that shows off her curves. There's no doubt about it. Lucia is only looking this good for her new arm candy.

"Hating me is like hating chocolate. Impossible." She sticks her nose up.

I raise my eyebrows at my friend, rolling my eyes, I pass my fake to the bouncer, "Might I remind you... I despise chocolate."

"We all have our flaws."

The bouncer passes me back my ID, along with Lucia's, it worked. Holy shit. Maybe now I will have the courage to look at it. I shove it into my wallet behind my school ID. I'll look tomorrow.

The instant I open the door, the sound of the building comes pouring out, colorful lights move around the room like a spotlight. The base from the music is vibrating the floor from under my feet. I haven't had an ounce of alcohol, even still I feel like I'm tipsy.

"Where the hell did you get these made?" I stand close to Lucia, talking loudly in her ear. This bar is so different from what I'm used to. There's a large dance floor, not just tables.

"That guy I'm seeing has connections."

Lucia grabs my wrist pulling me to the bar, not asking me what I want to drink. We've gone out so much I know she will order a cranberry vodka, and she knows I'll order a tequila and Sprite.

2

Nico

Gabe stops right in front of me, causing me to almost collide into him. "Dude." I look down at him with my eyes squinted, he's not even paying attention to me.

"She looks good. Just go over there. Sweep her off her feet." Gabe cracks his knuckles. "Who am I kidding. This fucking sucks."

I look at him with wide eyes nodding. "Alcohol?"

Gabe nods. Feeling the same way I am. Feeling fucking dread. The same music is blasting through the speakers. The same women are here weekend after weekend. I'm getting real sick of the same crowd. People really need to mix up their routines. That includes me, because I see the same damn people here every Saturday night.

Only difference from this weekend is that I'm getting a raise. There's only a slight possibility I might get killed. If they get their hands on me, they'll do more than just kill me, saying I'll be tortured is an understatement. I'm walking on a thin rope before I plunge to my death. It's all a coin toss, but hey I'm getting a raise.

My fingers wrap around the shot glass, watching the clear liquid spill over the top as I lift it.

Snake and a Lion, I wonder who will have the upper hand in a fight to the death.

One tequila, two tequila, three tequila. My insides feel like they are ripping apart, that was terrible. Absolutely terrible. I take a deep breath shoving my hands into the edge of the bar trying not to puke. I can do Vodka, but tequila? No way in hell is this staying down. Every time

I breathe, I can feel my stomach wanting to push it back up. I wish I had PTSD with tequila, and that's why I'm struggling, it's not. I'm just weak.

"Hi baby." I glance over my shoulder seeing Lucia place her hands on Gabe's chest, giving him a kiss.

Gabe's entire body tenses when she touches him. I get it the circumstances suck dick, but he's doing a good job pretending. The sight of her touching him makes me cringe. I don't know how Gabe does this so well. Even though this is everything Gabe didn't want to do, he has his arm wrapped around Lucia's shoulder, he's kissing her cheek and whispering into her ear. Watching that is enough to bring the tequila back up, I'm fighting like hell.

Cheering erupts from behind us. I turn around ready to break up the fight between guys again. It's not guys fighting. A girl with long light brown hair, it hangs all the way down to her ass. I shake my head bringing my focus away from her body watching her pin Gabe's ex-girlfriend by the throat onto the wall. There's a small amount of blood dripping from the ex's nose.

"Fucking say it again! I dare you." The voice from the girl pinning her to the wall comes out as a clear loud growl over the music.

I push myself through the crowd. It's Cameron, I know it is. Her dress is white, with one strap over the shoulder, at the curve of her body there are two holes in the side of the dress. Her ass is practically hanging out of the bottom. I know she tightens her grip around Ashley's throat when her shoulders flinch, her bicep flexes, and her forearms flex. She's impressively strong.

"Hey Cameron, put her down." Lucia stands next to her, talking in a calm voice. "Tequila?"

Cameron let's go. After seeing Cameron do that, I'm not even surprised she can hammer down tequila, while I'm over here trying not to die. Not only is she stronger than me, but she probably can also handle her alcohol better than me, and that's saying something.

I turn around looking at Gabe mouthing 'What the fuck?' her power was insane. She had no remorse. I walk through the kitchen in the back, downstairs, through a dark hallway, then push open the door. I would take the door by the entrance, the stairs are a hell of a lot less steep, but the entry way on a Saturday night here is ridiculous.

"What?" Dad snaps, not looking at the door.

I try not to look, there are girls sitting on the couch in lingerie, sitting in a position where I can see everything they have to offer. Bricks of drugs are sitting on the tables, dads counting money. Two of his goons are standing on both sides of the door, with their arms crossed keeping watch.

"I need the key to the guest room." The guest room was used in the past as a room to have girls in. My father tried to treat it like a saloon, that thought makes me nauseous. Even more so considering the fact he's married to my mom.

"Bones."

My dad's tall skinny goon, I guess you'd call him an assistant, stands up dropping the keys in my hand. I turn around fast, before he can ask me any questions, because I know he has about fifty questions and demands to roll off his tongue any second.

As of late Gabe is very good at reading my mind. Wherever I need him to go he's right there. He pulls Lucia out of the way from the door, I unlock it pushing my body weight into the door. I don't know when the last time this room has been used.

I turn on the light, thank God it's not set up the way I'd imagined it to be. It has a booth along the right wall, with a stationary table in the center. It's decently big, but it's still squishy as fuck. There's not a speck of dust on any surface. Along the wall on the left there's a hallway, as tempting as it is to go on an adventure to see what's done there, I have a sick feeling that dad has a bed back there. I stand leaning against the wall on the left before the hallway. This booth fitting four people is going to be impossible without putting someone on my lap.

Cameron is the last to walk in the room, she shakes her hand off probably still feeling Ashley's face under it. "I'm so sorry Lucia." She doesn't acknowledge either me or Gabe, I'm not even sure if she's registered other people are in here.

"What did she say to you?" Lucia asks softly, like she knows not to tread too rough.

"She said shit about you. I heard her calling you a whore and I snapped." Cameron's hands are shaking. "I tried not to."

"I didn't even know who she was." Lucia laughs, she turns to Gabe, "Why is it the girls are always the whore."

"Uh." Gabe pauses. His eyes shift to me. "That's because she's my ex."

Cameron looks at Gabe, the skin around her eyes tightens as she squints, finally noticing the other people are here. "You have a unique taste." Cameron raises her voice, her eyes are on the floor between me and her, she doesn't look at me. "Can I please have some ice? She has a hard fucking face."

I push myself off the wall with my foot, I place my arm on Camerons shoulder as I gently push by her as I leave the room. I need alcohol, she's going to be a hard one to crack. I don't know what the fuck my dad was thinking. I step behind the bar grabbing a bucket filling it with ice, four cups, and a bar towel for the ice. I scan the bar well cringing, the only bottle the bartenders don't have right now is tequila. *Of fucking course.* I grab it knowing full well that it's going to kick my ass.

I body chuck the door, using the bottle of poison to pull down the door handle to open it, "How did you learn to do that?"

"My family." She says simply, like everyone is just supposed to know. She doesn't look at me, she takes the towel out of my hand, dropping ice in it, setting it on her knuckles.

I look down at Gabe, shaking my head. Cameron has a smoking hot body, but what I've seen from her face, it's average. Her average looking face made this entire situation a lot less entertaining.

My phone buzzes.

Yours is hotter.

Mines emotionally unavailable.

Cameron is sitting here looking at her hand, she's completely zoned out. If it's hurting her, she's giving zero sign about the pain. She could probably kick my ass if she really tried. She doesn't even have to try that hard, she could kick my ass. I'm confident in myself, she would easily lift heavier than me at the gym. It's intimidating as hell. Her being that strong is enough to suddenly not be attractive enough.

"Why do we get our own private room?" Lucia asks, breaking the quiet.

I pull my eyes from Cameron. She can probably feel me staring. "My dad owns the building."

"Is there a kitchen?"

I nod. "What do you guys want?"

Gabe and Lucia both say chicken wings, and mozz sticks. I give Cameron the longest minute to tell me what she wants, she doesn't speak. She stays completely quiet. I pull out my phone texting a random ass server that has (weekend nights) by their name so I know I will get my order.

This is awkward. So very awkward.

"Yeah, I'm going." Cameron stands, "Thanks for the ice."

Lucia tries to protest, but Cameron just leaves in the middle of her pleading, totally ignoring her. It's really hard not to laugh. Cameron gives no shits, and I'm completely for it.

"What just happened?" I fall onto the seat, forcing Lucia to slide over closer to Gabe.

"You're fucked Nico." Gabe smirks. "Good luck with that one." Gabe nudges Lucia's arm, "He likes her."

"I will slit your throat." I mumble. Liking her is so far off.

"Good luck." She mumbles. "I can't handle her moods."

I laugh dry. "She just pinned Ashley against the wall by her throat from talking shit about you, reframe from trash talk."

"Calm down. It's not like the first time she has pulled something like that." She looks at Gabe, "Can you tell him to chill?"

Gabe puts his palm towards me, then faces it down towards the table. "Yeah man, just back off." I exhale a deep breath of air. He really doesn't need to be playing into this right now. It's completely unnecessary. The next few months of him acting like this is going to be my own living hell.

I need to be getting paid more to be dealing with Lucia's shit more than I already have too.

I put my hands in the air pretending to be defenseless. "Sorry. Sorry. But seriously, try to get us together, please."

"The only time I ever see her is at lunch, and on Saturdays when we drink." Lucia rolls her eyes.

"Lunch time it is."

"That means you actually have to go to school."

Her tone pisses me off. I do not want to be a part of this, not at all.

3

Cameron

The one day school finally fed us something tolerable for lunch, is the one day I have absolutely no appetite. On Saturday I was completely ashamed of myself. The red I saw, it wasn't a flash like how it normally is. It was like a curtain over my eyes, it dangled in front of me. I had her by her throat, then she smirked at me, and I felt my grip getting tighter. That bitch was feeding me on, and it worked. All because she called Lucia a whore. I'm lucky the cops never showed up, I would have been busted with my fake. That guy said his dad owned the bar that I just got in a fight in, and I felt even more shameful.

People saw me flick a switch. There were so many people around, too many of them were afraid to step in. Even if I try to be good, everyone is still afraid of me. I'm a ticking fucking time bomb just waiting to lose its temper.

I wanted something to stir the pot, but not that.

Lucia's boyfriend comes up behind her, I toss my chicken strip on the tray trying to not look at his friend. I succeed until he steals the seat next to me. I can see him from the corner of my eye, I still refuse to look at him. I lasted the entire time I saw him on Saturday, and never even acknowledged him, so I don't know why he decided right next to me was a safe spot. Especially after what he saw me do.

Lucia's boyfriend is about 5"10 so only an inch taller than me. He has tattoos, I remember seeing a giant Lion on his bicep, it was so beautiful. His friend had a different Lion in the same spot, it was more orange, it was showing its teeth. His friend is at least 5'11, he's muscular, but not in a way that's boastful. If I'm being honest, both guys are out of Lucia's league. They both have a class about them that outshines her. The way she speaks is very condescending, and they carry themselves with dignity. I never even looked at his friend's face, and I know he is already too good to be seen with Lucia. As brutal as that sounds.

I don't look at him, I just reflect my voice towards him. "Sorry about what happened. You said your dad owned it, and I panicked. I'm nineteen, it would have been bad."

He leans in uncomfortably close to me, his breath is on my neck. "Who do you think made it for you?"

I laugh through my nose. "I'll try not to strangle anyone else." I whisper in the middle of the table, trying effortlessly to get my voice to both him and Lucia's boyfriend. I really need to learn their names.

"That would be best." Lucia bites the words out.

I slouch, she's not wrong. I did destroy our night. That was the very first night I ruined. I've never gotten into a fight at a bar before. Probably because it was my family's bar. They hover over me. I talk to a girl, they know she's into it before I even do. I'm on a tightrope there. Last night I never had the hovering, and it showed. I apparently can't be left unsupervised.

"Can you not be a bitch?" What *am I doing?* All their eyes go wide looking at me. "I stuck up for you. I was apologizing, time for being a bitch is over." *Oh my God the words just kept coming.* It's just like when she was pleading for me to stay, my legs wouldn't stop walking.

Her boyfriend leans in, "Can you please talk to her with respect?"

I let a laugh roll off my lips, "This is too much for me." I laugh again. "Like what the fuck, grow a pair man." I grab my tray, stuffing a chicken strip into my mouth holding the other one between my fingers. She can't even stick up for herself.

I take it back. He is not out of her league, not at all. I have no respect for guys who do that, and even less respect for women who can stick up for themselves but have guys do it for them.

"Here." I see his friend standing next to me opening the swinging door of the garbage can.

I turn to face him looking at his chest, moving the chicken strip from my mouth. "Sorry that you met me twice and both times ended like." I guested towards the table. "That."

"I went through it after you left, it's annoying." He laughs. He does have a nice laugh, even if it's fake as all hell, and completely forced.

I look at him trying not to smile. His hoodie is only half zippered, his chest muscles are so strong I can see them in his shirt. His jawline is damn near perfection. His hair is messy, but neat all at the same time. His perfect olive skin is giving off pretty boy vibes, but if that were the truth, he wouldn't be standing less than a foot away from me. Not after Saturday, he would be gone. He's dangerous. At the table, he never would have gotten as close to my neck as he did if he was scared of me. A pretty boy would be scared shitless of me.

"Well thanks for being understanding." I take a step forward to walk away. His voice trails me making me turn around to look at him. My feet are turning into cement, refusing to leave his sight. *What the fuck is wrong with me.*

"Wanna stay out of the bar scene and do something else on Saturday... with me?" He doesn't look at me, his dark eyes are looking everywhere else in the cafeteria but at me.

"Like what?" I smile small, either he's testing his limits with my anger, or he's stupid. I'm going to go with the latter and say he's probably stupid.

He shrugs like he's taken off guard, expecting me to suddenly have a list of plans.

"I mean, yeah? Sure? Give me your phone." He holds it out, forcing me to walk closer. My feet wouldn't let me walk away, but walking closer to him is easy. I juggle his oversized phone with one hand, my chicken strips in the other, putting my name and number in without saving it as a contact, passing it back.

"Great. If I don't see you by Friday, I'll text you." His phone gets wrapped with his fingers, gripping it tightly, his forearm flexing.

Seeing the muscle move in his arm, makes my mouth water.

I run up to Lucia skidding on the floor in my runners crashing into her locker door. She jumps back in complete fear, her eyes are wide, breathing staggered.

"Guess what?" I kick the locker next to me with the outside of my shoe, she jumps back again.

"Lucia?" I say her name softly. "What's wrong?"

"We got in a fight, and you came out of nowhere." She closes her eyes, "We are in the middle of the hall so there will be witnesses." She closes her eyes tight.

"What are you—" then it dawns on me. She's scared of me. Just like everyone else.

A part of me just wishes I could get in arguments with people without them fearing for their life.

I turn around without making a sound. I had good news. I was proud of myself.

Are you home?

Yes

I use my key to unlock Charlie's door. I have a separate key chain for everyone's house. Each key has their initials. My key chain looks like a prison ring. I even have one for Archie and Hayley's, after high school I left for London, I spent a year living there. I really wanted to think about what to do for school before I applied. I tried to give my key back, but they refused. It makes no sense for me to have it, but they were very persistent on me keeping it just in case.

I held myself together until I stepped into the safety of Charlie's home. I shut the door and tears stream down my face.

"Oh." Charlie puts whatever she was holding onto the counter, sitting down on the couch in her living room, I follow. "So, what's wrong?"

Charlie isn't exactly the person I would go to for comfort, but everyone else I would go to is either working, or they are drowning in toddlers. She's probably the one out of my father's closest group that I'm not close with, that doesn't stop me from crying. I speak but whatever I say sounds like a bunch of letters, nothing remotely close to English.

"K what?" She tries to smile.

I'm so overwhelmed. I can't even handle myself, and if I can't deal with my emotions, how do I expect anyone else to be able to handle me? One minute I'm good, the next I'm unable to breathe because I'm so far into the abyss of feeling.

"On Saturday I went to a bar with Lucia, I got into a fight. Then yesterday we exchanged words, and today I ran up to her, she was scared of me. She thought I was going to hurt her."

"How did you get into a bar?"

I open my wallet tossing her my fake, she examines it then passes it back to me.

"That's impressively good." She laughs, then she's quiet for a heartbeat. "Wait. Cameron, do you have feelings for her?"

"No, she's a terrible fucking person. She got a boyfriend, and her personality changed. She's different. Why can't I control my anger? I was doing so good, then I snapped. No one even stepped in. My strength just overpowered my mind. I don't want people to be afraid of me." I sniffle.

Lucia was a terrible person. We weren't even really friends. The only reason I called her my best friend is because that's what she called me, and we saw each other every weekend. I never went to her house. We never did anything but drink. I kept my distance when I realized all she did was talk about other people. It's probably stupid of me to be crying over this. I'm not crying because of her, I'm crying because I'm confused about *me.*

"I was in juvie." Charlie blurts out, making me almost drop my jaw. "I beat a kid with a baseball bat, it was this whole thing. Growing up in the system fucked me." She sighs, "Us training you as intense as we are, isn't helping. Do you want to lay off, or have more rest days?"

I shake my head, "That's all I have." And I start crying again. "It's weird that I feel confused when I have nothing to be confused over?"

"Ice cream and movies? I did this a lot when Liam cheated on me. Adam or William sat through the torture with me."

"I pass the torch onto you." I wipe my nose on my winter jacket regretting it.

She passes me the ice cream and a spoon, I don't even check the flavor before digging my spoon in, "Can we keep this a secret? I just don't want everyone to know. That's a lot of people trying to comfort me, telling me I don't have a problem, when clearly, I do."

"Cam." Charlie doesn't look at me, "Believe me when I say we all have felt the way you are right now."

I stab my ice cream annoyed. Everyone talks about the past without talking about the past. No one will tell me anything. I know they are all hiding something from me. I just wish I knew what. I've tried to dig. I've searched every single one of their names and absolutely nothing showed up in the search engines. If I knew, maybe I would feel less the way I do. Maybe I would have a way to control it.

I live in a blind rage every single day, I've never seen anyone else react so quickly the way that I do. I watch people get angry, and they just use attitude, then walk away. With me I use attitude, and my entire body feels the rush of my emotions. It's exhausting feeling everything as deeply as I do.

"What way am I feeling? How do you know the anger? How does Dad know how to control me?"

Charlie looks down pausing, "Erik knows from being a cop. Cameron, I don't know what you're looking for, but I don't have any big answers."

Yes, she does. If she didn't, she wouldn't have dropped to that conclusion. I stand, grabbing my bag walking out of the house.

I can't fix what's broken inside of me if I don't know what caused my dad's anger. I try to repress my anger, but because I'm a passionate person it comes out in my emotions, and I cry. I want to stop crying, I want to stop choking people out. I never should have started working out, I wish that I never learnt that it temporarily helps me. At least if I never learnt that I wouldn't have the strength to hurt someone that triggers me.

My phone buzzes.

It's Nico. Are you okay?

I don't respond. I'm assuming Nico is the guy from the bar.

I step through the doors of my gym, William has a gym downtown, in the middle of office buildings. I have no idea what caused him to open it here, but it was a hell of an investment. All the people in the surrounding buildings use it before and after work, some even on their lunch hours.

"Why aren't you in school?" William faces me, his arms crossed.

"Just let me work it off please. I need to just work it off." My hands shake, I'm so angry. Charlie pissed me off more. William doesn't flinch to my shaking hands. "Please."

He nudges his head giving me a small smile, "Go work off some steam Cam."

And that's what I do. Very loudly. If I can throw a weight, that's exactly what I do.

4

Nico

"So does this mean I can break up with Lucia?" Gabe rubs his open palm on his forehead. "I'll go back to my old job. I can't stick up for her anymore man. I can't stand her."

If I could feel empathy, I would be feeling it for Gabe. She is annoying. She's a bitch, and she's super self-absorbed. I'm self-absorbed, because well look at me. She takes it to an entirely new level, she sees someone glance at her direction in public and her voice raises four decimals in sound, she makes herself known by laughing loudly, moving dramatically just to keep whoever was looking at her interested.

I shake my head, "I think it means we have to make them be friends again. What exactly did Lucia tell you about her."

"She didn't tell me shit. I said her name and her eyes got wide. She's terrified or she's doing a hell of a job pretending. I'm not asking her without people around, that means I actually have to see her in private." Gabe falls against his back on the lockers gracefully, mumbling "This money better be worth it." Before he clears his throat shouting across the hallway for Lucia's attention. He's really good at keeping this up in the public eye.

I feel like no amount of money is going to be worth this, and that's even if I succeed. If I don't, Gabe just wasted his time, and the last bit of sanity for nothing. I know exactly where Cameron is, I always know where Cameron is. I know what classes she has at what time, I know when her lunch is, I know she does fuck all but study on the week days, Fridays she goes to see her family, Saturday she binges, and Sundays she doesn't do anything but stay in that dorm, probably hungover. I wish I didn't know any of that, and I wish this job was for someone who has a life, it would at least bring some entertainment.

I make my way towards the cafeteria, Cameron and Lucia are no longer friends, so Cameron is going to be sitting at a table with a guy with bright red hair. Luckily for me, him and his mom both work under my dad, and I became 'friends' with him. I wait for a group of girls to move out of the way and finish eye fucking me. I spot Cameron once they clear. I let out a deep breath seeing that my assumptions were right on who she's sitting with. She's fucking predictable.

"What the fuck is on your tray?" I scrunch my nose looking at the chunks, I think there's Bell pepper and black beans, it straight up looks like vomit.

"I'm half sure it's Chili." Toby looks down at it, breaking his and Cameron's conversation. "I was trying not to think about it. Thanks. I appreciate that."

"How do you guys know each other?" I swing one leg over the bench beside Toby, my face is towards Cameron, on the other side of the table only wanting her answer.

"He's my uncle's nephew, but my uncles aren't really my uncles, so he's not really my second cousin, because I didn't grow up with him, so I guess family friend?" Cameron bites her chili dropping her spoon, "I need to start bringing my own lunch."

"Don't forget, your uncle is your stepdad." Toby chimes in, waving his spoon eyes locked down on his tray.

"Fuck you. Only one dad for this girl." Cameron talks with absolutely no emotion in her voice.

Maybe it won't be hard to get her to open herself up to me on Saturday. "Do you want to go to a museum or something? We never really got the details down." I know museums are her weakness, I know everything about her.

"Yeah sure, whatever." She stands with her tray, "Message me like three hours before, so I can actually have time to mentally prepare New York on a Saturday." She leaves, at least that didn't go terrible.

Toby looks at me with wide eyes, "Oh you're fucked. She will never go for you."

"You don't worry about it. How's your mom?" If he wants to joke around with me, I'll kick him where it hurts.

Toby glares at me and stands without saying a word. I can't even remember why the hell I had a conversation with his mom, it had something to do with this school. She spoke to me and stumbled over her words. I was on a high horse. Minus the fact that she is in her forties, and I'm not even twenty yet. Actually, what the fuck am I talking about. That is something I'm proud about. I wouldn't go near her, because she's far from my type. Even if she was hot I wouldn't, there's way too much money riding on Cameron to screw around with family — even if it is distant.

***

Cameron stands by the entrance of an old building, this place looks like it's straight out of the 1800's, it's old, made from bricks. I really don't know how people see the beauty in this place. All I see is bricks. There are at least 100 stairs to get to the main entrance, I'm trying so hard not to pant. I shake my opinions off about this building, walking to Cameron, she has a dark blue hoodie on. The hood is up, and long brown hair curly strands are coming out the front, tight jeans, and brown boots that almost go as high as her knee. Her bangs go straight across her forehead, sunglasses covering half her face. The sun is at the perfect level that it shines perfectly in her face through cracks of the buildings on the other side of the street. When I said she looked average, that was me looking at her as a paycheck. She wears makeup in an obvious way, but there's beauty under all those layers of cover up. She looks so casual right now. She tried to look good. She could easily make someone speechless without even trying. Her being intimidating to the average person, just amplified with how she looks right now.

"Doesn't this place close soon?" I ask, rubbing my hands against the fur inside my jacket pockets. I have no idea what she thinks tonight is, so I have no way to know how to play tonight. I'm getting nervous. It's hard not to look at her and see a dollar sign. She needs to at least tolerate me. No one can tolerate me. This is going to be a challenge in itself.

I'm fucked. This entire operation is fucked. The Basilisks won't even get their chance to get their hands on me. Because I'm going to fuck it up.

She smirks, nodding her head to the side of the building. I follow, I'm probably being led to my death, but I don't give a fuck. She takes the lead, leading me back down the millions of stairs that I just climbed up. I stuck in a large breath of air watching her do the stairs with ease. I feel my heart wanting to beat out of my chest already. I hang my head catching up to her, then walking around the left side of the building, past big garbage dumpsters, to a ladder that is half dangling in the air.

"Come here." She commands.

I don't know what the fuck is wrong with me because I listen.

"I'm going to jump on your back. I've moved the garbage bin before, but that's too much work."

I flinch my head back, looking at her. These garbage bins are huge. She rolls her eyes pointing to a smaller green one on wheels under it. She grabs my arm dragging me to where she wants me to stand. I brace myself watching her walk around me, I bend over, letting her jump on my back. Thank God I'm strong enough for this, she's not big, but she's built like a fucking bus.

My point is proven, she grabs onto the ladder connected to the building that's dangling in the air pulling herself up, she just did a pull up, while walking her hands up the ladder like it was no big deal.

"Okay Nico. Move. Move. Move."

I listen once again, watching her bounce, then the ladder falls a good three feet. Cameron is still wearing the sunglasses, but her cheeks are crinkled and she's squinting her eyes hard. She exhales then starts climbing.

I'm following her. I'm too intrigued now to turn back.

After what feels like 500 feet we are finally on a roof. I hope that was an exaggeration, going down is going to suck.

"Do I even want to know how you know about this?" I ask, watching Cameron open her bag, almost worried about her mental state and the discovery of the spot.

"I got bored, saw a ladder, so I claimed it. Simple really." She pulls out a bottle of alcohol. "When life gets me real fucked up, I like to drink up here, watch the sunset."

"I see you're using that fake."

She shakes her head. "My dad actually." That's all she says, she doesn't say anything else.

"Are you close?" I know all this, but I'm just going to be dumb.

She smiles and nods.

Okay, this is going to be ridiculous. The entire point of this is to make her gain faith in me and trust me. Her conversations are all dead ends.

I grab the bottle from her cracking it open. She grabs a cup with a straw, adding in pop from a bottle, topping it with vodka.

"Don't drink too much. That climb down is dangerous if you do." She giggles quietly. "We can be normal in a bit and drink on the land with the peasants soon, I just wanted to feel this for a bit." She walks away screwing the lid on the bottle of vodka stuffing it in her bag.

I follow her with my eyes, we aren't that high up, office buildings are higher, and in fact a lot still have their lights on. How often does she do this? Has she seriously never been caught? There's so much around us that's higher. I really don't see what's so great.

"Just a feeling of everlasting life. We are high enough that we can see the sunset, we can still hear the horns and the sirens, but we can't hear all the pissed off people. Right here there's no crime, there's no hate, no failed desires, we are just in the middle of it all." She sits at the barricade looking into the distance. "This metaphorically is the center of my universe. I grew up down there, there's an office building behind us with the gym I train in. I saw this spot from there, it's where I got this idea."

I sit beside Cameron taking the drink from her. "You know people are watching us then?"

She laughs, "Don't look, but my phone buzzed a couple of times. My uncle or uncles, maybe spying."

"They don't care that you are technically trespassing right now?" I take another long drink, passing it back.

"They know where I am at all times. My dad used to be a cop, and something about him making a few bad enemies? I have a tracker. It's fucking annoying." There's no emotion in her voice. She's stuck looking out on the street. She's standing far enough back that no one on the ground would be able to see her.

Is that the cover story they chose to go with? Erick being a cop could never cause that many enemies, especially almost twenty years later. She genuinely believes that lie.

"Enough about me. She smiles, passing me the cup. As I make my way closer to her. "Tell me about Nico. What makes you tick."

"Don't stop. You're the most real person I've met in a long time." And that's the truth, and it's fucking scary, I can't see her as a person. She's not a person to me, she can't be, or I die.

It's not like I didn't die the day I was born, living in a state of feeling numb. Where nothing is real, emotions don't exist.

"What's your favorite food?"

"Um." I pause. I don't have one. I've been beaten down for so long that as long as it doesn't look like the school cafeteria's food, I'm happy. "Pizza?" It's the first food that comes to mind, and I don't even know the last time I ate it.

"I don't believe you, not even for a second."

I sip, awkwardly long. This was not supposed to turn into her learning about me. There's nothing to learn about me. Maybe this is her way of trusting me? I don't know, I don't like it. I close myself off for a reason.

Her hand touches my elbow, "We will go to a new restaurant once a week, no this is New York, twice a week until you find something. Unless I suddenly suck at school, then I'm bailing on your ass."

"Take out. I'm really good at school. When you fail, I'll help you study." She's done a shift, she's talking now. I have a bit of hope for once. Maybe death won't be my only possibility.

Who am I kidding? I'm dealing with the fucking Basilisks, if I think I'm making this out alive, I'm insane.

"I'm taking history, cue the museum." She turns to look at me with a devious smile, "They say those who drink on top of this roof are doomed to be lost souls, sucked out by the people who built this building. In the cold blistering nights."

I blink staring at her. This does not seem like the girl that attacked Ashley. This girl is so light and happy, maybe it's the alcohol. Before she started drinking, she was cold, not even speaking in actual sentences.

"No? Not scary?" Cameron lifts half her lip. "Damn it."

"I'm not scared of anything. Step up your game."

"Fucking A. Mission accepted."

"What is this? 2010? No one speaks like that anymore."

"Shut up. I spend a lot of time with my family, okay." She grins. "They're old."

There's absolutely no way she doesn't know about her family and the Basilisks. I need to find out without asking directly. She seems way too smart to be living in the dark.

5

Cameron

I only took him up to my happy spot so I could calm down. I've been so overwhelmed the past few days. I needed to breathe. The second my feet hit the cement in the back ally my heart throbs against my rib cage. "Please don't use that spot to pick up girls. That's my spot." It's my happy spot, it's where I can go to breathe, and I needed to be able to breathe for once. It always makes me feel better. I feel free when I'm up there. "It feels like I'm not suffocating when I'm up there." I didn't mean to say that out loud. *Shit. Shit.*

"Never." His response is so quick. He doesn't make a face. He doesn't react to my accidental words.

It wasn't until we were on the roof, when the sun hit him perfectly, I let myself see him. He's beyond hot. Dark messy hair, dark eyes, olive skin, he picked me up like I was a weightless feather. I saw him in the cafeteria, I *really* saw him tonight. The way the sun hit him, he looks... Haunted. His eyes, they're so... dark, there's no color but brown, there's no sparkle.

Nico's face is hard. He's so serious. He needs to chill. His entire body is stiff, it looks like he hasn't relaxed in years, if that. Does he seriously not have a favorite food? When I asked him, it looked like he was shitting bricks. It took way too long for him to even say pizza, and his eyes were searching for a response. There's damage, and there's Nico. Nico is on an entirely new level.

I bend over, reaching into my purse for the vanilla vodka, dumping a diet soda into it. I eat my calories. I refuse to drink my calories. Especially when there's alcohol, and I drink the way I do, I'm very large amounts.

"Shitty street food?" I look up at Nico, as I stand up.

He sighs, "I mean, if you're forcing me to eat, we may as well start now."

"Oh good. Because I have diddly planned for the rest of the night." I nod my head towards the street leading him back to the conversations that we were too high up to hear.

"Diddly?" I almost turn to Nico to glare at him. He speaks with zero excitement. There's no sign of life in him. By the looks of his eyes, I wouldn't say that's a far off assumption.

Even if I end up hating his ass, I'm befriending him only so I can try to make him smile. Even though it seems like an impossible task, I'm putting it upon myself to try.

The first food truck we found is tacos, we both ordered chicken at the same time. Alcohol is making my head fuzzy, there's so many people on the streets, it's fucking cold out. Bright side, we both paid for our own food. I hate going out with guys like this because I always assume they think it's a date. I hope to hell Toby said something to him in the cafeteria, because being more into girls than guys, can be awkward when they assume you're on a date. It's never a date, and usually I'm the only person that knows that it's not a date.

The steam from our food is short lived, within a few minutes the steam completely disappears. "Are you from here?" I ask, my mouth stuffed full of food.

Nico doesn't mind that I have no manners. He chews then waits to speak like a normal human being with manners would. "Born in LA. I've been here for four years."

"Keep a secret?" I'm getting close and personal with him, because he's a robot, and I want him to feel things, eventually. No one deserves to live in robot mode. I'm going to expose myself for him to be able to feel things.

He looks at me with a blank expression.

"I love this city. I'm from here, but eventually when I'm settled down, married with kids, I would love to live in the suburbs. Just get away from all the crazy. Live in peace and quiet. Hell, I'd be happy with a small town in the middle of nowhere."

"That seems impossible." He pauses, "You'd be missing this shit every night."

Within a split second, I feel my body being ripped from the bench we were sitting at. Everything happened so fast, a loud crash, and people yelling.

I land on my feet, Nico's hands on my hips, standing behind me, his chest is brushing my back. My mouth drops looking at a car sitting on top of the bench we were just sitting at.

I dropped my taco.

"What the fuck." I let out a staggered breath, taking a very large sip of my drink. *At least I saved that.* "How did you — how did you see that?"

"I'm slick." He shrugs. "I have fast reflexes."

"You are now my bodyguard." I say quickly turning my head towards him, watching his eyes turn even darker than they already were. "Thanks for seeing that. But seriously. You have Edward Cullen reflexes. Are you a vampire?" I gasp for air. "Do you sparkle in the sun!"

Nico looks at me with his mouth separated, his nose scrunched, and his eyebrows raised. "What the actual fuck are you talking about?" His fingertips tighten on my hips with his confusion.

"Oh my. Oh my. You are coming over and we're watching *Twilight.*"

"Am I going to need more alcohol?" His voice is flat already regretting this.

"Oh yeah, another bottle for sure. And snacks." I jump away from him, with a shriek. This will get a reaction out of him.

"Next time you ever get excited over a movie, I'm plunging myself off the Manhattan Bridge." Nico still says flat. No emotion, and he's drunk almost an entire bottle of vodka.

I laugh. I love seeing people's reactions to this movie. It was even better when I made my dad, and all my uncles sit through it. I'll take any reason to watch this movie on repeat. I shut my laptop, laying down on my bed. I don't have a roommate. Apparently, Spencer 'made' arrangements for me not having a roommate. I know he has no control over that, I think my dad paid for me to have the room alone. I don't know how I got away with this, but I love it.

"You are lacking a personality." I cringe at my words. That sounded worse than I intended. "I just mean, I'm going to keep showing you movies until I see who you really are. No mask."

Nico looks down at me, his back against the wall. "The mask stays on." He leans down closer. "Always."

My eyes open wide watching him come closer to me, until his lips are on mine. I turn my head not skipping a beat.

"Sorry."

"It's fine." I let out a gentle laugh. "It's the alcohol. Go to bed, I'm not sending you out on the street after you saved me from a car."

"Pretty positive that the driver of the car knew you were going to make me watch that." He nudged his head towards the laptop, "And wanted to save me."

There's a personality. A small glimpse, it's there, I just have to dig deep to find it. "We're prettier alive." I whisper pulling him down to the bed beside me, covering us both up.

"No. Don't." Nico mutters under his breath.

I open my eyes, it's so dark in the room, there's a streetlight shining its light from a crack in the window. The curtain moves slightly, sending a gust of cold wind into the air.

"Leave her alone."

Is he on the phone? I roll over grabbing my phone brightening the screen. Nico looks pained, his forehead is creased with lines. He's asleep, completely unconscious.

"Get your hands off of me."

I drop my phone on the mattress. The light shines up on the ceiling for a few seconds before it fades away making the room dark again. I don't know what to do, I don't know how to help him.

"Dad. Why are you doing this?" His voice breaks, his heart is breaking.

Even in the dark, I can feel his body tense on the mattress next to me. My breathing is staggered, I want to know what's happening in his mind, I want to be able to help. I can't do anything from out here. His body relaxes for a split second, I use this as a chance to rest my head on his chest, wrapping my arm around his shoulders giving him a one arm hug. I heard you don't wake someone who's having a bad dream, but he looks like she's suffering all alone.

He jumps. I hold onto him tighter. "Cameron?" His voice raspy.

"Sorry. I got cold." I don't even know if he knows he has these dreams, and if he does, I don't think he wants me to know he has them.

"Move for a second."

I do, he leans over wrapping his arms around me pulling me into his chest to hold me tight, but not tight enough to break me. I'm almost surprised he's holding me like this after I pulled away from his kiss.

Minutes pass, my eyes getting heavier.

"Thank you." Nico's chest vibrates from his words.

I fall into my slumber with his chin resting on my head, and his fingers making circles on my back.

Nico

"Tell me she fell in love with you and the jobs almost done please?" Gabe crosses his arms, resting them on the table in the cafeteria sitting down.

"Nope. I kissed her and she turned." I really have no idea how that didn't work, she wasn't all over me, but she was completely absorbed by me. I don't get it. I leave out the rest about her cuddling me, even though she never pulled away, I'm worried she never wanted me to hold her.

"What? I'm straight and I'd be flattered if you kissed me." Gabe rests his chin in his hand, "Don't do that though."

"I'm so hungry I want to cry." Cameron falls on the seat next to me, dropping her tray with a loud *thud,* staring at us both. "I did cry all period actually. I'm so hungry."

"Okay. You're sitting here. Cool, cool, cool." Gabe looks at me with a smirk.

"Oh fuck. I'm sorry. Lucia will be so mad." Cameron quickly corrects herself, turning her body to stand and step over the bench seats.

"Don't worry about her." I open my pudding cup, liking my fingers clean from the splatter. "I'd rather not listen to gossip about you. Just stay. I'll protect you."

I only ever feel rage, or nothing. And when I hear Lucia talking shit about Cameron, it makes me feel rage. Not blind rage, it's annoyed rage. When Cameron said I never had a personality, she wasn't wrong. I genuinely don't. I was brought up for one thing, and one thing only. The only reason why people keep me around is because they're put on jobs with me. I'm not one that people voluntarily want to be around, and I'm okay with that.

I'm dead inside, whatever.

Cameron mutters, her mouth full of food clearly not listening to what I just said.

If I'm not mistaken, her eyes are locked on a girl's ass. She's wearing leggings that pull up her butt, making it lifted and rounded. She looks like she wants to pounce.

Oh my God.

I kick Gabe under the table, letting my eyes trail towards Cameron and the girl. His face lights up from humor. No wonder she never kissed me back. No wonder she's sitting here after I cuddled her without it being awkward.

"Oh. I dated her too. Bat shit crazy." Gabe grins ear to ear.

He in fact never dated her. He's probably never even seen this girl before. Gabe is trying to push Cameron closer to me, but if she's a lesbian, I'm doing the wrong thing here. I need to change up my plans. I clearly can't get her to trust me as her boyfriend. I need to get her to trust me as a friend. A heads up from my father would have been nice, this could be easier from this angle. *Of course, this is the one thing I don't know about her.*

"You have questionable taste in girls." She goes back to eating, paying attention to us again.

He laughs, "Says the one who was just drooling."

Cameron shrugs.

Lucia approaches the table quickly behind Gabe clearing her throat loudly to announce her arrival. Cameron tenses beside me at the sound of her voice. "What are you doing babe?"

"Eating." He says so matter of fact.

"With her. Tell her to leave."

"Nope. You should just make up."

"Never." Lucia walks away with a huff, Gabe glares at me, grabbing his tray following her.

"It's weird." Cameron shakes her head. "Lucia claims she's scared of me, then continues to back talk me. If I was scared of me, I would stay in line and not cross my path with attitude."

"Are you okay?" I ask.

"Honestly, yeah. I feel better not having her around. She's been sucking my happiness since sophomore year. Her being scared of me is something that happens a lot in my dating life, and friend life. By the way, her being 'scared' came out of nowhere." She uses her fingers to quote the word scared. "She's seen me do a lot worse. But whatever, no sweat off my shoulders. I'm good with no gossip."

"It sucks losing a friend though." I don't know what I'm doing. I'm trying to dig for her side of the story without seeming like I'm too invested.

"We never talked about anything. Every weekend we drank, and we would go shopping once in a while. We sat together at lunch, but we didn't know each other. I already know you better than her, and that's saying something."

She stands to leave as her alarm on her phone sends it shaking across the table. "When do you wanna have dinner?"

"Tonight. I have about 300 restaurants in Manhattan I want to try."

She smiles, a real genuine smile, full of happiness. "It's on me tonight."

She's too smart for her own good. Even if she doesn't suspect anything, she knows something is off.

And her intuition is 100% right.

"Over twenty restaurants are within a few blocks from us. What do you want to eat?" I watch Cameron looking down at my phone, shifting back and forth.

"I don't know."

"What looks good?"

"I don't know."

I close my eyes. She's *that* kind of girl. We are downtown Manhattan with endless restaurants, we both have fake ID's there's nothing in our way, and she still can't pick.

"Italian? Mexican? Asian? Burgers? Seafood?"

"I don't know." She pauses, looks at me then back at my phone, "We could do— no, not that. Or... no."

"Cameron. Fucking pick."

"No. You." She passes my phone back.

"Okay. Pasta."

"No, I was kind of hoping for a fat stacked burger. I also kind of don't want that either though."

I place the palm of my hand to my face, closing my eyes. "Have you ever dated a girl?"

"Yeah why?"

"How did you decide what to eat?"

"We didn't, we usually just didn't eat."

I close my eyes even tighter. She's making me feel an entire new level of annoyed. It's not even anger, I kind of want to laugh at her, but I also want to scream at her. I turn without looking back at her. The burger place isn't too far from us.

Cameron's feet patter against the sidewalk as she runs up to me very dramatically swinging her arms. She's going to whack someone in the face.

"Sorry. I'm annoying. You just kinda gotta tell me what we're doing, where we're eating. I go along with it. I just don't want to make you eat something that you don't want." She shrugs, taking a small break from talking very fast. "I'm not sure how I turned out this way. Everyone is like '*Be a force of nature. Tell people what they're going to do.*' I'm just too nice."

She talks a lot, when I think she's done she takes another breath.

"I like to think I'm a force of nature, I'm very excited over *every-thing*." Her body does a small shake.

I look at her with wide eyes, then bring my attention to the sidewalk, feeling her trailing behind me.

The restaurant has a 1950's theme. Cameron likes history, this restaurant is either going to be a good idea, or a very bad idea, probably reminding her she has homework to do. I saw pictures online, walking into this feels like we time traveled. The floor is black and white checkered tiles. The booths, and the chairs are all red, the tables are silver and shiny. Servers are dressed up in costumes, pictures of famous people from that time hang up on the walls. To top all that off, there is a light blue 1955 Bel Air in the middle of the restaurant, with a plaque reading the make and model.

I tell the host we need a table for two, looking over at Cameron watching her entire face light up as she looks around. *So, this was a good idea, noted.*

I sit in the booth, watching her look around with big round bright eyes.

"My family owns a 1920's speakeasy bar. It's the same feeling as this." She smiles at the server coming up, ordering a drink.

She doesn't say anything else. She just looks at the menu, her hands on her lap, she's not taking much space in the booth. Normally her smile takes up more space in a room than what she's taking up right now. She's shifted into an entirely new mood. Lucia did say something about her moods jumping around. That's Lucia's opinion. Her opinion is kind of shit.

She pushes the menu away from her. "Sorry. I'm a lot to handle, I was just in a good mood. I feel safe around you, so I don't hold *me* back, and I'm sorry." Her voice is so sad, she won't look at me, I see her chin quiver.

It feels like she just punched me in the stomach. Feeling safe around me is what I wanted, hearing her say it, takes the air from my lungs. I wanted her to trust me, and now that she does, I don't want her to. I want nothing but to push her away, the closer she is to me, the less safe she is.

"Don't apologize." I have to push the words out. I'm choking on them.

"Wanna share a milkshake?" She looks at me. Her mouth is in a faded frown, and it almost kills me that she needed to apologize for being happy. Her apologizing for that makes my lungs feel like they're collapsing.

"As long as you pick the flavor." I smile, why does smiling hurt so much?

Cameron sucks in air, "You smiled! Can we do caramel?"

I nod, whipping the smile off my face. I can breathe again at least, she smiled, and my lungs opened.

"Smile more. It looks good on you."

I'm never smiling again.

I pull out my phone texting Gabe.

We need to have a meeting with my dad. I'll get you to break up with Lucia.

I think I'm getting closer.

***

I glare at Tiny. He's far from Tiny. Every overweight guy is called Tiny I swear. They think the irony is funny, it's overused. It's not funny anymore.

"Nico" Tiny says, looking past me staring at the wall, he really needs to loosen up, no one's coming through the cement wall to get to my father. "He was so happy you contacted him."

"How long is he going to be?" I bark, my fathers never happy. Not when it comes to me.

"Hour at most."

"We'll be upstairs drinking."

"Eh, Nico." Bones steps in front of the door. His name suits him. He's skinny, no muscle, no fat on him. I have no idea how he's made it this far. "Any progress on the puttana?"

Gabe side steps him, opening the door behind him ushering me to leave my dad's office. I don't show any expression on my face, he just called Cameron a whore in Italian, and every single fiber in my body is light in sheer anger. I want to absolutely destroy him for that.

Tequila burns going down, it burns even more when it's shot after shot. I feel like I'm never going to learn my lesson. I don't know why I keep doing this to myself. Probably because it's the only thing strong enough to get me enough courage to talk to my father. It's most definitely the only thing that will prevent me from wanting to pull a gun on him. If I was drinking Bourbon, there would be no way I would be walking out of that room alive.

"I've never seen you like." Gabe looks at me, then down at the row of my shot glasses "like this before. Water for the dumb ass please. I'm positive you care about her more than me."

"You know we are only doing this job together. We're not at school, Cameron's not here. There's no act. Let's just get you away from Lucia."

"You really are dead inside." He shoves me the water. "No more for now."

"Are you done sulking?" Lucia stands beside Gabe. We both tense.

"I can't wait to break up with you." Gabe looks at her directly in the eyes. "You're all around unless you know that right?"

Lucia faces me completely ignoring Gabe "Quanto tempo prima che possiamo vedere il Leone?"

"Dad will be here soon." I say quieter than the music.

I need more time. I don't know how the hell I found a friend in Cameron. All I know is I did. Now I need to be a friend to her.

A game of telephone goes down the bar through the bartenders to reach us. I need to get this over with.

The same room I went down to get the keys from my father last weekend is the same room where we have our meetings. Our sit downs are held at another location, this is just the spot that we do the quick work at. The room is under the bar, it's public, and it's super fucking obvious that the bars a cover for what's really going on.

"Papa." My ass kissing sister runs up to our dad kissing his cheek. "I'm sorry, I come with bad news." Dad gesture for us to sit, "I couldn't get close to her. Three years of friendship and I've gotten nothing. I thought I had something, then she attacked Ashley, and got distant. I pushed her away."

"I know, you did your job the best you could. How's it going on your side?" Dad looks at me with intimidating eyes.

Cameron being into girls, it makes sense why Lucia was the first one to be in contact with her. Even though I was the one who endured the pain of the training. Honestly, when I found out Lucia was the one doing it, I guess I was glad to not do it. I figured when she became successful, there would be zero debate on if I got to live or not. I never once put up a fight when Lucia took my job. I gladly handed her my death sentence.

Dad thinks that look will scare me, he's the one that broke me. Scaring me isn't going to help. They call him 'The lion.' Past teachers have said I have absolutely no resemblance to him, strangers are usually shocked that he's my dad. I completely understand why. He's short, round, and bald. I might be mentally denying that I don't look like him, because I have nice hair and I don't want to lose it, but then again, I look at him and I feel the blood in my veins burning with scorching hot blood flowing through them. I was created to hate, and it's all towards him. He destroyed me.

"It's not going." I lie. "She won't open up. To convince her what you want her to do, it's going to be damn near impossible." I think she is starting to trust me, I think she is starting to open up. Dad will never know that.

"Does she know about the Basilisks?" His bug eyes bounce between me and Lucia.

Lucia looks at me, "I have no idea.".

"I don't think so." She's confused about her rage, if she knew what her family was, she would understand, I'm going off this, even if it's not true. She needs more time. If she knew what her family really was, I don't think she would love them as much as she does.

"Ninety days Nico. Or you're dead."

I'm not even worried about dying. I've been dead my entire life. He needs to come up with a better threat.

"If you can't do it, someone else will. Can you do it, or do you need some extra motivation?" He presses when I show no reaction to his threat.

"I can do it." I close my eyes. I don't want to do this. If I don't do this, Cameron will be put through excruciating pain. "No need to send more cars after us as a warning."

"Sorry to interrupt." Gabe leans forward. "Can I please break up with her now? Their fake friendship is beyond repair."

Dad nods, "You all may go."

I stand to leave when Bones grabs my arm, "Tick tock. Ninety days, or I'll be the next one up, you don't want that."

My hand is in a fist, every single muscle in my body wants to be thrown towards him, I want to hit him more than anything. Not only for Cameron, but because the tone he uses almost makes my screaming from a repressed memory resurface. That was the treat for Cameron. I didn't want to come. Three months. That's not enough time to save her from him. That's not enough time to save anyone from him.

"Get fucked." I mumble breaking out of his grasp, walking away.

I text walking up the stairs.

Are you free?

I fall against the bar. I'm way too spooked. That got under my skin. Nothing gets under my skin. I'm so messed up, I didn't even realize the time, I know exactly where she is, and I'm a moron for wanting to go towards Cameron right now.

"Six shots." Gabe sits beside me after ordering not saying a word to me. The shots come and he pushes three towards me. I don't hesitate, I need to numb whatever this is I'm feeling.

Yeah.

I'm just with my family. what's up?
Bad fucking night.
Can I come see you?

7

Cameron

"Why are we just finding out about this now?" Brittney waves the cover of a magazine in front of my face. "Cameron Watson, the New York state history essay winner."

She throws the magazine back at Spencer, he fumbles his arms around to catch the magazine. It's really hard not to laugh at Spencer's face, and the look of amusement on Brittney's as she watches him struggle.

Brittney hugs me, it's always an awkward hug, I'm five foot nine, she's five foot three, maybe five foot four. "I'm so proud of you Cam. You are everything you need to be, okay?"

I miss seeing her more often, now that I'm in university there's less time. In high school I never had to study as much, we spent a lot of time together, because I was able too. I honestly probably over study, but my dad just paid $800 per course, and I'm not ready to let him down. So, I study. A lot. My mom let him down, I cannot do the same to him. I know that's not my responsibility, the second I fail him, I know it's going to feel like he failed, again.

"Ass in here now Cameron." William shouts from the kitchen. He has a serious dad voice. I think I might be in trouble. I don't even know what I did.

I listen to William knowing for a fact that he's not in the kitchen alone, if I did do something, there will be an audience. These people are always together. I don't get it. It's been this way since before I was born apparently. If one is there, there will be at least two other people trailing behind. I don't know how they can always be together. I need time alone. I think that's part of the reason why I always need to study. It's just alone time. Maybe it roots from me always having people around? I don't know how they don't get exhausted from so much socializing. It's like they don't need to recharge, ever.

April is eating a bowl of chips, she has it cradled in her arms. She's been eating like shit ever since her husband randomly sent her divorce papers. This is her second divorce, first it was Josh, and now it's this guy. I never liked him, so there's a very high possibility I just called him *that guy*. I never bothered to learn this name. The marriage lasted an entire six months, after dating for three years. She got two kids out of that relationship, it was another, *you're pregnant, we better get married.* I don't know how she's had such a hard time finding someone, she's so beautiful inside and out. It gives me zero hope someone will love me and my emotional disaster tendencies.

"Rooftop. Spill." William leans into his arms, "Is this like a friend thing, or you're experimenting with guys?"

I make a frowny face, my eyes opened wide staring at him. I'm definitely not in trouble. It's just awkward boy talk. "Ick."

"Oh. Come on Cameron." April drops the oversized bowl, "He was a solid twelve. If you sleep with him, your expectations for men will be impractically high."

"For your information, I've slept with guys before." I grab a handful of chips out of her bowl, "We're friends. That's it."

Williams eyes go wide, and a shiver takes over his body. He doesn't even look at me, he just walks into the living room shaking his arms, trying to get my words off of him.

April laughs. "You broke him." Her face lights up, happier than I've seen her for a while. "Hey, have you heard from your mom?"

I shake my head. I forgot I told Liam that she can call me. Of course, April heard about it. Liam, April, and Dillon are siblings, you can't really say one thing without the other knowing about it. If one of them knows something, William knows. It took me a long time to figure out the clicks. This family loves each other with everything in their heart. There are people in the group they love more than others. Once you think you have it figured out, you realize the clicks overlap, and suddenly you vented about someone, and every single person knows. There's too many people here, if someone has an issue, they all need to be straight forward or it's a game of telephone, and nothing is said the way it was intended in that game.

"Are you okay? Liam was so confident she was going to call you. He tried so hard." Her voice is tired.

God I almost feel bad for pushing Liam into that position.

I know what I'm about to say is going to reach mom. "Honestly. I have enough family. If she wants to choose her new shiny kids who didn't cause her to go screw up her life, then so be it. I don't even care." I bite my lip, "You can tell her that yourself."

April smirks, "I chose you. When I told Liam that, brother looked me right in the eye and said 'good.'"

I look at April with wide eyes, what do I say to that? I don't want anyone picking sides, she did. The two people who were Lizzy's best girl-friends, picked me without thinking about it. I look down trying to hide a smile.

Theo rests his chin on my head, after a solid few minutes of quiet. "Don't shit yourself when your dad comes in."

I groan. My dad probably caught wind of my article days ago. I'm really starting to hate Spencer working at my school. This means my father has had time to prepare. When my father has time to prepare, it's overboard. I love it. I'm so much like him, his friends couldn't believe how crazy he went with my celebrations, eventually they stopped bugging him and joined him. That means since my aunts and uncles taking part in his celebration backfired on them. Now that they've done it for me, they have no choice but to do it for their kids. My dad owns half the bar with his brother Adam that his parents used to own, but other than that, he's the unpaid family's event planner. I have a lot of cousins, like a lot. An entire eighteen of them, all in New York. You wouldn't think my dad is this type of person by looking at him, the tattoos, the way he towers over every single person on the street, and the crazy amount of muscle on him, he looks scary as hell. It almost makes it better. Him planning a big, combined birthday bash for multiple kids all at once makes him happy. He's in his element.

I don't know how he became so big on family, but I hope to God I can continue the Watson bloodline. He deserved so much more than me, even if he will not admit it.

"What's wrong?" Max grabs my shoulder, giving me a squeeze for reinsurance.

I move out from under Theo, wiping my eye. I cannot handle these waves of emotion. I'm tearing up because I'm my dad's only kid. It's not even my fault, and I'm almost crying. It might even be what April said to me moments before, I need to learn to control my feelings.

I clear my throat before speaking, "Sorry. I just have a lot of shit going on."

I'm surprised that Theo, and Max still come around even though my mom's MIA. There used to be a picture of those three, and Brittney when they were in their late teens hanging on the wall when my parents were together. The past few years Brittney has made her choice and chose me over mom. If mom chose Liam and her new children, Brittney thought she should make a choice too. Liam, Max, and Theo have split their time between all of us. Of course, they're still here. Every single Friday. They show up. That's all a person can do is show up.

Children's voices fill the house, then grown-ups voices follow behind. There are so many kids I'm not even sure what kids belong to what adults. One thing I am sure of about my siblings, my mother hasn't told them I'm their sister. Those three kids are the only ones that don't come on Fridays. They have their own play dates with other kids, because unlike me they have cousins that are the same age as them. There would be twenty-one kids here, but there's only eighteen. There's only eighteen because she's keeping me from them.

It probably has to do with my anger, even though I would never hurt someone on purpose. It takes over me, but even I have my limits on who my anger is directed towards. Not a single one of these kids have ever seen me mad, not a single one has ever feared me.

My dad walks into the kitchen with a tall white cake box. "I am so proud of you."

Josh opens the box revealing a three stacked high cake. The first two layers have *The American History Magazine* written in blue, with lines from my article written on it. The top layer is tall, it's the same size as the magazine would be, the 'pages' are white fondant, with black icing written in my words. The baker copied every single word on the fondant for the first two pages.

My mouth drops, the hand cramps the cake decorator must have gotten.

"A short story on immigration to New York." Dillion crosses his arms, smiling down at me. "I thought for sure I would have fallen asleep. It made me feel things."

"Those are emotions dumb ass. Can someone take a picture of this cake so I can eat it?" Josh looks at me, "For real though, twist in a romance, you got yourself a book."

"I've already written it. This was a summary without the main points. I wanted to see everyone's reaction if it got picked."

Dad looks at me with the biggest smile on his face, in fact they're all looking at me like that. The book I wrote about was about a couple coming from Ireland in the 1800's. I wrote about the terrible living conditions they had to endure, I wrote about them staying hopeful because they love each other so much, and nothing could go wrong if they were together. I put the love that I hope one day to experience in my book. I highly doubt it will happen. What I told Nico about me wanting to live in the suburbs away from the city, was completely true. I just left out how many kids I want.

I want so many kids. Four, maybe five. I'm a lot to handle with my moods. I know a rational person wouldn't be able to handle me on top of that many kids. Who would probably inherit my moods. So, I wrote about the fictional love I want. I've never had my heart broken before. It was all pure innocent love that I poured into my characters. Love that I watched between my aunts, and my uncles. I want to love someone that way, I also want to have kids to love the same way my dad loves me. I chose romance, because fictional characters can't break my heart. It makes me feel something when I'm writing it, and when I'm rereading it, there's no strings to it. There's no risk.

"Cake." I feel my phone buzz with Nico's name lighting up my screen.

I instantly sent him my dad's address. William, and April are going to make this so fucking weird.

Spencer passes me a piece of the cake. It's layered with caramel between the cake slices.

"Tequila and Sprite?" Liam looks up at me, holding the bottle.

I look at him, he has a smile on his face looking down at me. I set my cake down and walk up to him wrapping my arms around his chest squeezing him. He sets the bottle down, hugging me in return. I didn't know what else to do, I told his wife to call me, she didn't, she lost a friend putting him in yet again another bad situation, and he still shows up. Absolutely zero obligation to be here, and he's here.

"I'm sorry." I press the words out of my chest saying it quietly under everyone cutting into the cake.

"My kids will know you. I promise Cam." He whispers, before clearing his throat. "Tequila?"

I guess I'm drinking.

I take a step backwards, and another one, turning away to the porch without being seen. I open the door, and Nico is pacing back and forth, this must have been a really shitty night. I'm honestly surprised I'm the one he called and ran too.

He looks up, his jaw is locked, the pressure his teeth are feeling is probably painful. That only lasts for a minute before he lets out a breath pulling me in for a forcefully strong hug.

"Hey. Are you okay?" I hug him back asking softly.

He doesn't say a single word.

"Okay. You're coming in for a drink." I break my hug running my hands down his arms. "There's cake."

"Cami." He says quiet.

He just gave me a nickname. Don't look like I'm melting. Stay cool.

"Does that shitty sparkling Vampire movie have a second one?"

I nod.

He lets out a long breath from his lips. "Can we watch it later? I just... I don't..."

I move my hands in his, feeling the weight of his heart in my chest. He doesn't have many facial expressions, he looks cool and collected, it's the way he's talking. Something is really wrong. I squeeze his hands, trying to comfort him when I have no idea how too. "We can watch something else."

"No. That one. It will be our movie. Please."

"Breakfast in the morning. We can watch it all day tomorrow. For now, we must drink." I have no idea what's going on, all I know is that he came to me, so I need to try to help in any way that I can.

He nods.

I open the door, Nico steps in behind me, his hand still in mine. Everyone turns to face us. Every single adult minus all four of the Taylor's look like their eyes are going to pop out of their head.

Nico stops in his tracks standing beside me, "Everyone here could kick my ass. That's lovely." His tone is nothing like it was outside, he's acting like he's one hundred percent, and it scares me how well he can wear his mask.

"Are you?" Spencer looks at me, then at Nico.

"Guys are thrown in the mix now? Okay, okay." Brittney puckers her lips.

"Wow. We're friends. Why is everyone acting more shocked about me having a boyfriend then you did when you thought I was a full blown lesbian."

"Yeah. She's not. She's been lying to all of us." William shutters.

April bursts out in laughter again at him being uncomfortable.

Dad scrunches up his nose. "You couldn't get pregnant that way. You dating girls was less stressful."

"Just friends." Nico's voice is strained. "I swear."

"I need a drink." I mumble.

Under Nico's breath he agrees with me, my gut is telling me it's for an entirely different reason.

8

Nico

My arms bleeding from her fingernails clawing their way into my skin. She's been fighting back. I'm positive my nose is broken, there's blood on my shirt, and I don't think it's her blood. She hit me hard. I heard a crack. I should have known her strength, I shouldn't have underestimated her.

Now I'm stuck doing it in her dorm room. I don't even know how I got us into this situation. I had a well thought out plan, now I'm holding her life in my hands. I tighten my arm around her neck. She's bent over completely vulnerable. The tighter I make the headlock the harder she punches my legs trying to hurt me. She's strong, I'm stronger right now, I'm completely overpowering her. She has no way to get out of this, she has no way to win this.

"Nico." Cameron cries my name. "I trusted you." She bursts out in tears, her body shaking.

"That was your first mistake." I tighten my arm more, moving my body to the side quickly, her body goes limp.

I let out a gasp dropping her lifeless body to the ground.

I sit up quickly gasping for air, my lungs are burning, my throat feels like it's closing off, my heart is pounding in my rib cage, I can't breathe, even though that was only a dream. I feel Cameron's soft blankets in the palm of my hands, I know it's her bed because the mattress is too soft. I still can't breathe. She's okay, I stayed with her tonight to make sure she's safe from everyone. If I'm with her, no one else will be watching her.

"Nico." Cameron sits up, she puts her hand on my back, she doesn't flinch feeling the sweat under my shirt.

I know she woke me up the other night from my nightmare, I know she knows about them, I just never acknowledged her knowing. She's not supposed to be this person. She's not supposed to care about me. Besides, I have nothing special about me that would make someone care about me.

I'm not supposed to care about her. Me coming to her tonight was for me to protect her from my father. She needs protecting from me, I'm the one who's dangerous. My father and I both are, I want to protect her from us. The reality is, she needs to be protected from me. There's just one issue. I can't seem to stay away from her.

I exhale, grabbing her knee from over top of the blankets, I just need to make sure she's breathing. "I'm sorry." I move my hand from her rubbing my eyes.

Cameron turns on her flashlight on her phone shining up the room, then passes me a water bottle from the floor on her side of the bed. The water is ice cold, it's helping me realize I'm awake, and my dream was just a dream.

"I'm here, okay?" Cameron takes the water bottle from me, putting it back on the floor. "Cuddle me. Share my good dreams."

I lay on my right side, feeling her back press up against my chest, I already feel my right arm going dead. I wrap my other arm around her middle, holding her close to protect her.

She has more than ninety days left. I don't know how I'm going to do it, but she is going to live her life.

***

"This is better than sex." My mouth is so full. There's so much cheese, large cube hash browns, sausage, veggies, and Chipotle to give it a kick.

Cameron laughs, "Oh, you've been sleeping with the wrong girls."

This sounds stupid, I can't wrap my head around it. Before we started to eat at restaurants together, I never tasted food the way I do now. It was just food. There wasn't any taste, no way to make it better, I never had a preference on hot and cold. I just ate what I could get my hands on to give me energy. Now I notice the taste. Before I was eating what I could as fast as I could in case it was time for another one of my lessons.

"I was thinking." I stop talking, this is a bad idea. It's also a good idea. "I live not far from campus. Do you want to come over tonight? I have a bigger TV." I take another large bite not looking at her, scared of the expression I'll see.

"A bigger bed to hey?"

I nod slowly.

"I'll get my shit together after we eat."

I normally wouldn't have been so sheepish to ask, but after that comment William made last night about her being into guys, I felt my chest get heavy. I know it shouldn't, we're friends. Being friends is pushing it, I was mechanically designed to hate her. When Cameron turned away from my kiss, I was just thinking it was because she's strictly into girls. Knowing that she likes guys too, it tightens my stomach up in knots and I want to punch something really fucking hard.

Since I've met her, I've smiled, tasted food, and felt— I don't know what the fuck I felt last night with her family when her said that, but I never want to feel it again.

At least today, and tonight I'll know she's safe at my place. I have security cameras at every entrance, sensors when someone enters my walkway. If I'm home alone and there's movement in a room, my phone gets a notification. Paranoid? No. That's what being *me* is like. Now I'll be spending less time looking over my shoulder and can have my own space.

9

Cameron

Nico holds his wallet up to a card reader on his house door. The reader is black, with silver buttons under it. I've never seen anything like this on a house. It's a high tech version of the entrance to a hotel swimming pool. There's a loud buzz noise, then the light flashes green. Nico body chucks the door, I don't even have my eyes off the light before it turns red. Outside his house there are so many trees. It looks like the view inside the house to the street is completely blocked. We're right down the road from the school, close enough to the main road where we can hear everything on the street.

I pull my eyes from the yard watching Nico walks inside, unsure of what to say to him. He's been different, I guess it started last night. I don't know how he would normally act in front of my entire family, so that doesn't count. After breakfast today, he's been well... weird. He will not look at me. Every time I glance over at his direction his jaw is locked together. His straight face looking more serious than before. The only time he acts relatively normal is when he has food in front of him.

I shut the door, the second I shut it, there's another buzzing noise, glancing behind me the deadbolt turns locking itself. My eyes trace the wall, seeing Nico's black runners kicked off. I take my boots off, resting the fake leather against the wall, so they don't fall in a puddle tracked in from the snow on the souls of my shoes. Nico walks and the sound instantaneously begins to echo through the house. I follow the echo though an empty hallway, to my left is the laundry room with a stacked washer and dryer. To my right is a two piece bathroom with a sliding door. Both rooms are completely empty, minus the bare minimum needed items. There's nothing in the hall, and by the sound of the footsteps, it sounds like nothing is in his house, at all.

I keep following the hallway, leading myself to a living room. Straight ahead is the kitchen and dining room. The dining room doesn't have a table. The living room only has a three person couch, one end table on the side of the couch, a long coffee table, a game console, and a TV all sitting on one basic white TV stand.

Not only does the house look empty, it feels empty. I didn't think houses got quieter than me and my dad living alone, he's proving me wrong. I'm used to going over to someone's house, hearing multiple adults talking, children fighting, or on the rare occasion, children getting along. It's anything but quiet. Nico's house is so quiet, it goes past being lonely. My dorm is lonely, at least I can hear voices in the hallway, here it's just quiet.

I sit pulling out my phone, it's time to scroll, I'm done feeling like I'm judging him now.

After what feels like an hour of me scrolling, I finally put my phone down, I look behind me ready to call out his name when a camera in the top corner of the room is pointed towards the front entrance. I squint my eyes looking at the opposite side of the room seeing another camera pointed towards the windows.

I'd be worried he's watching me, but the cameras are tilted at an angle where the couch isn't even in the vision of the shot. It's clearly at the entrances.

"I downloaded the next three movies." Nico's voice comes up behind me making my body jolt from being surprised.

I watch him looking down at his laptop, grabbing the HDMI cord from the TV plugging it in. He normally stands up straighter than this, his shoulders are slouched, his neck has a curve downwards, his entire body is slouched. He looks like someone told him his puppy died.

"Are you okay?" I run my hands over the fabric of the couch, feeling it tickling the inside of my palms.

Nico shakes his head, setting the laptop down, closing it halfway so the light won't bother us. "My dad just gave me an impossible task." He closes his eyes, scratching his jaw walking to the couch. He falls next to me grabbing the remote. "Wanna run away? Panama would be cool. I looked it up."

I look at him with wide eyes trying not to laugh. "My family would kick your ass."

Nico puts his hand on my knee tightening his grip, his fingers digging into my skin, not in a painful way, in a reassuring way. He's not showing any emotion, it's all in the way he carries himself. Maybe I've been reading this wrong. He might just not be able to say how he's feeling. His face is rock hard. There's absolutely no expression. It's all in his body language. I've been reading him wrong.

I bite my bottom lip, we always sit so close together without touching each other, except right now, his hand is still on me. *Do it.* I bend my knees to sit on them. Nico doesn't move his hand from me, putting the other arm on the side of the couch putting up his footrest. I use this window to slide closer to him, wrap my left arm over his middle, bravely I rest my head on his chest. He smells sweet, I can't pinpoint it, it's such a good smell.

Nico's body tenses, his chest rises, and I brace myself for him to tell me to move. The words don't come. Instead, his breathing becomes deeper, his heart rate slows down. I make myself more comfortable laying on the couch, using him as a pillow knowing he won't reject me now, his arm rests on my side.

We have the soundtrack to a movie that I know he hates, the living room is so dark, other than the lights from the screen I wouldn't be able to see a thing.

This is oddly comforting.

The credits come on, and Nico stands up to go to his laptop. He hasn't criticized the movie yet, so I know something is seriously bothering him. I want to know what's wrong more than anything.

"What's your family life like? You never talk about them." I ask picking at my nail beds, I need him to talk, give me something. "Parents, siblings?"

He exhales deeply, looking up at me. The TV is only lighting up half his face. "I have a sister. Parents are still together. Now if you ask me if I like them, do you want the truth?"

I nod.

"I hate every single person in my family." His lips go in a straight line. "It's complicated. Where was your mom last night?"

"She chose a different family. When's your birthday?"

"This isn't a game of twenty questions."

"I will find out, and I will make you a cake."

"Do you even bake?"

I pucker my lips to the side, "No, but I can learn."

He is one of the few people in my life I would put the extra effort into learning how to bake and learn how to decorate a cake.

"Do you really hate your family?" I ask, following him with my eyes back to the couch.

He nods.

"You can borrow mine. Holidays, weekends. You just have to walk in a house and pick an adult."

"Why are you like this?" he lifts his arm on the back of the couch, I don't know if that was him readjusting, or if it was him telling me to come back. Either way, I take it as my cue to slide in and cuddle him.

"I know what it's like not to have a mom. I couldn't imagine not having my dad. You have me, and I'll never let you be alone."

Nico doesn't say anything, he just bites his bottom lip, closing his eyes.

I give him a one-armed hug before my attention is drawn on the movie.

10

Nico

I scratch my handwriting out in my notebook, making long exaggerated lines, pressing my pen onto the paper so hard it for sure has the pressure from the pen on multiple pages.

I can't come up with a plan. The only thing that's logical enough is us packing to another country or moving to the mountains and completely falling off the grid. Neither one of those options are going to be suitable, because she would never leave her family behind. In the last twenty years, the Basilisks have redeemed themselves, they don't deserve to just pack their kids away to a long lost countryside. Even I know that they deserve more than that.

My stomach sends a sharp pain to my brain, trying to tell me I'm hungry. I don't care how hungry I am. I can't eat anything until I figure this out. My guilt has been eating away at me. I haven't been sleeping, every muscle on my body hurts. I've never felt guilty before in my life, I didn't know that I was capable of feeling guilt. On top of everything else that Cameron has made me feel, guilt is the worst. I want to tell her, I can't. I don't care if I die, I just know that if I tell her I'm dead, then the same people who fucked me up will be dealing with her. I can't have that. This has to end with me, one way or another. She's too good of a person, she cares too much.

This isn't even my mess. I know who caused it all, I saw them on Friday when I went to Cameron. I wanted to wrap my hands around their neck and strangle them. The worst part? They didn't even question a random person showing up to see Cameron, the girl who would rather be alone, she doesn't come with friends. No flags were raised, nothing seemed out of the ordinary to them. That makes me hate them more. They claim to love her, but they didn't even notice when something was obviously off.

After meeting, and getting to know Cameron, I hate that specific Basilisks as much as I hate my own family. My parents, Cameron's specific 'family' member, have completely fucked us.

And I will get my revenge. I want to be the one to watch the life drain out from their eyes. I want to see the act they've been putting on for the last two decades crumble, watch the truth come spilling out.

No one, and I mean no one hurts Cameron.

Right now, I'm the only soldier in the war my dad's started, one way or another I will end this. He never wanted me to have emotional thoughts, or feelings. It backfired, I'm angry, I hate. There's something else he never thought of happening. What I feel for Cameron is the opposite of hate, and I will not stop until she is safe in a good Basilisks arms. Even if I'm dead. At least someone will still be alive protecting her.

11

Cameron

On this side of the school all the classrooms look the same, on the other side of the school everything is a literal circle. The stage for acting students is built right in the center, and around the stage are all changing rooms, music rooms, anything for the performing arts. Over here it's just boring smart people stuff. Okay I take that back, half the kids in my class are far from smart. This college just takes anyone for some of the programs. I mean, I'm getting a degree in history, so it's debatable if I'm smart in ways that matter. Whatever, if I'm dumb, I'll flaunt it. I've been expelled from six schools, and I'm in university. When I say they take everyone, I mean it.

I scan the doors, looking at the numbers on top, this hallway looks like everything is just duplicating itself. I'm almost done this semester, and I still need to triple check the numbers on top of the doors.

There it is.

I open Spencer's classroom door. "I brought you a salad. They fucked up. I don't like steak, so you can eat it."

"What did you do to it?" Spencer puts his lips in a hard line watching my food. "Is this like that one time you and your dad put laxatives in my coffee?"

I cackle. "Cows are just too cute to eat. That was so funny though. You gotta admit that at least."

He looks at me with a long blank expression. "I almost shit myself for my interview here. It was already ironic that I applied to teach a criminal law class. I couldn't look at either of you for a week."

I stop laughing. "Why was it ironic?"

He takes the salad nodding to the desk for me to sit in his computer chair, while he leans on the desk half sitting, half standing. "I was a shitty person in college. Got into a lot of trouble. I sold illegal things, I killed someone."

I look at him with wide eyes not saying anything. Spencer doesn't beat around the bush, maybe that's why he's my favorite uncle. My mouth moved, words are having a hard time forming, "Wh—what?"

"It was a long time ago. Just promise me something Cam. You do not let your anger get to that point. You do not let anyone manipulate you. Your Dad has raised you into someone who you can't control, and believe me, who you are as a person helps me sleep at night."

"Why are you telling me this?"

"Charlie told your dad you were asking questions. He agreed, even if someone wanted to try to manipulate you, they wouldn't be able to. He trusts you, but the thought of you living through what I lived through is just too much for any of us. If you ever feel like you're in danger you need to come to us, okay?"

"You're just scaring me now." I try to laugh, but it comes off fake.

"Not trying to scare you, all I know is I keep watch of the students, I hear rumors, I know there's some kids here that were like me. You don't want to tangle yourself up in them. If it wasn't for Brittney, I never would have gotten out alive."

"Do you know who?" Not like I'll know them, I'm just nosey. It's like seeing police sirens, it's only natural to want to go to the danger zone. I really want to know who they are, and what they do.

Spencer shakes his head.

"Okay, so I only ever hang out with Nico. Got it."

"Yeah. What's going on with that?" He laughs.

I smile and my face heats up.

Spencer just smiles, "Can you tell him to show up for my class? I'm just getting insulted here."

"He's in your class." I rest my head on the head rest of the chair confused. I didn't know that. I don't even know what courses he's taking. Damn he doesn't tell me shit. I bite my bottom lip. "Thank you for being the first person to be honest with me."

Spencer smiles weakly. "It's not about us not being honest Cam, it's about reliving my past. Saying it out loud to someone who looks up to me, it's ninety shades of regret, and I haven't forgiven myself for any of it."

"I forgive you."

He looks at me with a smile, the lines around his eyes showing. I've always been told I'm the good in everyone, that's not why I forgive him. Well, maybe it is. I know who he is, I don't need to know the details.

I snap my fingers loudly. "Hayley's show is this weekend, isn't it? She would murder me if she knew I almost forgot. Is everyone coming?"

"It's twenty-one and over." Spencer opens his salad, rolling his eyes, "You always get the fruity dressings."

I bob my head from side to side, "According to the state of New York, I am twenty-one. I'll see you there."

Spencer chuckles, "Fake ID?" He looks over at me, his lips separated watching me nod, "Oh Max is going to lose his mind when he catches you." His voice is painted with delight. He shakes his head ripping open the dressing. "I really want to scold you, then I remember at your age all of us were glued to a whiskey bottle."

I roll my eyes, "Get me two tickets, I'm dragging Nico's sorry ass with me too."

"I'm going to assume he doesn't know?"

"That assumption is correct." I smirk. "Hey, could you dig up his birthday for me?"

Spencer looks at me confused.

"I just need to know, he won't tell me."

"I can't just go digging Cam. Ask him."

I puff out a breath of air seeing students opening his door for their class, "You don't think I tried that? Came up dry."

12

Nico

Oh God. I chew slowly. I watch Cameron freeze. she waits for a server to walk by when she leaves her line of sight. Cameron reaches her hand out to the napkin dispenser spitting the calamari out, she drops the napkin on her plate.

My jaw hurts, my tongue is burning.

Cameron's entire body shakes. "Too much lime."

"Is it supposed to be this chewy?" I ask slowly, trying to bite, it feels like I'm chewing on a dog toy.

Cameron shakes her head, passing me a napkin. "Spit it out." Her voice is low, trying to hold back her laughter.

I nod my head, frowning.

"Cami." I move my tongue around in my mouth, "Is my tongue supposed to be tingly?"

She looks at me, and laughs. "Oh fuck." Her eyes go wide. "Are you okay?"

I scrunch my nose, sticking my tongue out. "It just feels funny."

She looks at me, not amused. Biting her bottom lip, eyes wide. "Dumbass. Did you know you were allergic to shellfish?"

I look at her dumbfounded, still sticking my tongue out. I probably look like a panting dog. "I literally haven't eaten food until you demanded it."

She pulls out her phone resting her forearms on the table. "Is your throat swelling?"

I shake my head.

"Oh, you're fine then. If you can breathe, you're not dead."

"Wow. You're so caring. I love you too. Asshole." I mumble.

She blacks out her phone, a devious smile spreads across her face, "When you piss me off, I know how to deal with you now."

I lean into the table shoving the plate of chewy poison to the other side for the server to grab it, "I will find out what you're allergic too, I will make you dinner, and I will accidentally use extra. Don't underestimate me with a good time."

Cami puckers her lips, her face moves towards her shoulder "Oouu" A smile spreads across her face, "I like this." She leans into the table, "But seriously I'm crashing in your bed tonight, so you know, you don't like, die."

I nod an excessive amount. "Yeah. I'd appreciate that, thanks."

Note to self, I'm allergic to shellfish. Also, if I eat shellfish she will end up in my bed. I'm learning a lot tonight.

"I don't study much anymore because of you." Cami closes her eyes, "The weekend I met you I wanted something to happen to mix things up for me. I wasn't expecting someone to come into my life and distract me." She smiles looking at me, "I'm so happy."

"Are you still passing?"

"Yeah, exams are right around the corner though. You need to go to Spencer's class Nico. I can't be the only one trying here." She laughs.

"Okay, I'll go. As long as after tonight we don't see each other for a week other than lunch."

"Oh. That's not going to happen. Saturday night I'm seeing you. I have plans for us. But yes, I need to crack down."

I smile, conversation with her is just so easy.

"Are you dying yet? Or are you okay?"

"I'm good Cameron." I almost smiled even bigger than the first time.

***

All Cameron said to me was "Dress up, bring your ID." I'm in jeans and a button up shirt. I thought that counted for something, until I saw her in a short purple dress with her hair curled. The circles in her hair are super loose. She has a silver sparkly bag hanging from her shoulder, with the matching sparkly shoes. She looks over at me in mid laugh, her entire face lighting up even more.

She skips over to me, I don't know how she's doing that in those heels. "Don't hate me."

"We are at a five-star hotel, and everyone is making me look like I'm poor." That's an understatement, the girls are making all the guys look poor. The girls are all dressed up, some guys are wearing jeans, others are wearing dress pants. We don't just get into the entire dressy thing the way girls do.

"I think you look amazing." Cameron has pink cheeks from her makeup, they're turning pinker, until she looks away from me.

"Why am I going to hate you?" I take a step forward, I'm never close enough to her, I hate it.

"Hayley, my best friend from London, she's doing a traveling art exhibit, and she's in New York tonight." Cameron clenches her teeth together frowning, tightening the muscles in her neck.

"I don't do art." I look behind her seeing her large swarm of family members. "I don't do families."

She reaches for my hand, stroking the back of my hand with her thumb. "Please, I miss you."

I look down at my hand, feeling my stomach tie itself in knots, thank God exams are sooner than later, it's weird not having her in my space. I don't like it. I move my hand without breaking our touch, interlocking our fingers together. It's like I can't think when she's not *right there.* Nothing feels real, I've just been sucked into a non-existent world. There's no emotion, no taste, no sense of life. My battery is dead. Then I see her, and everything is brought back to life, the pain I endorsed is gone, the life I live feels like a faint memory. Things are just easier when she's in my personal space. I suddenly recharge.

I look up from her to the crowd behind her, rage pulses through my body looking at the Basilisk who supposedly loves Cameron. My spine suddenly feels like it's about to break from standing up so straight, my heart rate speeds up, I want to turn around and leave, I want to shield Cameron from them. I want to shield every person here from them.

"Nico." Cameron breaks her hand away shaking it. "I like my fingers not broken. Come."

I don't argue. She will not be more than an arm's length away from me all night, she will be right beside me.

"Hi sir." I approach Erik with Cameron positioning herself between us, she grabs my hand interwinding our fingers. "We never stuck around long enough last weekend to meet you. Or anyone really."

Erik takes a deep breath. "Are you still just friends?"

Cameron tries to say something. Erik puts his hand on the top of her head, gently shoving her back into one of the guys standing in the group to break our touch. I watch everyone roll their eyes, including Cameron.

"I don't like you." Erik says bluntly, getting a reaction from every person around us.

I mean, I don't blame him. I'm me. I do have to admit, that does sting a little bit. What do I even say to that? I'm so relieved I don't show emotion. I look at Cameron's crushed face. I need to catch my breath. She's genuinely upset. She doesn't say anything, she just grabs my hand again and drags me inside of the hotel.

"Cameron stop!" I scold her quietly so only she can hear.

Cameron stops walking abruptly, dropping my hand. Turning to look at me with wide eyes. I don't care if her family likes me or not, I don't want to be making things worse than they already are. Even if they don't know how bad it is.

"I'm going to go, stay with your family." Saying that feels like acid in my mouth when I know who's here with her.

"No. I want you to meet Hayley." Her voices shakes.

I take one step towards her, tucking a strand of hair behind her ear. "nessuna opera d'arte potrà mai paragonarti alla tua bellezza."

She breathes deeply, her hand reaches for my elbow, "What did you say?"

I shake my head taking a step back, "Maybe one day I'll tell you."

She holds onto my elbow pulling me forwards, "You're staying. You aren't going to say that in the sexiest voice ever, then just leave. Oh no." Her fingers link in mine. "We are going to eat some greasy ass pizza at the first place we see after this. Go to your place and fall asleep on the couch from watching movies."

I walk past her. I've been searching for something since I found out she's into guys and she just basically told me I turned her on, so I'm not leaving. I fucking refuse.

"Bene mia Amata, vieni?" I smirk feeling her arms linking up with mine, she is pulling on me so hard she's dragging me down.

I smile from ear to ear, letting out a laugh for the first time in my life.

Cameron stops walking, she looks at me, her entire face is light up. I think she's blushing. "You just stopped my heart for a minute."

I wish I could lean in and kiss her.

13

Cameron

Nico is beautiful. His smile is breathtaking, his teeth are so nice and white, his eyes squint. Even after I said something about him laughing, he never broke his smile.

My stomach is fluttering. Him smiling is giving me so many butterflies. Not even to mention how wonderful the sound of his laughter is.

"Cameron? What the hell?" The sound of Hayley's voice rushes over to me.

I turn on my heels watching her run up to me, whisking me in her arms, hugging me tight as possible. I hold onto her tighter, trying not to destroy my makeup.

Hayley is straight up my best friend. We send each other videos every single day, we randomly message each other venting about random shit. Half the time our messages go back and forth of us venting about completely different things. The rare time she and her husband Archie fought she called me, it was two in the morning, I picked up, we always picked up for each other. There's over twenty years of age difference between us. I was the flower girl at her and Archie's second wedding, I've never had such a solid friendship in my entire life. She's been my rock.

She still is my rock, now I'm finding that Nico can ground me just as much as she can. I never once thought I would find that in anyone but her.

Hayley steps away from me. Her dress is long and black, it's so sparkly the lights in here are dim, it's almost like it's sparkling even more. The sleeves on the dress are short, there's fabric next to her bare arms that are like a fan when she moves. Around her middle finger is a loop connected to the fabric against her arms. It looks like she has wings. It's the perfect dress for an artist.

"I need you to come back to London." She fans her face.

"Not happening." Nico pipes up, handing us a champagne flute. "She's not leaving me, and I don't do London."

"Oh." Hayley turns to him, grabbing a glass from his hand. "London would do you. Seriously." Hayley looks at me, with wide eyes, hiding her smile behind her glass, taking a small drink.

I'm counting my blessings that she's married to someone that she loves more than anything, because Nico looks like he would be tempted to play with fire. That shouldn't bother me, yet I'm taking every bit of strength not to crush this champagne glass in my hand. I need to walk away. What am I feeling? Is this jealousy? It feels like my stomach is on fire. I'm about to implode.

I take a step back, walking around Nico without saying a word, heading towards the artwork. I try to breathe to let my heart rate slow down, he isn't at my side yet, and it's frustrating me so much I want to break down and cry. I've never once in my life felt jealousy this intense.

I stop looking at a picture from across the room. My heart rate slows down, and I let out a laugh. When I was at Hayleys house last year in my year off, I went into her art room and started screwing around with a canvas. I cannot paint, that didn't stop me, I grabbed blue paint, and a paintbrush and I went for it. I drew a small table, with a teddy bear and a girl sitting at a table for a tea party. Of course, my bear didn't look like a bear, and the girl looked like a stick man that was all arms and legs because it was sitting on the floor. The table was taller than the girl. Hayley did her voodoo magic and painted two girls sitting across a wooden table both in blue dresses, a purple tea set, and a brown teddy bear. She made my idea into a masterpiece.

I feel the sparkles from Hayley's dress rubbing against my bare skin. "I got offered eighty grand for this." I let out a puff of air. "I said no."

I crank my head towards her in shock. "You deserve it. I'll send it to Nico's."

"Thank you. You could send it to my dad's house? Or my dorm?" I look at her squinting my eyes, "A place I actually live would be wonderful."

Hayley looks at me giving me a low effort smile and a laugh, "Oh shut the fuck up. Open your eyes." She turns around talking to other ticket holders.

Dad hugs me with one arm, "I'm sorry Cam. I don't trust him."

"Why because suddenly getting pregnant is a worry? He is my friend." I roll my eyes looking at the picture.

"No. I just don't trust him. Something's off."

"Start trusting him, Dad. I'm not going to just stop every relationship because you don't trust someone who comes into my life."

Dad nods. Not saying anything else.

"Sorry Cameron. Papers for Hayley, she needed signed." He looks away from a picture noticing my dad beside me. "There was a cool looking zebra thing back there. It was black and white stripes, so Zebra? I have no idea what's going on." Nico scratches the back of his neck, crunching his nose. He's way too good at taking the awkward out of situations.

Dad lets out a laugh. "I feel that." He walks away.

That was at least something right?

I lightly nudge my shoulder against Nico's arm slowly walking past the art, taking champagne glasses off a server's trays as they walk by. I'm so proud of Hayley. She's worked her entire life at this. She's been pushing herself. She's locked herself away for days at a time to master a portrait. Archie would leave her food outside of the door and take the dirty dishes away, so she didn't have to leave the room. He left her absolutely no distractions, so she could create all of this.

Archie throws his body into mine, almost making me drop the drink. Thankfully Nico was on standby grabbing it out of my hands before it landed onto the ground. Wherever I need Nico, he's right there before I even say anything.

"I'm so proud of you guys!" I shriek.

Archie looks at me confused.

"She couldn't have done this without you. You're the reason for all of this. Thank you for everything you do for her." I exhale before I start crying.

Archie looks at me tenderly. "I didn't do anything Cam."

"Those days you reminded her to go to the bathroom, drink water, and to eat, did everything for her."

When I was writing my book, I forgot to pee, I went an entire day with no water by accident, and almost two days with no food. Having someone there when you're a passionate person, just to make sure all your basic needs are met, means everything. When you're like me or Hayley, getting caught up in something means forgetting we need to breathe in order to stay alive.

"I'll keep doing it." He looks at Nico, sticking his hand out. I grab my glass giving Nico a free hand to shake Archie's hand. "If you hurt her, my wife's a little psychotic." He walks away.

Nico looks at me holding down a laugh. "So, it wouldn't be out of reach for her to paint a picture with my blood?"

God, laughing for him looks so natural now.

Every piece of work looks so different from the next. Hayley can't choose what she likes to paint more of, she doesn't want to tie herself down to one thing. It makes her feel restricted, cuts down on her creativity. She has abstract drawings of towns on the ocean side, famous stores, and forests. One wall is an entire story. The first canvas starts off with a knight coming face to face with a dragon, the dragon slays the knight, then comes home to its little dragon family.

Her and Archie never had kids, the dragon family is the only thing in here that has anything due to a parent. There's a lot of pictures with a girl and two boys. I'm assuming it is her brother's Spencer, and Josh. There are kids playing hide and seek, I counted eight. It's one of those pictures where everything is camouflaged, so you have to hunt to find them.

I walk up to Britney, "What's the appropriate amount of time to stay before leaving? I've looked at every single one twice, I don't want to be rude."

She laughs. "Just go. We're heading out soon too, there's a line up waiting to come in."

I link my arm to Nico's walking out the door.

After tonight I'm fully convinced that the only way you will find good pizza is if the company doesn't have a neon sign in the window claiming to be the best pizza in New York City.

Nico picks up the slice of cheese pizza, it's shiny with grease. Both of us lick our lips staring at it. "I'm trying to ignore the fact that you're way too overdressed," He speaks with his mouth full just like I do, and a sense of pride washes through me, I'm destroying him.

"I'm so sorry that Hayley is delivering her painting to your place. I have no idea what she was thinking."

He looks at me with wide eyes, "That was weird right?"

"Not to mention, my dad. I'm so sorry Nico. Everything that could have possibly gone wrong tonight did."

Nico reaches across the table, wrapping his fingers around my arm, "Cami, I'm fine with parents not liking me. It's no sweat off my shoulders. I was more bothered by how upset you looked."

I give him a weak smile. My dad absolutely destroyed me saying that. One thing I don't like about that man is that he holds grudges. I'm surprised he was even at the art show tonight, something happened with him and Hayley twenty-five years ago, and he still doesn't particularly like her. Hayley put in effort, Archie tried to get to know him, Adam tried to talk to dad to put whatever it was between them behind him, nothing worked. Being a girl my friend groups in middle school, and high school, went through phases where we were no longer friends. Once our friendship broke the first time, my dad lost all respect for them. Suddenly me trying to make plans with them when we were back being friends became nearly impossible. Maybe that's why I forgive so easily? I could never imagine holding something against someone like that. Now I'm worried that Dad will never change his mind about Nico, I'm worried he will never give him the chance he deserves.

"Cameron." Nico whispers my name, "Maybe one day he will change his mind."

"Yeah." I give him a tired smile. "Let's drink."

Nico smiles at me before flagging down the server. My heart stops beating in my chest, my breathing is cut off for a moment, making me gasp when air is welcomed in my lungs again. When he smiles, it's like the entire world just stops moving.

I fall on Nico's bed. I wasn't prepared to stay the night here again. I tried to go back to the dorm. We both drank a lot. He wanted to make sure I was safe. He was very persistent. So, I came home with him. I'm wearing a black shirt of his. It's black like everything else he wears. I never really paid much attention to his clothes until I opened his closet. Everything he owns is either black, dark grey, or dark blue. I don't know how I never noticed it before, he needed a splash of color in his wardrobe like yesterday.

Nico falls on the bed beside me. "I had so much fun tonight."

I roll over facing the wall covering myself up, I thank him for coming with me, for the pizza, the alcohol. There's a lot more I want to thank him for, I don't know how to say it, I don't know how to admit it to myself. So, I don't say anything past the pizza parlor. I stay silent.

I feel Nico grabbing the blanket, covering himself up. Instantly the warmth from his body radiates towards me. The mattress creaks ever so lightly, I feel him shift. He's facing towards me, tonight he's staying further away from me than normal.

I don't like that.

One of our phones buzzes on the end table near his bed making the room shine bright. Our eyes meet, his dark brown eyes look broken, it looks like he's shattering into a million pieces right in front of me. I lay on my back, still looking at him.

The phone goes off again, I give him a weak smile.

The room turns dark, I feel the warmth getting closer to me, right before Nico's lips land on mine. I don't pull away this time, I search for his shirt, grabbing a handful pulling him in as close as he will possibly get to me. Then I let our lips touch for the very first time.

I push him down on his back, not pulling our lips away from one another. I open my mouth slightly feeling his urgency, his tongue strokes mine, and I readjust myself, climbing on top of him.

Nico's body quivers weakly under me, as I sit directly on top of him.

He's so hard my jaw shakes, making me pull away gasping for air.

His hand strokes my panties, I use one arm on the mattress, and one on his chest to keep myself levitated to give him room. I kiss his lips tenderly, then I kiss his neck, licking him, biting him softly, when his fingers enter inside me making me instantly moan.

He moves his hands fast, moving his fingers inside of me, I'm not even sure what he's doing, but it's making my head fucking spin. Another moan erupts from my throat. I frantically move, taking him out of me, taking his sweatpants off, and moving his boxers down. He springs out, I stroke my hand around him, spitting, stroking again I climb on top of him, kissing him, guiding him into me.

Nico grabs my hips slamming me into him. "This is a terrible idea." His words don't even sound like words mixed in with his pleasure from my rhythmic moving.

I lean down kissing him, then moving my lips to his ear, "There's nothing terrible about us."

Nico flips me over onto my back, he kisses me slowly, then moves faster, making me grab the sheets on the mattress feeling my eyes roll to the back of my head calling out his name.

"Mia ama, sono stato addestrato per ucciderti, tutto di noi é cattivo." Nico kisses me, letting his lips hover over mine.

I dig my nails into his back, "That's what got us here." My words are shallow with pleasure.

He laughs, and that sound alone is almost going to drive me towards another orgasm. "Ti amo."

He speeds up, my nails fall from his back, landing on his bed, another orgasm takes over my body, one after another. My legs are shaking. Nico pulls out, I sit up quickly before he has the chance to move. I guide him into my mouth, stroking him, his hands are in my hair, he holds on tight to me as he lets out a moan saying my name, his entire body tenses and I swallow every drop from him.

I wipe my mouth, pulling him towards me, "Come here."

Nico doesn't hesitate. We're lying in bed wrapped up in each other.

"We can't do that again." His words are quiet.

I don't say anything, I just nod, because I do not agree with him, not at all.

It's quiet between us, it's only our breathing, and I'm scared he regrets it. "I'm sorry." It comes out like a whimper.

"Two beds for now on, okay? Distance ourselves a bit."

Yeah, he regrets it.

I close my eyes tight trying to hold down my tears from surfacing.

14

Nico

"What the fuck is this?" I stare in disbelief.

Bones stand in front of me, "Tick tock."

I have my hand in a fist, stepping forward to knock his ass out when Tiny lights the fire behind me. The heat rushes up my back, distracting me from Bones ghostly face. I turn my body watching the flames move around the circle quickly igniting all of the fire starter.

It's a literal ring of fire. I can't pull my eyes away.

"Stop!" I scream, holding onto the metal cage. Tears soaking my face.

These bars are thick. The metal has turned completely black, and it's rough on my skin. It feels like pieces of metal are falling off, it's cutting into me. I look down, through the spaces of the bars that's under me. There's something on the ground, it makes a complete circle, I have no idea what it is. I think it's small chunks of wood. I'm levitating in the middle of it, at least thirty feet in the air, dangling by chains hooked up to the roof. I was trying to move around looking for an escape, the cage was moving too much. Every time I move, the cage swings.

Bones pushes a button on the wall. The cage jolts as it lowers, the chains are making a high pitch squealing noise. I want to cover my ears. If I let go of the metal, I'm scared I'm going to swing too much from the movement. They lowered me about halfway, the squeaking stopped. Tiny waddles over throwing something burning onto the wood circle. Within a second the fire roars. Thick smoke circles its way up to me, followed quickly by the heat. I'm coughing, I can hardly breathe.

"You're sixteen, stop fucking crying!" Bones screams at me. He mimics me coughing.

"No more than five minutes." Dad screams as he slams the door behind him.

'Why is he doing this to me? Why does he do this to me? No other kids get put through this. Why me?' I think to myself. Counting the seconds in my mind, until I'm out.

I retreat my hands back to my body. My hands heated up. The slight movement from me pulling my hands away has the cage rocking. I'm way too light for this. The bars under my feet are heating up even faster, I physically can't sit, because it will burn my entire lower half. I can't stand anymore because I'm coughing and sending too many movements, it's already hard enough to stay balanced from the separated bars. I squat. I need to center myself. My shoes are melting under my feet. I can't see inches in front of my face. I cough again hard, causing me to lose my center of gravity and falling over. My side instantly alerts my brain of pain. I don't react the way I should pain anymore, I suck in smoke, bracing myself as I rip my side off the bar. I let out a scream feeling my skin burning. Feeling the heat through my melted shoes.

It feels like I'm melting.

I blink. Dad can't be serious. My training was meant to break me, not to make me relive my PTSD.

"Who is it?" I ask Tiny, trying to completely ignore Bones.

"Cop. He gave the Lion info on some drug smugglers. Boss was done with him. Cop had too much on us, and he dies." Tiny shrugs.

I feel like I'm going to puke. I raise my hand to my mouth. All the smoke is going directly up, not much of it is lingering down with us. His screaming fills the air. My heart gets heavy, pounding hard and fast in my chest. My palms are sweating, my hands are shaking, my knee is bouncing in small motions. I close my eyes. I need to distract myself.

Cameron's face flashes in my mind, I hold onto her as tight as I possibly can. I focus on her, instead of what is happening here. She's so close to me, I just want to touch her face. I just want to be able to tell her I love her in a language she can understand. I want to explain to her that I said separate beds because this is what I want her distanced from. I need her to be distanced from me. I need her to know that I will go through any length to protect her, from becoming what I am. I think of her drinking the milkshake, I think of the sun hitting her face just right on the rooftop. I see the look on her face when I laughed for the first time, I focus on her being in my arms.

His screaming pulls me back into reality, making Cameron's face turn into dust, completely blowing from my mind.

"You look— uncomfortable Nico." Dad appears out of nowhere. "You're going soft. I have to make sure you're on track with the plan, or this will be her. She will sit in that cage until she agrees, then some."

"I'm sure I can find something worse." Bones smirks looking at the cage. "I think you found his weakness."

My words come out quickly. "Absolutely fucking not."

I back up looking at the controller. It makes no sense. There's a green button, then a yellow, and red. Tiny prompts me that the yellow goes down, and red is up. Whoever made this, is an idiot. I press the green one for a few seconds before letting go. The chains are so loud screeching against each other, I'm fighting with my mind not to relive that memory.

"In order to have a weakness, you need emotions." I mumble.

Cameron still has time, I don't know what game dad is playing, I'm not putting up with this shit. She will be free. I don't care what I need to do. I'm pissed. I'm ready to go to war, even if I'm alone. Nothing like this will ever happen to her, I don't care what it takes. The woman I love will not have her life controlled by him.

"I'm getting impatient." Dad barks at me, he always tries to use big voices around me to scare me. Nothing scares me now, and he can't wrap his head around that.

"Patience is a fucking virtue, Dad." I smash the green button with my palm letting the cage fall. From the corner of my eye, I see the chains come to a complete stop hovering inches over the fire.

I move my head over my shoulder, I don't need to see what is going to happen next. The room is filled with high pitch screams, then suddenly, the screaming stops.

"See. No weakness." I walk past him leaving the room as quickly as I can before the smell of burning flesh makes my stomach turn even more.

I need to feel peace, even though I don't deserve it.

She is my weakness. She is the only thing that's important to me. This wasn't supposed to happen like this.

I need to see her.

It's selfish for me to want her to save me.

I'm every single type of fucked up right now.

15

Cameron

My exams are in two days.

Two days.

I still have seven semesters after this one. I'm not even sure how I'm going to survive it. This is stressful. More than anything I just want to sleep it off. I love school, I love studying, I love learning, this stress is a lot. I can't stop crying. I'm stressing myself out even more. I have so many more semesters left.

A loud alarm sounds in the hallway, making me jump four feet off the mattress. My heart stopped in my chest. I exhale a long breath with my hand on my chest feeling irregular heart palpitations. That scared the shit out of me. It was so quiet, now the loudest war alarm I've ever heard is sounding. I move off my bed standing up to my door looking out the peephole. There's a red light making a full rotation in the glass. I lock my door, ignoring it. If it's a fire, the floors are not hot yet. I'm fine.

It doesn't sound like a fire alarm.

I sit back down trying to do my flashcards, but I can't focus. That alarm is seriously loud. I turn on my phone, checking to see if I have a notification of some sort. This is New York, it could be anything.

This is not a drill. A robot voice goes on the PA. I didn't even realize there was a PA system.

I call my dad, there's no answer.

I call Spencer, he doesn't answer.

Red and blue light up the dark outside, there's no sirens coming from the cars, it's just colors.

The PA sounds again, *do not leave your dorms, lock the doors.*

My breathing becomes shallow. My hands are shaking.

"Answer." My voice pleads.

"Need a break from studying?" Nico asks, his voice light.

"Somethings going on at the dorm." Panic thick in my voice, my heart is beating faster than ever before, I didn't even know that was possible. I have to yell to be heard over the alarm.

The PA sounds again, telling us not to leave the rooms.

"The police are outside. I'm scared."

"Okay Cami, listen to me." His voice is so calm he's almost making me calm down. "Slide the other bed so it's blocking the door."

Screaming from the main floor echo's all the way up to me.

"Do it now. I'll wait." He sounds like he's out of breath.

I set my phone on my blankets, rushing over to the other bed. I drag it by the footboard towards the door, running around to the other side of the bed, I push it at the headboard, blocking the entire door with the twin size bed. That's not going to hold, it'll have to do. I have no choice.

I pant, picking up the phone. "I did it."

"I'm not far from your dorm. Go around grab anything with your name, or anything that your identification could be pulled from. Be fast."

"Why?" I ask even though I'm already stuffing my laptop in my backpack, along with my wallet, filled with my credit cards, school ID, and fake ID.

"Because that shit's important, and you will be staying with me for now on. I need you to climb out your window. You need to jump." His words hardly sound like words right now.

"Nico" I hiss, I'm on the second floor, he's crazy. I must have heard him wrong.

Over the alarm I hear loud thuds, screams that soon fade. I hear loud pounding, then more screams. Whatever is happening is happening right down the hall from me. I grab my textbooks and stuff them in my bag.

I open the window, my body is telling me to stay, that's a long way down. But my mind is telling me to leave. Nico is right under my window on the grass. His face is lit up from the police lights. I want to fight whatever is going on, I also want to escape towards him. I try to breath my way through, until my door rocks hard. Whoever is on the other side is fighting against the lock.

"Cami." Nico's voice shakes on the other line. "Keep your feet pressed tight against each other."

I hang up my phone, stuffing it into my backpack, I put it on leaping out the window.

I close my eyes, feeling myself being pulled down by gravity, I try to listen and keep my legs close, I'm falling out a damn window, it's hard not to flare my limbs out.

I land hard, on my feet, instantly being held against Nico, and feeling the brick wall stopping us from moving further.

I slowly open my eyes, staring into Nico's dark eyes. I'm okay. I never died, I don't think.

I pull my eyes away, watching police officers, after police officers passing back and forth talking to each other, holding up radios, watching what's going on around the building.

One watches us walking close, "Were you in there?"

I nod, "Doors are getting kicked in. Why is no one in there helping!" I take a step forward, feeling a pain shoot up in my foot. I fall against Nico letting out a cry.

"My foot. Oh my God." I let out a whimper. "Why did you tell me to do that?" I look around Nico, my face is suddenly frozen. I think I'm crying, and the winter air is turning my tears into ice. I'm numb, I can't feel a thing.

"You falling means you were safer." Nico wipes my face with his sweater.

It's three am. My eye bags have eye bags. My phone has been going off constantly, every single person but my mother has texted me multiple times and called me. My dad even called Hayley to see if I talked to her once I didn't respond to him.

He's not happy I never came home, he's even less happy a boy talked me into jumping out a window on the second floor.

Max got a hold of me, he wasn't working, he demanded answers. I was the only person who got injured. There's just a lot of shaken up girls, and a lot of broken doors. My door was the last one that was broken, whoever it was fled after my room.

Now I'm sitting here with a clunky ass boot. My foot has swollen so much, and now I'm on crutches until I can walk. This pain is intolerable. Walking is a nightmare. I'm tired. Nico looks like he's about to break down. He hasn't said a single word to me in over an hour.

I close my eyes, I'm tired, in pain, and I'm bitchy. It's three am. He doesn't need to be talking right now. He sat with me at the hospital, he pushed my wheelchair to the X-ray, he held my clothes when I went in, and he waited by the door for me to come out. He showed up at my dorm when I was terrified, he's been right beside me all night. I swear, I couldn't function some days without him. This is definitely one of those days.

"I know you said no sleeping together, but can I please stay in your bed with you?" My voice is tiny.

Nico stands in front of me at the couch, he bends down, hovering over me putting his arms on the back of the couch, "Hug my neck."

I do, he straightens out, and I carefully put my legs around his middle, digging my face into his neck. He smells musky. I know I'm in pain, I know we're both tired, it's just hard to fight the urge not to kiss his neck. The only thing that's stopping me is knowing he would absolutely hate it if I did. I really don't want to add to his regrets, again.

He stops, bending down on the bed letting me let go.

I let go of his neck landing on my back rolling over, not saying a single word. I almost forgot he regretted it, until now. I tried to remember some of the words he said to me so I could translate it on the internet, but I don't remember anything he said. I'm not even sure what language it was. All I know is hearing him speak another language was sexy as hell. Speaking other languages is attractive, I think it's the fact he's opening up to me I found appealing. As soon as he starts to open up, we come to a sudden halt, and he closes off again.

The door opens, the light in the hallway almost blinds me from the darkness in his bedroom. I blink watching Nico come into my line of view, shutting the lights off. He's in a different shirt. We've spent countless nights together since we met, and I've never seen him without a shirt on.

I wouldn't have cared before, but I've slept with him, and now it just feels weird not to see him without a shirt.

"I'll get a key cut for you tomorrow." He lays in bed facing my back, wrapping his arm around my middle.

"I'm not staying."

"Like hell you aren't. Not after that. Thirty days at least please." He presses, there's not a chance for me to even try to argue, he's dead set on me staying. His tone is not leaving it up for debate. "You'll be safe here."

I want to argue. I don't like this idea. I don't want to stay with him. I want my own space, my own alone time. I don't want to live with him. I don't have time to stay awake arguing. I have an exam in a few hours, and I need to try to sleep off whatever the fuck happened tonight.

16

Nico

I toss my fork on my tray. I have one class. One fucking class, and I need to eat this damn food every single day so I can try to get closer to Cameron. I just can't stop eating lunch here, even though she's in my bed, she'll put it together that somethings off if I'm home all day.

"Woah bro. Are you okay?" Gabe stairs at the table across from me.

I don't look at him, I haven't spoken to him since my father decided he could break up with Lucia. I haven't spoken to Lucia since then either. It's been peaceful. Seeing her that much was almost sickening.

I almost hate Cameron. Ever since our rooftop at the museum she's made me feel my feelings. I despise it. If I'm sad, I want to cry, if I'm angry I want to fucking scream, if I'm happy, I smile. I laughed for the first time around her in years. I want to say I hate her, I wish I could mean it. I don't. I don't have it in me to hate her. What happened last night was because my father was trying to send me a message that I'm weak, and he has complete control over the both of us. She is nothing but a pawn to him.

She's not a lion, she's not even a snake.

And my father is going to make sure she picks the winning team.

I fucking hate the Basilisk that exchanged their life for hers.

"No." I let out a weak sigh. I'm weak. I'm vulnerable now. "Did you hear about last night?" I look at Gabe for the first time in weeks.

He cautiously looks around us, "I was in the building with Ashley. On the third floor, we were both ready to destroy them."

"My father's goons stopped at her door."

Gabe pulls his eyebrows in, looking at me in shock. "I haven't heard anything."

He wouldn't. He's no longer a part of the job anymore.

Cameron falls at the table, landing into me hard. My reflexes quickly grab her, pulling her into me. She looks up at me with tears about to pool over her eyes, "I think I failed that test. I'm in so much pain. I was passing, so I'm not worried." She pauses, taking a staggered breath reflecting her pain. "I'm sorry if I was bitchy last night."

I help her readjust in the seat, so she can rest her elbows on the table. She looks at me again, I swipe a stray tear with my thumb, rubbing her back with my free hand.

"What happened to you?" Gabe asks, his question hovering over us. He asked so quickly, I couldn't even acknowledge and reject her apology.

"He told me to leap, so I did." Cameron exhales deeply, "Out the second floor. It's just a bad sprain, but it may as well be broken at this point."

"Last exam is in an hour?" I watch her nod. "You are not leaving my bed. You need to relax. Got it?" I shove my tray towards her, "I will fight you." I reach into her bag seeing her bottle of pain medication, I shake it, dropping it on a napkin laying on the table within her reach.

She leans into me slightly, I think it's her way of saying thank you? I don't fucking know.

Gabe looks at me exhaling his cheeks full of air, his face is written with an expression telling me I'm fucked. "What are you going to do?"

I look at him frowning, shaking my head, my eyes are locked on the ceiling tiles as I find my words. "I have no idea."

Cameron picks at my food, completely distracted by her mind, she never even clued into our conversation. I wrap my arm around her, pulling her into me kissing her hair, I look at Gabe, his expression is as dumbfounded as I feel. "I have no idea."

After saying it twice, I realize how bad this is.

Every day that passes it's getting worse.

Her time is cut short, there's nothing I can do other than fight my way out of it.

Tick tock. Bones' haunting voice echoes in my head.

17

Cameron

"He told you to jump out of the window, so you just went for it? Fuckin' YOLO." Dad shakes his head in disbelief. The veins in his neck are throbbing. "Jesus Cameron. I hope you're in so much pain."

"I am." I whisper.

I'm not just in pain from my foot. I'm in pain from my crutches digging into my sides. My foot was so swollen last night I don't even want to know how big it is now. This boot is awkward. It's wintertime and I'm struggling trying to get around outside. I'm so mad I listened to Nico. I'm almost convinced the x-ray lied, and it's broken.

Dad can't even look at me. So, I look at the wall behind him. This is the house he had when mom moved in. We're on the main floor, because well, he's too angry to let me use the stairs to get to the other living room with the TV in it. I'm just thankful this house has a fireplace in it, the crackling is saving a tiny bit of the awkwardness.

The cracking isn't saving us from much awkwardness by any means.

"Why?" his voice rises, "You have never been this stupid before. What is going on with you?" He stands, looking at me dead in the eyes, I look away not being able to make eye contact with him. "You are grabbing your shit, and you're coming back here."

I snap my head looking at him, feeling anger bubbling in me, "No. You don't have a say of who can or can't be in my life. You live so far away from the school."

"Watch me." He yells even louder.

I don't jump. I don't react. I just sit here, watching him get angrier and angrier. "Stop trying to control me. Did you say the same shit to mom before she left?"

The words fell out of my mouth, his face crumbling right in front of me.

"Dad, I'm sorry." I spit the words out, "Daddy." The word leaves my mouth in a whimper.

He exhales, shakes his head, turns around and walks toward the door, before he opens it, he says, "I know the dangers hidden in this city, smarten up and listen to me when I say I don't want you near him." The house shakes from the door closing hard.

Tears pool in my eyes, I'm so stupid.

I grab my phone, ordering a ride.

I fall into Nico's door unlocking it with tears falling down my face. I slam the door letting my body collapse against the wall letting out a scream, I toss my crutches across the entryway in anger, my back slowly sinks, until I'm sitting on the floor. I've never hated myself so much before. The look on my dad's face, the pain each time I take a step, the struggles I had today trying to write my finals, everything is going to shit.

I try to calm down, then the lies keep piling up from everyone. It all started from mom. Everyone has been avoiding their past by refusing to answer any of my questions. Dad knows the danger? How?

What dangers are lurking in the city? Why does my dad hate Hayley as much as he does? The scars on all of my uncles bodies, Charlie, Hayley, and Brittney all have the same ones, they're small, circular what is it from? I've asked, and everyone just shut the conversation down so fast by changing the subject, or pretending they never heard me, making me feel like a moron. I ask questions, and they make me feel crazy by deflecting me. How is everyone so rich? I ask, and all I get is "It's been passed down" or "Parents life insurance." I'm so tired of this.

I just want one person. One person to tell me what's going on. I feel like I'm going insane trying to Google my family to find answers. I want to know why I have a tracker on my phone, and not like every other teenager who just checks in with their parents.

I take a shaky breath, I don't see red this time, and I break down crying.

"Oh shit." Nico shuts the main door, he kneels in front of me, I don't look at him. Instead, I watch the snow on the souls of his shoes melt into a puddle. "Stand up."

My crying slows down, I listen to him. I'm refusing to look at him, I'm stuck looking at the floor, no one is going to see me looking like this, especially him.

"What happened?"

At least he never asked me something stupid like *are you okay?* I would straight up punch him if he asked me that. I stand leaning against him, letting him hold me. I'm tired of the never ending lies from everyone.

"Why did you tell me to jump?" I wipe my nose with my sweater, still not letting him see me.

"The screaming, I couldn't get to you, I needed you to come to me. I'm sorry it was stupid, I had no idea what was happening, all I knew was I needed to protect you. Is this about that?" His voice is so light, so tender, so caring. I melt into him, finally getting the truth out of someone.

"This is the after effects of getting into a huge fight with Dad."

His hands intertwined in my hair. He's looking down at me. "What about?"

I sniffle my nose slowly looking up at Nico. I don't say a word. I don't need to. He pulls my head into his chest holding me, keeping me safe. I don't know what it is about him. He can control me without even trying too. He takes the mood right out of me. All the bad feelings in me slowly leave when he enters the room. I let out a shaky breath in his chest. He answered me, he never gave me a bullshit answer that was irrelevant, he never dodged my question. He gave me an honest answer. He was worried about me.

He tells me to get changed. I can't move from his chest. I've never felt security from another person like this, I've never felt so protected.

Suddenly my vision of spending my life with a girl shifts, all I see in my future is Nico.

I look up at him again, I've never seen his eyes look like this before. They're dark brown with a ring of gold. The gold makes his eyes look so much lighter. He has so much emotion on his face. The more I watch him, the harder he has to fight to keep a straight face. His eyes are no longer almost black. He no longer has a cold hard expression on his face. It's hard to look away, because I don't know how long his eyes will be this color, it's so beautiful.

"We still have to watch the fifth movie." I whisper sniffling my nose.

A smile breaks across his face, as he backs away from me creating space between us.

I kick my shoe off my good foot swallowing hard. Whatever I was feeling, whatever those thoughts were just now, need to stay in the very back of my mind.

I always get so screwed up after sex.

18

Nico

Somehow, we ended up on the conversation of Christmas, and now I'm standing face to face with a life size plastic snowman with bright lights, in Brooklyn. I hate Brooklyn. It's the knock off version of Manhattan, with less to do. Cameron tugs on my arm, drawing my attention away from the plastic snowman. I turn around facing where she's pointing, closing my eyes trying to get the little spots created by the light to fade from my vision. The only reason why we came here was because she wanted to go for a drive, so one expensive ass cab ride later we arrived.

There's a horse carriage, I don't even get to agree before she limps over to it. Walking down a neighborhood, with her in a boot was probably the stupidest idea we could have come up with. Thankfully, this will get her off her feet. Her jumping out the window seemed like the most rational thing to do. Actually, it still seems like rational thinking. As guilty as I felt when she was in the hospital, the truth is, I had no idea what was going to happen when they got their hands on her. I still don't know if they were going to take her or leave her. She's fine, well kind of. I will make the same choice again. I've even came to the second-guessing thoughts that maybe it wasn't my dad. Then I realize, if it wasn't dad, they never would have stopped at her door. They never would have done it the night dad accused me of her being my weakness. It was all too coincidental.

I feel guilty on a daily basis now. That's another new raw emotional response to add to my list. I know what would have happened if she was in that room when they pushed the door open, that still isn't making me feel better about the pain that she is in now. I wanted to take the pain away. There was nothing I could have done differently. I couldn't tell her the truth, so I had to let a part of her hate me. I can't tell Erik why I made her jump out the fucking window, so I need to let him hate me.

Maybe it's better if he hates me, I'm only going to destroy her anyways. If he didn't hate me, I would feel even worse. Cue more guilt. I honestly don't know how much guilt I can carry around with me.

Cameron digs in her bag, I race up to the carriage, stepping in front of her passing the guy two $5 bills. Like hell she's paying, for anything ever again. Ever.

I step up the ladder, turning around grabbing her hand to pull her up. She grabs onto the railing hesitantly pulling herself up the stairs. Her boot is bigger than the damn stairs. I can't believe I was put in the position to do this to her, right after what my father put me through. I had no time to come to terms with what happened to me before Cameron called me.

She sits down beside me, watching people line up, paying for the shortest carriage ride in history. We're only going down the street a few blocks.

"I was thinking." She slaps her knees with her mittens looking at me, "Do you do anything for Christmas?"

Oh God. "I don't have anything to do with my family." *If it's not work related.*

"I'm definitely not inviting myself to that then. You're coming with me." She smiles at me.

Every time she smiles at me, I feel my internal temperature skyrocket. It legit feels like I'm melting from the inside out. "That's a terrible idea."

"Probably. But it'll be fine. There's a shit ton of people. We rent a hall. Dad won't even see you. What could go wrong?"

I know how her Christmas' go. It's all the family she's normally with, and her mom. They mix in a few extra friends, it's a crowd. Which means, I'm going to be stuck in a room with two people I hate as much as my parents, plus her dad who probably wants me dead. I don't know how I'm supposed to look at her mother and not ask her how she doesn't love Cameron. Everything could go wrong, absolutely everything. I look at her pleading to let me off the hook, she smiles again.

She doesn't know it yet, as soon as she smiles at me, she gets her way. I'm mentally cursing myself out.

"Oh, there's lots of people here now. No arguing, there witness to agree that your silence is a yes."

The woman sitting next to her says something, drawing Cameron's attention to her, her body shakes from laughter before scooching over to me, letting them adjust.

She's practically sitting on my lap at this point. I'm tempted to put her on top of my lap and wrap my arms around her tightly.

The carriage jolts forwards, making her squeak. Her face lit up from the lights around us. Her eyes are twinkling, her smile is brighter than the colorful lights, she watches people on the carriage. She watches their reactions to everything, while not missing a single thing from the other side of the road. She moves, just slightly and a floral scent comes up from her jacket, making my heartbeat speed up to a rate that really can't be healthy. My stomach ties itself in knots, I can't stop watching her.

I lean in, whispering in her ear, "Ti amo."

"You make me wish I took another language in high school." She laughs. "What did you say?"

It doesn't matter. "Only time will tell."

Only it won't. I can never tell her. As far as the Lions concerned, she's a job. Only one of two things are going to happen, and her loving me by the end of this, isn't going to happen. I'm either going to be dead, or she's going to hate me so much I'm going to wish I was dead. Neither one of those leads us to the happy ending that I surprisingly want.

She shivers, I don't hesitate to wrap my arm around her pulling her in even closer, feeling the carriage turn around to look at the other side of the street.

Me feeling this way about her goes against all my training.

I was trained to not have emotion.

I was broken to not feel anything.
If she dies, I die.
End of story.

19

Cameron

Last night I stood staring at the Rockefeller Christmas Tree for hours. I couldn't take my eyes off the lights, I couldn't stop watching the people around the tree, I couldn't pull myself away from the Christmas cheer. I was so cold. The lights were too pretty to not look at. I one hundred percent looked like a tourist. It's not something you can photograph. You can't photograph the lights as they sparkle, you can't photograph the people's emotions. I had to stand there and soak up every last detail.

I wanted to be like Buddy the Elf and start singing so loudly. If I was able to dance around, I would have.

I've always been so numb at Christmas, something inside me has shifted this year. I'm less numb, I'm still dreading family time with my mom, but I'm less numb.

I'm just going to assume it's because of Nico. I think it's a really safe assumption.

"Yup this is an entire hall... for your big ass family." He takes a deep breath, he's already overwhelmed.

"I wasn't kidding. There's a lot of us." I sigh.

I've always loved how big my family is, I can't keep up with so many people. I'm thankful for having everyone, there's just a lot of people to follow up on. When you try to have your own life, it's way too easy to accidentally forget to call someone.

"You are going to need this." Josh passes Nico a glass of alcohol, it's probably whiskey and ginger. "Drink it."

Nico jugs it back at an impressive rate, William's wife passes me a drink without saying a word before she walks away. She's a blonde blur leaving as fast as she came. If it wasn't for her warm smile, I probably wouldn't even have registered it was her.

William, Max, Theo, and Dillon are all married to someone other than the regular faces in my family and I hardly know them. They rarely come around. Well to be honest, I can't really blame Dillon's husband for not coming around their wives. They are all the type of girls to get their nails done, and eyelashes done twice a month. Dillon's husband will not hesitate to organize a 'girls' night', but only one night. He gets overwhelmed by women.

I feel that. I hate girls.

But I also love them.

It's complicated really.

"I'm assuming my mother's here?" I grip the cup hard.

"Yeah… so, do we just light her car on fire, or just her?" Hayley speaks from behind me.

I spin on my toes giving her a one armed hug. "Move here please."

"I'm thinking we do her car, so it looks like an accident." William speaks up behind me.

"Give me three good reasons to come back." Hayley smiles.

Nico clears his throat, "Cameron." Hayley laughs. "Famous New York pizza, and Cameron. It would get me here, just saying." He puts his free hand up in defence in front of him.

I roll my eyes pushing Nico backwards away from the group so we're standing alone, dad just walked in, and he won't approach us if we're alone. As much as it looks like I'm avoiding him, I'm not. I haven't spoken to him since the other night. It's super immature on both of our parts. I don't know how I'm supposed to talk to him. I don't even know what me and Nico are, I can't ignore what we do have because of my father's disapproval. I get it, he cares about me, I'm nineteen, allow me to have some freedom. Everything in my body is hoping Nico isn't a mistake, and if he is, dad needs to let me make that mistake on my own.

Nico looks down at me with a weak smile, ever since he picked me off the floor crying, that light brown color has been in his eyes. He puts his free hand that's not holding his drink on my elbow, "Cami. I can go. I'm not going to get in the middle. I don't want to cause more issues than I already have."

"Don't go. We both lost our tempers. It's my fault I made it worse." My bottom lip quivers, it takes every muscle in my body not to cry. "I accused him of mom leaving us because of him. He only stayed with her for me. I destroy everything in my path."

Nico wipes a tear from my face before it has the chance to fall, "You don't destroy anything. If you ask me, you put things together."

"Minus my parents' life." I try to press him on what he meant, I feel someone walking up to us.

"Sorry man. Didn't know she was bringing a plus one." Dillon hands the green reindeer onesie to me.

I walk away listening to Nico reassuring Dillon that he will survive. It sounds like Dillon agrees. Then they both start laughing. The sound of Nico laughing sends a chill up my spine. I need more of that sound.

After changing, I shove my clothes in my bag body pushing on the swinging bathroom door open to see Spencer waiting for me.

"January 3rd."

I look at him confused, still stuffing my sweater in my bag.

"His birthday, I had to bribe the girls in the office. He'll be nineteen."

Oh my God, I forgot I asked to find out Nico's birthday. "Thank you. Thank you. Thank you!" I leap the best I can, giving Spencer a hug.

His birthday is in a few days. I have no time to plan. I don't even know who his friends are, he likes everything we eat, I can't even pick his favorite food. As long as it doesn't live in a shell in the ocean, anything will suffice. I can't do something just for us, I'm not his girlfriend, that's weird. It's right after new year's. I have to make sure he doesn't overdue the alcohol on New Year's Eve. If that's even possible. This is going to be impossible. My thoughts are running way too fast for me to handle.

"You're overthinking this." Spencer says quickly, like he's reading my mind. "Talk to him, women. Use big words."

"It's just a birthday. I just have to make it perfect. No pressure. It's fine."

"That's definitely not what I was talking about."

"What were you talking about?" Dad stands beside Spencer, with his hands in the front pocket of his jeans rocking back and forth.

I hug him without thinking, apologizing profusely, feeling my eyes burning with tears. I'm so sick and tired of feeling one emotion, just to start crying. I want to feel something without crying. I blink hard and fast to stop the tears from falling before I pull away from our hug.

"You brought him I see. That's great. It's really great. Fabulous. If you get hurt one more time in his presence, I will not hesitate to blow up his house." He sides steps me walking into the men's bathroom to change.

Well... that went... good?

I quickly find Nico in the crowd, watching Josh hand him drink after drink. He's slamming back alcohol. Not that I blame him. Spencer gives me a shove in Nico's direction.

"Joshy, can we not poison him please?" I link Nico's arm with mine.

"Your best friend is making me do it. Apparently, rath of Erik, bad." He responds shrugging, "Rath of any Watson bad."

"Very, very bad." Nico nods his head fast.

"Good I have you in your place then." I talk between a locked jaw looking up at him.

Josh and Nico smirk at each other. At the very least, he's getting along with someone, and that's good. I'm kind of surprised at how well they are bonding, I'm not going to complain.

Josh leaves us, I drag Nico to a table. I've been watching for my mother in the corner of my eye, she doesn't once look over at my direction, she watches for her other kids. Liam, Max, and Theo are all with their kids. I want to say it's because of mom they don't come around very much, but they all spend so much time with their kids. They used to have 'daddy meet ups' at the park to make dad friends. They're that involved. That sounds terrible in my opinion. I'll just pump out a bunch of kids, then wait till they're in school to make friends. It can't be *that* hard. Can it? They must have been over dramatic?

God, I hope they were just being over dramatic and I'm not naive.

"Cameron." Nico speaks softly. "Is that your mom, what happened with you two?"

I tell him the truth, that she wasn't ever really a mom, that she left the first chance she could and completely started over.

He faces me in his chair, bending forwards so his forearms are on his thighs, "If we need to leave, just say the word."

Brittney stops at the table with a plate full of chips, and chocolate, she sits down and eats without saying a word to us. I haven't seen her since Spencer got all confessy with me in his classroom, I see her differently in such a good way. I don't know the full back story on Spencer's past, but she stayed with him. I already loved her, now it's amplified. I know my mom's my mom, but Brittney's the only mother figure I've had. Spencer killed someone and she was still right there beside him. They've stepped up my expectations for relationships. Anyone I date is going to have to jump through hoops, and it's all because of how hard they love each other. I can guarantee that Spencer was probably really hard to love back then.

Nico puts his hand on my thigh, still sitting forward, "You're too quiet Cami."

"I just feel off." I whisper.

I'm not lying. A shiver shoots up my spine, and my stomach ties itself in knots. I thought I was just nervous from being in the same building as mom. It feels like I'm going to puke. It's not just that though, there's something else. I thought it was over seeing my dad, I talked to him, I said sorry, and the feeling is still eating at me. I can't tell Nico because he'll think I'm crazy. My intuition is screaming at me that something is wrong. I want to do nothing but cuddle up in his arms on the couch.

"You get no personal space tonight." I keep my voice low, grabbing onto his arm, pulling my chair so I can sit even closer to him.

The table is quickly surrounded by all my aunts and uncles, and their plus ones. The only ones who never brought someone this year are Josh and April. Funny since they used to be married, and they're both dateless.

Nico smiles, then says "List them off please."

I introduced him to absolutely no one the last two times, and I have no idea who he's met already here while I left him alone. "Adam. he's married to Charlie, but she's not here." I turn around looking, I thought I saw her earlier. "Whatever, she's one of the blonde ones. Liam, my mom's husband. The one with the guy is Dillon, his husband's Shawn. William is married to Julie. Spencer, Brittney, Max, Theo— their wives are over there." I wave my hand in their general direction. "You met Hayley, and Archie. you'll always find them like that they know personal space less than I do. Then you recognized my mom, the one that's deliberately trying to avoid me."

Nico presses his lips together, not impressed.

Dad sits beside me ignoring the fact I'm holding onto Nico's arm for dear life.

"Just breathe Cameron." Nico leans in whispering, "Today will be over soon enough."

I exhale looking at the people around me, I've never felt like this at Christmas before, I normally just fit right in, this year has shifted. I'm so thankful he has the power to calm me down. I don't know what's wrong with me. I hate this feeling.

Only a few more hours until we can leave.

Nico moves his hand down to my thigh, squeezing it making me feel grounded.

20

Nico

Cameron shuts the door, obnoxiously kicking off her shoe, running her boot over a towel that's laid out on the ground, before limping away to the bedroom. It's only been a few days since her accident. It feels like weeks. Her foot is still swollen. She winces when she puts her foot on the ground as she walks. She doesn't verbally say it's bothering her. Anymore. It might not even be so much of the pain that's making her struggle, the boot is bulky as hell.

I've come to the realization that I hate two of her 'family members', that's including her mother more than my parents. I thought it was an equal amount of hate, nope. Cameron's family takes the win. The rest of her family though, they're amazing. I also realized I care about her family. I don't care about anyone. I'm fucked up. I fucked up, this entire situation is fucked up. Meeting everyone has made it so much worse for me, and so much harder for me to even think about doing what dad wants me to do to her, to them. I knew her mom's relationship was rocky, but to that extent? I don't know how anyone could ever not want Cameron in their life, she makes everything better. Cameron's smile alone turns a terrible day around. I can't understand how the rest of the world looks at her and doesn't want to hug her. If I was allowed, I'd have such a tight grasp on her at all times.

I noticed a black car parked outside my house. I noticed it all day when my alarms were letting me know continuously of street activity. It also didn't help that I was checking the camera's nonstop checking to see if we were going to be walking into a trap. I thought maybe it was a neighbour's car, company, or family, or whatever. Until it wouldn't leave. It was parked there all bloody day, just watching, waiting.

Cameron screams down the stairs asking if I'm coming. I quickly yell back, ignoring her sudden mood changes. I love her, but chill damn it. All day she would be happy, then a second later she'd be upset. I'm getting whiplash.

Not that I'm in any position to bitch about her moods. Especially right now.

My phone buzzes, I know it's the person behind the wheel outside. *Tick Tock.*

Time's a precious thing, and you're running out.

Anger boils from my toes, all the way up my neck, my blood runs hot, my hand folds into a fist, and before I know it, I drill my hand into the door, feeling a shooting pain up my forearm.

I shake my hand off, kicking my shoes, turning around and walking down the hallway. The pain I felt quickly faded, at least I know I'm still immune to physical pain. I still have two months, there's no way Cameron would side with me, her picking me over her family was never in the realm of possibilities.

I don't want her to side with me, she can't know what it's like to be me.

I grab a different shirt, and pajama bottoms, shutting off the bedroom light, walking to the hallway to quickly change. She won't see my chest, or my back. Ever. I will never let her know what has happened to me. I couldn't stomach it, and if she did see it, I would want to tell her because she would be asking, and if I tell her, my job is over. Me coming up with a plan to keep her safe is over.

She was only supposed to be a job. Her uncle wasn't supposed to be feeding me alcohol and spending time with me. Her best friend wasn't supposed to deliver a painting to my place. I wasn't supposed to fall in love with her. None of this was supposed to happen. She was a *job* that was it.

I open the door again, guiding my way through the dark room. Listening to her speak, "I'm done with this boot, I don't even care."

I had a feeling that was coming sooner than later.

I look over at my bed, it's dark, I can't see shit. I almost laugh, me telling her anything doesn't work. I said separate beds. I don't even have two beds. I don't even know what I was thinking when I said it, and I'm so thankful now is the time she has decided to be stubborn. She never even asked me about the second bed. Her comment about me not having personal space earlier. She was testing me. I clearly failed, because she's laying in my bed looking like she owns it. It's not just tonight, it's been every single night since we slept together. Every night since I tried to put distance between us, she's been pushing herself to get closer to me.

That's terrible. The most dangerous place she can be is next to me, but on the contrary, it's also the safest. We have blurred every single possible line, and that was exactly what wasn't supposed to happen. Not after I knew who *she* really was.

"Shit." I mutter, "Can you turn your flashlight on please?"

Cameron does as I ask, the room is surprisingly bright, minus my closet, where I need to look. I run my hand over the top shelf, waiting to feel the long rectangle box. I grab it, looking at the snowman wrapping paper, I toss it on the bed in front of her.

I definitely did not wrap that myself. If I did, it would have turned into a comedy show. I've never once bought someone a gift, let alone tried wrapping paper.

"What is this?" she sounds shocked, I also hear the smile in her voice. She doesn't hesitate to rip the wrapping paper open.

Her face drops looking at the silver chain, with blue diamonds. It's over the edge for her; I know she would still wear it, even if it's hidden by a sweater. I didn't know what else to do. We have a movie. I wanted her to have something from me. Just in case I do come up with a plan to save her, and things go south for me, then I can still be there with her. I want to be prepared for every possible outcome, and that means I need to prepare to comfort her if I'm not physically on earth anymore.

I've turned pathetic.

She puts the lid over the box, staring at me, her face is lit up by her phone creating shadows. "Thank you." She goes quiet, rubbing her forearm with an open palm. "Wh—what are we doing here? This was expensive Nico."

I want to be able to kiss you. Is what I want to say, I know if I do anything along those lines, it'll only hurt her more. If she's hurt, she will not listen when I plead with her about her future. "That was a thank you for everything you've done for me."

"I haven't done shit." She pats the bed, putting the box beside her on the end table. "Why didn't you go to your families? What's the story? I know I keep asking you this, it just feels wrong to not know parts of your life."

I crawl over her falling on my side of the bed, interlocking my fingers behind my head using them to prop me up. "I have a sister, she's terrible. Like, terrible. My dad's a horrible human. My mom's even worse than him."

"What do you mean?" She's laying on her back, only her head turns to face me. She moves her hand, so her fingers can squeeze my thigh. Her voice is much softer than her grip.

Is she protective over me?

"My dad survives off money, and revenge. My mom is the mastermind of the revenge. My sisters, just self centered, and a kiss ass." If I say much more, I'm going to spill everything, so I really hope this is enough for her, at least for now. "Thank you for dragging me to yours today. Get some sleep."

She shuffles on the mattress rolling on her side, her back facing me. I roll over, forcefully pulling her into my chest. She starts giggling, and every single emotion is heightened. "You told me, you were going to be in my personal space." I whisper into her ear,

Her fingers run over my arm, instantly giving me goosebumps, "My bad. I'll do better next time."

The smile in her voice makes me hold onto her tighter, she says goodnight. I'm going to be laying here for hours awake. Now that I can finally feel something, I'm going to soak up every second with Cameron, even if she's sleeping.

I ate my cereal, watched cartoons, and I fought with Lucia. She's always in my space. Just because she's older she likes to think she's the boss of me. One day I'll show her.

One day I'll be as big and strong as Dad, then she'll really regret it.

This morning started normal, until my father pulled me out of the house by the hood on my sweater not telling me where we were going, he opened the SUV door and shoved me in the passenger seat. I pull my eyes up from my Gameboy, there's so many cars in LA.

I can't wait to be that person who's ripping down the freeway in a nice bright Lamborghini. I'm going to be untouchable. It'll be powered by NOS, and I'll never get caught because cop cars are slow. Everyone will be slow compared to me.

Dad takes a sharp turn, I lean into the door from the force of the turn, looking back down at my game.

The SUV stops, dad takes the game out of my hands, my door opens, and he unclips my seat belt. Tiny grabs my arm, pulling me out. The pressure from his hand is hurting my arm. He scares me, so I can't say anything. If I'm scared, everyone tells me I need to man up, so I stop saying it. He's holding a kennel that my dog Sadie used to have.

I smile, I wonder if we're getting another Sadie?

Dad comes beside me, finally Tiny drops my arm from his hand. Tiny pushes the door open letting us walk in. It stinks in here, the air smells dirty. I can't see anything, it's too dark. Someone's behind me, I think it's my dad. He holds a lantern giving off hardly enough light. I can't see anything, so I stay close to Tiny.

Creaking of a door sounds ahead of me, followed by a voice, a man, cursing out my dad. He's saying a lot of words that I know I cannot ever repeat.

"Son." Dad leans down to look at me, his talking is drawing my attention away from the man in the room. "This is your job. You get to work with me now."

I smile.

"I need you to open that dog kennel. You remember how we would take Sadie out right? Push the clamps down, then open?"

I nod.

"I need you to do that again, only this time I need you to stand behind the kennel when you open it."

'Why wouldn't I let the dog jump on me?' I think to myself turning around.

The lights flicker a lot of times before they are dimly turned on. I can't see much still. I blink, closing my eyes hard, then opening them wide. I think I see something on the ground? I bend down, listening to a man yelling even louder.

"Do it Nico." My dad's voice raises.

I quickly move my arm down in front of the kennel from behind, something fuzzy brushes up against my arm. 'It must be another Sadie!' I quickly unlock it seeing small, but large animals rush out of the kennel all at once.

Screaming fills the air. My eyes can see a bit better now. The man that was talking mean to my dad is on the ground, he can't move, his legs are chained down. Squeaking from the animal I set free is getting louder. I blink again.

Really big mice?

I back away, watching the mice bite the man on his leg, his body flares, he starts screaming, and so do I. I want to run, but my feet are stuck into the ground.

What did I do?

Oh no. Dad is going to be so mad.

I'm being drugged by my sweater, my arms are flaring, I can't breathe, I can't stop screaming.

"Nico enough!" Dad screams.

I sit quietly with my hands folding together on my lap, somehow, we're back at home in the driveway.

"You always wanted to work with me, now you are. This is the Nemean Mafia, you play a bigger role. You will find Cameron, and you will make her one of us."

I want to ask why, but my mouth won't move. My throat hurts, my eyes hurt.

"The Basilisks will die, or they will give her up to me."

I sit out of bed, breathing deeply, brushing my hand trying to get the feeling of the rat off of me. My heart is beating so fast, I can't breathe, I'm trying to catch my breath, no air could possibly fill my lungs as fast as I need it too.

"Jesus Nico!" Cameron sits up brushing my back with her hand. "What do you need? What happened?"

I look at her, it was only a dream. Only it wasn't, I was twelve.

"Shower." I need to get away from her as fast as possible. I can't think of what my dad will have me do to her.

21

Cameron

I have no idea what spooked Nico so bad, he won't talk to me. He woke up in a freak panic, had a god only knows how long of a shower. I tried to stay awake until he came out, time on my phone kept passing, I fell asleep. I woke up and he was cooking. He then had another shower, left the house with his gym bag, came back, had another shower, then sat on the couch in silence.

He's just sitting there staring at the wall. I'm used to people having nightmares, Hayley has them all the time. I stayed in the room next to hers for a year, I have no idea how Archie is sane after that. But this, this is different. It's like Nico is gone. He always glances up at me, he hasn't looked in my direction once today. We passed each other, he reached out to me, his eyes never landed on me. I did see how dark they were. His eyes were almost black.

I slowly walk up, I'm not scared of him, not by a long shot, I'm almost scared how he's going to react to me.

"Hi." I kneel in front of him on my knees, his eyes are completely dark like they were before. His body flinches towards me, I stay still. There's nothing he could do that would ever put me on edge.

The light brown color in his eyes reappears the instant we make eye contact. He lets out a breath that looks like he's been holding for hours. His entire body moves with his lungs emptying. He leans forward, his head on my shoulder, not saying a word.

I start to stand up, his arms wrap around me making sure I don't leave. I lean down, making him rest on the back couch cushion. He will not let me go. I close my eyes, there's a lot of weight on my foot right now, and this next position is probably going to make it worse. The pain will definitely be worth it. I bend my knees one by one, placing them beside his thighs, straddling his lap, holding him as close as I can. The only thing I can do is breath through the pain as I hold his head to my chest.

"You're okay, I got you." I whisper in his ear softly. I'm not this person for people, I don't know what the actual fuck I'm doing. I haven't had to be there for someone if it wasn't Hayley in a very long time. All the other adults just 'deal' with their emotions.

His hand moves on my back to the sound of my voice, so I continue. "You need to eat some of the food you made. We can watch movies. We can make popcorn. Whatever you need?"

"Can we restart the vampire movies?" His voice is so raspy, he needs water.

I pull away looking into his eyes, his eyes are still light brown, there's no hiding the sadness that's in him. It looks like whatever grief he is holding onto just keeps growing. My eyes drop down to his lips, and before I can even register what I'm doing I brush my lips against his. I'm not sure what one of us seals the kiss, my cheeks heat up, I pull away.

His arms wrap around me, "Please be patient, we need to be careful. I want you. I'm going to make sure I have you. Just wait for me."

Do we need to be careful? Careful of what?

My Dad, teen pregnancy, failing grades.

Okay, maybe there's a few things. I don't think he's talking about any of that.

His phone rings loudly. I reach beside me grabbing his phone, it lights up, it's a notification from his stupid security camera.

"Make popcorn please." He drops his phone back on the cushion beside him.

I stand, being careful not to put weight on my foot, so I use the couch arm to balance me. I refuse to keep wearing that bulky ass boot. Nico looks down at my foot not saying a word before walking away.

"Actually." His voice comes closer to the living room as the front doors open. I can hear cars driving outside. He reaches for his phone. "Can you hold off on the popcorn for about an hour. I have to go, I'll be back. Do not leave this house." Nico looks at me with a dead serious expression.

"You're not my father?"

He runs his hand through his hair, "I know. I'm sorry. I will not be gone long, if you think of anything that we need, or that you need, text me."

"What's with the cameras?" I blurt the question out. "Do you watch them when you aren't here?"

He wrinkles his nose, until the question dawns on him, his eyes get wide. "Don't flatter yourself. It's not you I'm watching." He walks away pausing mid step, "We live in New York, the crimes are terrible. You like history. History always repeats itself."

22

Nico

I drop the package on the table in front of my mom. She hides behind my dad, if Nemean ever went down, my dad would take the fall for it, even though she is the mastermind behind all of it. Every single torture technique has been on her. Dad handled the drugs, but she has handled the pain this mafia has endured for the last twenty-five years. She is the one who's responsible for my pain and suffering. I was only conceived because of her plan.

I don't even want to know what would have happened to me if I ended up being a girl.

She's a monster.

"What the hell is this?" my voice radiates throughout the house.

"Merry Christmas to you too." She mutters. "Basilisks doing well I'm assuming?"

"Who does this belong to?" I tip back the package, letting the baggie fall out, landing onto the table.

It's pale, there's no color left to it, I'm not even sure what race the person was that belonged to this finger. She's sending me body parts in the mail. Fucking body parts. Who in their right mind does that?

"No one important. Are you staying all day? We missed you yesterday."

"Yeah. Fuck that. Whose finger is this?" I press. I honestly don't care who it belongs to. I'm scared it's someone that Cameron cares about. I know none of them would go down without a fight. If something did happen, Cameron would never know.

She looks at me looking up at the corner of the room. "I think his name was Mark?"

My mom stands no more than five foot seven, she has long black hair, she's gotten a bit rounder over the years. I'm honestly just hoping her ankles suddenly give out. Looking at her my blood pressure rises.

"His name isn't important." She looks up at me, glaring at me. Her eyes are completely dead inside. She looks how I looked just weeks ago. "Until you turn Cameron in to us, you will have body part upon body part delivered to you."

"The logic in that makes zero fucking sense." I push out my jaw, trying to not snap at her. "If she opens it, there's no way that I will be able to do this. She will get scared off and run."

"Maybe you should have thought of that before you wistfully saved her from the break in. This wasn't part of the plan Nico. You break the rules, so now we will too. You now have thirty days."

"Thirty days? I had three months."

"Oh." She grins. "It's a new timeline. See, new rules. Thirty days until you bring her, or her entire family dies. Either way she will be with us."

Dad walks in, I can see the gun under his arm, he's not making it hidden at all. "The Basilisks will soon learn they never won."

Mom laughs, it's a real laugh, I have no idea how she's twisted enough to find any of this funny. "Oh dear, what did we call ourselves back then?" She snaps her finger, "We paid out every news company in the states." She pauses, "I can't for the life of me remember."

"McKinnon's." Dad replies quickly.

"That's right." Her smile fades as she looks at me. "We bought Machine guns from your girlfriend's uncle. If there's any issue between now and then, we will use them on anyone who steps in our path."

I take a deep breath exhaling through my nose. They have made this so much more complicated. I can't get her to safety on my own.

"We aren't the Baker Cartel son." Dad speaks, I can't look at him, I know he's only bringing this up because of Hayley and Archie. "We won't crumble, they stepped on our drug trade, they slaughtered our men. Your purpose of life is to bring her to us. A deal was made, so it's only fair."

"Thirty days." I say out loud.

Thirty days.

I need to go home to her.

Lucia walks into the kitchen, she takes one look at the finger and her entire face goes from tan to ghostly white. "Is that Cameron? I mean, it wouldn't be the worst thing if it was."

I turn around walking out the back door, if I go near my sister, I'm going to throw myself at her. I wouldn't even feel bad about it either.

23

Cameron

Nico wants me to stay even longer. I want my own space, he will not stop nagging me to stay longer. He's saying I have to stay another month on top of me already having weeks left here, he's not even asking me, he's demanding me to stay. I'm so angry. I want my own space back.

You cannot just tell me what to do, you cannot just take away my freedom. My hands are shaking, tossing my clothes from the clean hamper, back into my bag. One piece of clothing lands in the bag, and Nico tosses it back on the bed.

I'm so frustrated tears start to pool down my face. I keep trying to pack, while he unpacks for me.

"Cameron. Enough." Nico says sternly. I can't even look up at him. "Sit down."

I wipe my face with the back of my hand, I'm pretty positive my cover up is tear stained. I'm so used to crying out of frustration my breathing isn't even interrupted. I'm shocked I haven't yelled at him. I don't even want to.

"I'm not asking you to stay for you, I'm asking for me." His voice turns soft, he lightly grabs my arm, preventing me from tossing the exact same hoodie in the bag for the tenth thousand time.

"More like demanding." I bite at him, I may not have it in me to yell at him, but that's not stopping my attitude from coming to surface.

Nico goes silent. Not a sound leaves him, not even the sound of his exhaling. He's still holding onto me, so I know he's not dead. I look up to him watching him, his eyes tighten. Followed by his jaw, I see it flexing.

"I'm not asking for you." He exhales. "I can't believe I'm saying this. I like having you around."

What the hell was so hard about that? Holy hell, that almost infuriates me even more. It's called emotions. I suddenly remember why I ventured to girls, guys are so emotionally unavailable. "You also like having your coffee pot around." I bit. I have no idea where I'm going with this.

"The dorms aren't safe Cameron!"

My eyes open wide, that tone, the volume of his voice, his grip on me, my tears are frozen. I'm Frozen. If this is how people feel around me, I have guilt weighing on me. I cannot move, I can defend myself, I'm a brick wall, but I have no reflexes right now. I'm still not scared of him, whatever is bothering him, he needs to get under control and stop deflecting it on me.

"I'm so sorry." He finally let go of my arm.

I turn back facing the bed, tossing my clothes into my bag, I can't even sniffle my nose, I can't cry the tears that are flooding in my eyes.

"Call me before you go to bed." His voice is weak.

I walk out of the room with my head down, I don't know what's gotten into him. I'm so over it.

An hour later I drop my bag on Brittney's counter, exhaling a huge breath watching Hayley take a shot of whatever alcohol is in front of her. It's clear, my wild guess is that she's pounding back tequila. She slowly pulls the shot glass away from her mouth watching me intently.

"What is wrong with you mate?" Her accent is so thick, I've gotten used to it, I don't even notice it anymore, until she says something only British people would say.

"He's a dick weed." I exhale again.

She pours me a shot glass, looking at me, then looking at it. I don't even have a second thought, I walk over to it hanging my head. I raise the glass to my lips, feeling the intense burn run down my throat.

I wipe my lips with the back of my hand, "Not only is he trying to hold me hostage, he can't even admit that he wants to admit that he likes having me around." I shake my head, "Why can't guys just admit their feelings, and be open to feeling something?"

"Guys your age are trash." Brittney skips into the kitchen. "Children are asleep, and no one bullied me today."

I can't even help it but to glare at both of them. They both met their husband's when they were my age, Brittney was actually younger, I think. "Yes, because you guys are prime examples."

"Archie had a hell of a time admitting that he loved me." Hayley pours three more shots.

"I had a falling out with Spence, breaking our engagement off." Brittney shrugs. "It was when things were going hard for him, that talk he had with you." She waves me off grabbing her shot glass.

"He told me you helped him."

"Oh, I did. He just wasn't keen on the idea of help."

I roll my eyes, "Whatever. Still bad examples. And Nico doesn't love me, I honestly don't think he has it in him. I tried to get some emotion, but nope. Nothing. I'm done. I don't even know what I was trying for."

Brittney and Hayley just look at each other.

The one downfall of Hayley being my best friend, is that she's also best friends with everybody else. Not only can she silently communicate with me, but she can also do it with Charlie, and Brittney. It's kind of a nightmare, because I'm not at that level with them. It usually always leaves one of us out in the cold. Currently it's a blizzard out here, and I'm freezing.

"Yo. English." I take my shot, letting out a squeal as the alcohol burns my throat. I don't do shots, especially this many.

Hayley rolls her eyes, waving her hand, "Take it from the wise."

I interrupt her, "Okay Grandma's."

She swats me with the back of her hand grinning. "We all have a habit for falling for broken men. That's why your father was so spooked. Our reputation, is kind of shit."

Brittney speaks, "Emotionally unavailable."

Hayley continues, "Check."

"Sexy as fuck."

"Check."

"Met boyfriend at college?"

"Check."

"Mom and dad never met at college, uncheck that." I push my shot glass away from me, I'm already light headed.

"No." Haylcy shakes her head, filling the shot glass up, assuming I was asking for more. "They met in the back of his cop car."

Hayley bites her lip hard, closing her eyes, it looks like she's silently screaming. I think Brittney just stomped on her foot.

"What?" Hayley says defensive shaking off her foot. "I don't like the bitch, so ima rat her out."

Excuse me what? The words finally settling in my mind.

"Talk to your dad." Brittney spits the words out annoyed.

"Absolutely not. She's nineteen, she can handle the truth. She was mixed up in drugs, he drove her home, then not too long after, you were conceived." She shrugs. "Bloody hell, it's really not that big of a deal Brit."

I watch Hayley, waiting for her to take back what she said. "Thank you. Why didn't you go dropping truth bombs before."

Finally, some fucking truth. That's all I wanted. I just wanted a little bit of honesty. It doesn't answer anything but damn it's something.

"You wanted her to come back, I didn't just in case it changed your opinion. Back to this Nico kid. Did you sleep with him?"

I lift the shot glass Hayley poured for me, slamming it back.

Hayley giggles a little bit evil under her breath.

There's a knock at the door, grabbing Brittney's attention. "Good the sitters here to get me out of this conversation. We're going out, you showed up, so you're coming."

I smile, shaking my head, "Nah, I'm going home."

24

Nico

Ten o'clock. She's still not back. I can't text her. I can't call her. I told her I like having her around, that was a huge thing for me. The way she just looked at me before she stormed out, it was like she was ripping my heart out and stomping on it. I wish I never fell for her, she deserves so much better than me. She deserves someone who would go through the length of hell for her. I'm just going to destroy her, and everything she's built. Everything she loves, everyone she loves is going to be destroyed, and it's all because what if I'm not strong enough? I'm not manly enough? I was designed to not have an emotional response, I don't know why I thought I could suddenly be on her level. I don't know why I thought I could be enough.

Nico D'Oria will never be enough, and I don't even blame her.

I don't know how I'm going to get her back. I don't know how I'm going to make my dad's plan work because now I've fucked up even more.

My phone rings, it's a chirp, meaning it's my alarm. I open it watching someone in a black hood drop off a box. I toss my phone not in a rush to get up, it's another body part. Just in time to make me realize how much more time she doesn't have. I've gotten two deliveries today. They're going to come more often now. I'm going to be panicking more and more now.

I can't stalk her at lunch, that would be weird, and I'm not even in a class this semester. I can't just show up and force her to talk to me.

My phone vibrates, then chimes. It's a phone call. My heart stops. I panic, flaring my arms to reach it, even though it's just beside me.

Everything inside my body twists when I see Gabe's name appear.

"Yeah?" I answer.

"Broooo." He holds his o's obsessively long. "Are you and Cameron together?"

"No. She went back to the dorm." Saying that makes something inside of me feel like it's shattering. I can't even start to describe this pain.

"Ashley got a call, so we went outside with some of her shit. Stay away, this has to be a test."

A loud explosion echoes in the background, screaming, and crying sending shock waves in the air. I'm already on my feet running out the door. Ashley is in the background yelling something along the lines that they didn't have time to get to Cameron's room.

I hang up my phone, holding onto it with everything in my body, blood is rushing through my veins. My breathing is deeper than I've ever felt, my heart is pounding in my ears. I'm so close I can hear the screaming. The air wreaks of the building burning. I look up, seeing a huge cloud of smoke erupting into the sky. Sirens are getting closer, or maybe that's then echoing off the buildings. Either way they're coming.

My legs take me faster. Until I'm standing at the door, pushing through girls who are coming out, fighting for their lives. I try to patiently wait, watching everyone in the crowd, she's not here, she's not coming down the stairs. I touch the door, instantly feeling the heat. I shake it off, using my foot to foot to prop open the door, the heat consumes through my foot from the medal of the door. Ignoring the screams of someone telling me not to go in. I still don't see her in the crowd.

I'm trying to peacefully pass people in the stairwell scanning faces, making sure I don't miss her. Everyone who is running down the stairs is panicking as much as I am to get up stars.

My girl is in here, and I'm not letting her burn. The door for the second floor is hot, the fires on the other side.

I just have to make it to her room.

I exhale quickly, grabbing the handle, pulling the door open. Flames come charging at me. I lay down on the ground to get under the flames, and I roll. The air is so thick. I can't see where I'm going. My eyes are burning, my lungs are burning. I can just see enough to see the flames. I'm trying to keep my memories from the cage deep down in my mind, this smoke making it nearly impossible.

Stay focused Nico.

I stand up putting my back to the side of the wall, feeling the temperature rising with each step. I'm sweating more than I ever thought was possible.

I'm going to die here.

I cough, I try not to freeze, the pain is so much. The breath I take is nothing but a wheeze. Breathing hurts.

I still follow the wall, waiting for a small clearing to get to the other side of the hallway. I'm across from her door, flames are between us, I just need to get in there.

I take quick breaths, there's no other choice.

Go Nico. GO.

I push myself off the hot wall feeling a heat wave in my pant leg, my body falls against her door with every ounce of power I have left in me.

I brace myself with my hands, feeling the heat getting worse, and worse. I fall hard, the door gives out causing me to crash onto the floor.

I stand in her room, letting out a scream trying to pat the fire out from my sweat pants, shaking my leg isn't enough, it's not going out. The flames are getting bigger. I look down, the flames have engulfed my sweatpants at my calf. My toes wiggle, I forgot shoes.

Your sweater Nico. I snap out of it, taking my sweater off, suffocating the flames.

My body collapses, I fall on my stomach, trying to lift my head up to find her. Cameron isn't in her dorm.

My leg turns numb, I try to keep my eyes open, the air is too thick, and I can't breathe.

Cameron

"Mid night booty call or what?" Hayley glances down at my bag, that's basically vibrated off its seat at this point.

I exhale, biting my lip, I know it's Nico. I don't want to look at it, because I've drank enough, I will end up at his place the second I hear his voice. Then I'll be pissed off about him being emotionless, then it will be a never ending cycle of disappointment. I will always forgive him.

The same number has called me every minute for the last forty minutes.

My phone vibrates again, "Uh, hello?" I squint my eyes looking at the table.

"Holy fuck Cameron!" The voice sound relived. "It's Gabe. Get to St Mary's Hospital now."

"How did you get my number?"

"Are you drunk? Whatever doesn't matter. There was a fire, Nico's in the hospital. Get here now. I'll meet you at the main doors."

The blood drains from my face. I can't breathe, it feels like everything is caving in on me. My eyes pool with tears, I lay cash on the table. I don't even know if it's enough to cover my tab. I stand trying to say words, nothing will come out.

I run outside, waving down a cab, opening the door, demanding that they hurry.

I left Nico hours ago, how did something already happen to him? I said I was done, I meant it. I'm just going to go see if he's okay, or alive.

Then I'll leave.

The traffic is ridiculous. I can't breathe at a normal pace. I try to slow down, I'm making myself light headed from the constant deep breaths. The time on my phone keeps ticking by. Time is moving fast, and we aren't. I see the time moving, I feel like I'm Frozen in space. I see Hayley texting me asking what happened. Brittney is asking if I'm okay, at least I think they are, I can't take my eyes off the clock.

I don't know what happened. I don't know where the fire was, I don't know anything.

I jump from the sound of Gabe's voice. "How much does she owe?"

The cab driver responds, I watch Gabe pass the money through the open passenger window, I can't move.

My door opens, before I can register that I'm running inside, the cold air kisses my face.

Gabe runs in front of me, opening the door. He reaches out to a girl, grabbing her hand, I follow. I want to run past them, but I don't know where I'm going. I don't know if I'm going to emergency, or if I'm going to the morgue.

Please don't be in the morgue. Please.

Gabe stops at the elevator, he presses the number five, I can't stand still my leg is tapping, my fingers are tapping on my thigh, and I'm crying again.

"Your dorm exploded." Gabe says heavily.

It takes a few minutes for my mind to process.

I look up at the roof, more tears filling my eyes. Nothing else is said.

The elevator opens to a sign that reads *burn unit*

I walk out, looking both ways. On my left is nothing but rooms with shut doors, my right has a desk, with nurses at it.

"Are you here for Nico?" A woman asks me, looking over my shoulder, I'm assuming she recognizes Gabe. "Leave your bag here. We will keep it behind the desk for you."

I pass it to her, I just need to get in there.

She hands me a yellow gown, and a blue mask. Putting the gown on we can both see my hands shaking uncontrollably. I put the mask on recoiling when I try to breathe. I'm recycling my air in this thing, I need to breathe normally, not fast and shallow.

My mask is already wet from my tears. I try to tie up the strings on my gown behind my neck, I stop trying letting my hands fall to my side.

She steps behind me, I feel the gown getting tighter. "He's getting treated right now, you can wait if you want."

I shake my head.

The door opens, and the doctor pauses, Nico's eyes are pinned tight, he's not making a single noise.

"Oh my God." I run up to him, pulling my mask off and kissing him.

Nico's hand grabs the side of the face kissing me hard, his fingertips run over my skin.

The doctor says something about starting again.

Even with my eyes closed I know the second they start, because his body tenses.

"I'm right here." I speak in a broken whisper.

The smell in this room is terrifying. I'm trying not to gag, I'm trying not to scream at him asking why he was there. I know he was only there because he was trying to see me. He could have died.

I close my eyes even tighter, thinking about everyone who probably died in that fire. The life that was just taken away pointlessly.

The doctor stops again, Nico searches for my hand. I pull my mask up feeling the exhaustion from the drinks, and the stress weighs down on me.

"That was good. I know it didn't feel like it. The next four days are going to be hell, you'll be home soon." The doctor stands. "I'm going to check up on other patients. You need a break." His voice is directed at me. "If you need anything, let a nurse know."

I really want to acknowledge him, at least Nico was looking at him when he spoke. I can't take my eyes off of Nico. If he was in the morgue, I wouldn't be able to survive. The guilt, losing him, I wouldn't be okay.

The door shuts, finally I find my words. "What were you doing there?"

"Gabe called me." His voice is so shaky from the pain, he sounds like a different person. He put on a good front. "It's not Friday, so I knew you wouldn't be with your family."

I run my fingers through his hair, he moves his head, I'm supporting him with my forearm from the pillow.

"I couldn't find you outside. I got upstairs, and the flames were everywhere. I had to get to you. The relief when you weren't in your room."

"You could have died." I try to say softly, it comes out angry, full of rage pulling my hand back to my side.

"I didn't."

I turn around ripping the mask off my chin, it's pointless to even have it at this point. This room is depressing. Not like it's supposed to be exciting.

There's a sad looking chair in the corner. There's a TV, and a window. That's it.

I'm sleeping on that chair, I guess.

I lay on it, kicking my feet over the arm, using the other side to support my torso, I rest my head on the back, closing my eyes.

"That looks uncomfortable." Nico sighs.

"Since you run into burning buildings, I can't leave you alone." I bark at him.

He mumbles, not in English. Again. He groans really loudly, making me stand up. He moves over on the bed. "Come here."

He moved over to the left, he just moved his singed body over for me.

"No. I have bacteria and shit." I argue.

"It's fucking wrapped. Come here Cameron. Or you can go to my house."

I walk over to his side of the bed kicking off my shoes.

"You won't get any sleep here, but you need to sober up."

I look at him before crawling in.

"You ran up to me and kissed me, so you're not sober." He has no emotion in his voice, no pain, nothing.

"You'll be here for new year's." I whisper.

He shrugs.

I crawl into the bed, there's no space, I can hardly breathe here from the plastic side digging into my back. "Gabe was here. Should I go talk to him?"

He shakes his head.

I'm not expecting Nico to be anything but lively right now, obviously there's something major going on. I think I really hurt him by leaving the way I did.

"Do you need me to call anyone?" I pause. "You probably already did. Never mind. I feel so helpless, can you tell me what you need? You almost died because you thought I was home, just make me do something, anything."

Nico moves his arm, making me readjust, he wraps his arm around me, holding me into him.

"Nico please." I look at him, basically begging for his attention, anything to tell me what he wants me to do or say.

"Believe me Cameron, I've felt worse. Just lay your head down."

I do as he says, even though I'm in jeans, my sweater is bulged up, I have a plastic bar digging into my back, I feel my eyes getting heavy.

26

Nico

The doctor came and left. He gave me shit for letting her on the bed, I don't really care. Honestly, it's nice not being completely alone for once. She woke up when my bicep flinched from the pain, and she got off the bed, holding my hand, squeezing her eyes closed. I'm pretty sure she hoped this was a bad dream, and not real.

Sorry babe, it's real.

It's not even the pain that's getting me, it's the itchiness that's getting me. I guess my sweat pants melted onto my skin or something. I've honestly been too distracted to even really catch the full report on my condition.

Between Gabe and I we called Cameron so many times, and it's eating me alive not to know where she was. I know her routine to a T, and on Wednesdays she stays home. I don't know what's bothering me more, not knowing where she was, or the fact she came in and kissed me like she meant it, then pretended like it never happened.

All of my thoughts are distracting me from what Gabe said. How could I be so stupid. How could I just run into her building? My father wouldn't have sent any of his goons to set the fire if she was in the building, he obviously knew she left. He set it to see what I would do. If I never showed up, then it would be easy to assume that we weren't close enough, and I don't care if the Basilisks die. Me running in proved to him that we are close enough that I can convince her. Me wanting to save her life just destroyed her life.

If it wasn't a message the Lion wouldn't have sent another body part to my house. Ashley was less than thrilled about grabbing that box from my doorstep. It couldn't really wait, it wouldn't take long for a dog to sniff it out.

Cameron is just sitting on the chair on her phone typing to someone. I'm half surprised she never recognized Ashley from the bar, since she had her by the throat pinned up against a wall. If Cameron did notice her with Gabe, she hasn't said anything.

"They're asking if you need anything?" she doesn't look up from her phone. Her makeup is still on from last night.

"Cami go eat, go sleep."

She shakes her head not looking up.

"Cameron." I scold.

"I'm staying, just like I'm staying when you go for surgery tomorrow. I'm not leaving."

Now that I actually love a girl, she pisses me off. Ironic. "You need to take care of yourself."

"You come first. Stop." She bites into her words. She's been doing that a lot with me lately. I just hold up my hands in my mind and walk away slowly.

I want to tell her it's really no big deal. I've been through so much worse. I can't. I really want to, but I can't.

"My dad hates us. Jumping out of windows, running into fires. He called us dumb." She finally puts her phone down. "Can you eat? There's a French place not far from here. I think it was on your list."

"Before nine."

"I'll make you a deal. I go home, shower, grab your laptop, bring us food, and watch movies? I just need a brea—." Before she finishes the word, she puts her head down. "I'm so sorry, I didn't mean it like that."

"Grab my wallet, take my debit out. Get yourself home, buy a movie online, download it. Take your time." I look down at the blanket covering half my body.

I can't look at her, it's not that I don't want to, she's pretty even when she looks the way she does right now. Every time I look at her, I feel something inside of me break because all I can think about when I look at her, is the way that she kissed me, and how she tasted. Then I think of the way she left, not taking a look back, she was gone. I've been left before I know it's easy to walk away from me, I was hoping for it that somehow it would be a bit of a struggle for her, I was hoping she would at least look over her shoulder before she left me.

"I'm sorry." I shake my head, trying to come up with words. I have so much I want to express, just no way of saying it. "If you don't come back, that's okay. You were really fucking angry yesterday. You don't have to come back."

She stands, walking to my wallet. "I still am. Then I thought you were dead. I'm mad at myself for being here."

She walks out, again without a single glance back. Leaving me sitting here in even more pain.

I'm trying. I don't know what I'm doing. I was designed to not have feelings, the lion made sure of that, the scars under my shirt are a reminder. Her leaving makes my chest heavy, my air supply is cut short. If she doesn't come back, I don't know what I'm supposed to do to protect her. I had to give her a choice. She needs to make the decision on her own, and if she doesn't come back, it'll just make it harder for me to protect her, not impossible, just harder.

27

Cameron

I can't believe I said that to Nico yesterday. *I'm mad at myself for being here.* Way to kick him when he's already down Cameron. The entire day, all night he couldn't even look at me. He never once spoke. I downloaded *Harry Potter*, I brought extra food, I felt so damn bad, I can't even blame him for basically ignoring me. I'm not mad at myself for being here, I'm mad at myself for seeing him and throwing myself at him.

If it was as easy as not caring, I wouldn't be here. If I didn't care I wouldn't be sitting in his room, at the edge of this damn seat waiting for him to be pushed back in here after surgery. I haven't left this room, and I don't plan on it. I'm going through hell trying to not let my imagination get the best of me. It's really hard sitting here with the absence of his bed. It's taking way too long, no one has been in here to update me. I'm panicking.

The one thing that's really bothering me, not a single person has shown up. His parents, his sister. No one. It might look like I'm only here for pity. Hell, he's probably assuming that's why I'm still here.

It's not.

I genuinely care about him.

Of course, it took him running into a burning building to find out. I don't think I've ever felt this way. He pisses me off. If he wasn't in so much pain, I'd probably push him in front of a bus because he frustrates me so much by not communicating.

Yet, I'm still here. I'm sitting at the edge of my seat waiting for him to get out of surgery. I've been preparing for him to be dead since Gabe called me. I'm pretty sure he's still alive.

I need him to be okay, I need him to not be dead.

I just need him.

He ran into a burning building because I'm too predictable, he knew I was home, he was trying to protect me in his own weird way.

I wipe my eyes just in time for the door to open.

"I know. It's tragic I'm still alive." Nico's voice is hoarse, he doesn't look at me, his eyes are glued to the roof.

I jump out of my seat tapping my feet on the ground. It was just a skin graft. He looks so tired, his eyes are heavy.

"I made them keep me in recovery longer." He still doesn't look at me.

The Doctor looks at me, "I'm assuming you'll be making sure he uses this cream on the donor site, and that he shows up to change the dressing."

"No, she won't be." Nico shakes his head, his voice sounds even more exhausted.

"I will." I speak quickly.

"Make sure he relaxes, he has to come in every three days for two weeks. Do not let him scratch anything. Pain medication when he needs it. The donor site is on his back, don't let him get either one wet."

I nod in agreement. "When can he go home?"

"We'll watch him, but probably later today."

I watch the doctor leave the room and look at Nico smiling. "You get to go home today." My eyes light up realizing neither one of us will be stuck here tonight for New Years.

"Yeah. I know. I have ears." He bites his words at me.

I bite my upper lip. I probably deserved that. Actually, I didn't. "We can stop being so fucking toxic and speak to each other with respect."

Nico slowly turns his head on his pillow and looks at me with no expression.

"What is wrong with you?"

"I don't know Cameron, maybe it's the fact I just had skin removed from my back onto my leg. Or maybe it's the fact you have been jumping down my throat for the last two days."

I hate this. I get mad at him for showing no emotion, and when I get angry, I just say shit that I automatically regret saying. I walk to his right side of the bed, bending over hugging him, he doesn't hug me back. He lays there stiff as a board.

I rest my head on his chest, "I'm sorry. I want to be here, I want to help, I want you to be okay."

He wraps his left arm around my body, holding me as tight as he can right now. "I'm not okay. I don't know what I'm supposed to do." His voice shakes.

I lean up, looking at his dark eyes, they're broken. I don't know how long he's been falling apart right in front of me. I've missed it all. He put up a front and completely fooled me. I spend all of my time with him, and I never saw *this* expression before.

I place my hand on his cheek, he turns towards my palm. "What is it?"

"I'm starving." He whispers.

I don't press him, I give him a weak smile. "I'll call my dad. Delivery on New Year's Eve is going to be impossible."

And just like that, we're done fighting. Or maybe it's a pending fight. I'm not sure. I don't even know what *this* is, and it's making me that more frustrated.

***

1. *Broadway*
2. *Comedy show*
3. *Burlesque*
4. *Fake a wedding for cake samples*
5. *Tour bus*
6. *Laser tag*

7. *Escape room*
8. *Helicopter tour*

Nico groans asleep on the couch next to me. Planning his birthday was hard before. Now it's almost impossible. I look at his left leg on the reclined foot rest, crossing out the escape room, and laser tag. While I'm crossing it out, I forgot I'm a poor college student that's never worked a day in my life, so there goes Helicopter tour.

I need to make this fun. After what I saw this morning, he deserves the best day possible. I don't even know where to start. I don't do this kind of thing. I don't even know how much adventuring he's done since he moved to New York. I don't want to take him to a repeat place. I want this to be special, I want him to remember me.

I want him to suddenly realize how I feel about him.

I'm using his birthday for selfish reasons.

Whatever.

At least if I make an ass out of myself, he'll remember it.

I toss the notebook over the couch behind me, listening to it hit the ground. I give up.

"Can I have water?" Nico's eyes aren't even open before his face crumbles. "It's so itchy." He groans, it sounds like a scream. "I'm so fucking tired of this." His voice rises.

I don't flinch, I think I'm immune to guys suddenly raising their voices. My family's fucked, people always yelled. "Do you want ice?"

"Yes." His voice is calm when he speaks to me, at least he can control it. "I'm sorry, I just, oh my God!" His words sound like a cry.

I get up walking towards the cupboard grabbing his insulated water bottle, filling it half way with ice, then topping it with water from the fridge. My guilt is eating at me. I can't even bring myself to look at the news to see who died. I could have been at the dorm. My name could have been on the list. I feel terrible that Nico is going to remember the way it was in the fire, I don't want him to remember the heat, or the smoke. I don't want him to be haunted by the flames. I don't want him to have a reminder on his body.

I walk back sitting beside him passing him the water, reaching for his thighs with my opposite arm. "I'm sorry this happened. I'm sorry I left, I'm sorry I wasn't home."

He looks at me with squinted eyes, "I'd rather you not be dead." He shakes the look off his face, "No Cami. I just completely lost it seeing the building, you didn't do anything."

"I just..."

"Feel guilty?" he cuts me off. "This was all me. You have nothing to be sorry about. Let's watch a movie, I need a distraction."

I lean into him, resting my forehead on shoulder before standing up, "I will never walk on you again."

Half way through the movie Nico's phone chirps, "Your dad's here." He presses a button, and the door unlocks. "It's open." He speaks to the bottom of his phone.

I stand, running towards my dad, hanging off half his body, getting a side hug, careful not to disturb the pizza, and the bag that's in his other hand.

"Are you okay?" he asks, quietly enough that Nico can't hear.

I nod my head, "I need help with his birthday."

Dad asks what I have planned, I walk away pointing to the book that's on the floor, so he can look without it drawing attention.

"How are you feeling kid?" dad walks so he's standing in front of the TV, he sets the pizza box on the other couch cushion, purposely trying to get me to sit on the other side of the couch to create space between us. My father looks at Nico with a soft expression, I don't even know what he's thinking.

Maybe Nico running into the burning building was a good gesture for him? Fuck if I know. I love my father, but Erick Watson is a hard one to figure out. He's so hot and cold about everything.

"I honestly don't know." Nico exhales. "This is nothing, but it's also a lot."

"No more burning buildings. No more jumping out of windows. I'm going to die if I get another call. Literally, die. So, stop." He walks around the couch, stopping to pick up my notebook before walking out of the house.

"I think he's warming up." I look at Nico trying to hide my smile.

"You could have told me it only took a burning building. I would have done it long ago." Nico reaches for a slice of pizza, "Move this, come back please."

I do as he asks, cuddling up next to him. I don't know where he was hiding before the night at the bar, but damn. I wish I got that fake ID months ago.

"Nico."

He stops mid bite, with the pizza in his mouth side eyeing me. My heart beats faster, I try to take a deep breath to calm down. He pulls it away from his mouth looking at me with big eyes. His mouth is full, I know he wants to say 'what' to prompt me to find the words.

"I love you." I let out a shaky breath.

Nico freezes, until he swallows his bite, not taking his eyes from me.

He doesn't say anything. I bite my lips, closing my eyes looking away. "Push play." I try to sound playful, the truth is I've lost my appetite.

He completely froze.

The rooms still silent, until I hear Hermione's voice.

I pull away from him watching the TV, I pull my feet on the couch hugging my knees resting my face on my arm. I really fucked up, I'm feeling heart broken, anger, sadness, relief, and regret all at once, and I can't let a single emotion show.

Heartbreak because he never said it back.

Anger because I told him how I felt.

Sadness because I thought I had a shot.

Relief because he knows.

Regret because we might lose everything we built together.

28

Nico

The last thing I want to do is have a shower. I wasn't even concerned about the aftercare when the doctors took the donor skin from my back. I don't want to take my shirt off in front of Cameron. I didn't even want the doctors to see my back. Them seeing my scars probably explained why I was so good at not screaming while they were picking at me in treatment.

Cameron looks at me tapping her foot holding duct tape, and a cut up garbage bag. This is going to be a bitch to take off. We don't even need to go this far, she jumped to every single conclusion about what would happen if the donor site, or my skin graft got wet. Apparently, they'd need to amputate my back. I rolled my eyes and laughed her off, until I realized she's actually scared of me not healing properly. So, now I'm just going to do what she wants, because it will make her feel better.

After all, I'm the one who didn't tell her I loved her back.

I turn around, facing the bathroom wall taking my shirt off. My eyes are closed tight, the air in the bathroom is cold. She's not touching me, she's not making a single sound. I open my eyes, looking to the left without moving my head, she's looking at my back with a soft expression. She's seeing scars from whips, she's seeing indents in my skin, and puncture wounds. The Lion always chose my back, because it's the easiest place for me to hide the scars from her, and everyone else. Her lips separate, I think I hear a small gasp of air. She's not asking me a single question. I'm so thankful for that, because I don't even know what lie I would be able to tell her.

She takes a step towards me, her eyes are locked on my back. She wraps her arm around my middle, stepping even closer, her free hand touches my back, the chill of the garbage bag sends a shiver down my spine as it brushes along my skin with her movements. I feel her head rest against my back. Then her lips touch my scars. My eyes instantly start to burn. It doesn't last long before she backs away, and the sound of the duct tape makes an uncomfortable noise in the quiet.

I turn around trying not to laugh, "You are going to have to take this off fast."

She smiles until she scans my left bicep, looking at a scar from a bullet. I know she's thinking about all the other people in her life that have matching scars. It's probably killing her that she doesn't know what it's from.

I turn around to face her, "Go, I'm about to get naked."

I unbundle my pants, her eyes travel down my body stopping on my hand. She bites her lip, so I pull them down just enough for her to see my V.

She backs up, running into the bathroom counter, then tries to fix her mistake by running into the wall. Her face lights up beat red. She's either super embarrassed, or insanely turned on, either way, I'm loving it.

She covers her eyes. Probably doing so, thinking that will cover her blushing. "Wrap your leg up."

I stop her by putting my hand on her shoulder. "I don't deserve you to take care of me."

"Wrap your damn leg up." She says stern her face no longer red, her hand dropping to her side, and her eyes locked on mine.

"Yes ma'am."

She closes the door, I love her with every fiber in my being. I never felt safer than I did for those few seconds of her seeing my body, without asking questions, or judging. Now that I know she feels the same way, telling her that her fate is already sealed is going to be easy, because now it's easier to manipulate her.

I can't fucking do that.

29

Cameron

It's Nico's 19th birthday. I don't even know what my dad planned, all I got was a text two days ago that said *'it's on. No questions.'* I'm kind of scared. I haven't said happy birthday to Nico, I haven't acknowledged that we have plans, nothing. We went for a walk in Central Park, we got coffee and sat at a bench watching birds like a bunch of old people.

Seriously, we're both nineteen, why are we like this?

His mood is a bit down today, and I can see why. His phone hasn't gone off once. If Spencer never found out the date for me, I wouldn't have been able to guess. There's absolutely nothing off about today, and it breaks my heart.

After seeing his back, and skimming his chest, everything in me shattered. Seeing the scars that Charlie has on her back on his. Nico doesn't have it as bad, but he has other ones. His skin was indented, he had so many sizes of welts on him. Scares overlapped each other. Not to mention the circular scar on his bicep, that everyone in my family has. I couldn't do anything but kiss his scars, the second I did I felt him relax into me. It was like, every guard he put up is slowly starting to fall down. I want to know what happened to him, I want to know how to protect him.

He's grown so much over the last two months. I made it my mission to find his favorite food, and I completely failed. Everything we had, minus the calamari he loved. He never even made it awkward after I told him I love him. I love him so much, my body can't function. My mind shuts down, then when he walks in a room everything is clear. My problems go away, he relaxes me. My anger issues are so much better with him around me. He makes me a better person.

I want to absolutely spoil him for making me feel the way I do.

K now. Meet you outside of the museum.

See you soon.

"Let's go get ice cream." I scream. I have no idea where he is, my voice must be heard. I fumble in a paper bag, pulling a hoodie over top of my head, ripping the tag off.

"K. No need to FUCKING SHOUT." He yells through the camera making me jump. His cackling comes through the speaker of the camera.

I finger the camera in the hall, it doesn't point in the bedroom, it's the thought that counts.

I glance in the mirror before walking out of the room, he's going to look at me and suspect something is up. My makeup is done better today. The blue necklace he bought me is visible under my hoodie, I never take it off. It's grown to be a part of my body.

Nico looks at the stairs raising half his mouth. "This isn't ice cream. This is history. And your dad's here. Why is your dad here?" His voice is flat, no emotion at all.

"Come!" I grab his arm walking up the stairs.

Nico doesn't complain, he follows me getting pulled up the stairs behind. I really hope this isn't a disaster. I have no idea what's going to be happening. I have no idea what that man has planned, and knowing dad, he's gone full out. I'm a little nervous after dropping the L bomb.

Dad spins, pointing down a hallway right before the ticket booth. It's so dark in here, the lights are hardly enough to light up. We walk past a sink on the ground, I'm assuming it's for a mop bucket. There are brooms, cleaning supplies, and wet floor signs next to it, just no mop.

Dad walks up the stairs and Nico groans. I wonder if his leg is starting to bother him now. This isn't exactly the relaxing the doctor told him to do yesterday when we got the dressing changed. The moving has to be good for him though. At least I'd think it would be. Even if he hates every second of it.

We reach flat ground, with a door in front of us, Dad shakes his head going up more stairs. "I haven't done this much cardio since my police days." Dad lets out a sigh.

"I've never done this much cardio." Nico groans. "If I can't lift it, I won't do it."

I roll my eyes, all the men in my life probably have the worst heart health.

We reach the top, Dad faces me, "I'll just clean up tomorrow. Don't hurt yourself, I forged a lot of liability signatures."

He goes back down the stairs, and I push the door open with my entire body weight.

The sun is blasting on the rooftop, making the shimmer from the balloons pop. Fake candles are lined around a blanket on the floor, a wooden woven picnic basket is sitting on a pile of neatly organized blankets, a bottle of alcohol is sitting in a metal bin, full of ice, pillows are surrounded by the blankets.

This is way too romantic after dropping the L bomb.

"What the fuck?" Nico sounds even more breathless.

I grab onto him again, pulling him towards the blanket, if I know my dad, there's a cake.

There's a small cake sitting on the blanket, made for two people. It's white with simple dark blue writing *Happy birthday.*

Nico looks at it, closing his eyes. His face slowly breaks into a smile. "How did you know?"

I shrug like it wasn't a big deal. "Spencer bribed the girls at the school. Let's see what is in the basket."

Nico sits down on the blanket opening the basket. Pulling out cloth napkins, paper plates, and a white cardboard box. He opens it revealing chocolate and peanut butter covered fruit.

"Cameron. I can't. What the fuck." His voice is soft, gentle, he's not mad, he's shocked. "I don't deserve this."

"Stop Nico." I reach out to his hand holding the box. "I'm sorry this is a lot. I had no idea what we were walking into."

"So much for me using the rooftop for picking up girls, that's your move." He laughs.

"Is it working?" I ask softly.

Nico looks at me, the golden ring in his eyes widens, almost transforming the color of his dark eyes. He leans in towards me, my heart's beating so hard I can feel it in my ears. His lips slam onto mine, pulling me on his lap. I stroke my tongue over his lips, feeling his mouth open, welcoming me in one of his hands is in my hair, the other is on my back pulling me in. I wrap my arms around his neck, trying to hold him as close as possible.

I feel a smile break out on both of our faces, we both pull away slowly, kissing each other quickly one last time.

"Non voglio mai che questo sentimento finisca, ma deve farlo. Mi fa male quanto ti amo. Mi fa male il fatto che sarò io a distruggerti." His forehead touches mine.

"What language is that?" I ask in a whisper.

"Italian."

"What did you say?"

He smiles weakly. "One day I'll tell you, but now we snack. So, get off me, there's food women."

"Oh!" I smile, swinging my leg off him, "Anything for the birthday boy."

He sticks his tongue out at me. "That's right. It's my day." He picks up the box, "I wonder how many people were spying on us."

I chuckle. "We scared them away, don't worry."

The sun is getting lower and lower, we still have a while before sunset. I couldn't have planned something like this on my own, I was too busy about not making it weird between us. Maybe we needed it to be a little weird, because the way he kissed me, it was like he was finally letting go.

"What are you going to do about school starting next week?" He drops the green leaves from the strawberry into the box.

"I'm going to have to ask my dad for his credit card. I need more clothes, laptop, bedding, everything."

"I have bedding." He says casually.

"I might need to, just for a few days. You live so damn close." I scrunch my nose up.

"Now I'm having a good day." He smiles looking down. "This is my first birthday cake."

I look at him wide eyed.

"Really. Never even had a birthday party."

My lips turn into a frown. "Next year I'll buy you a present every day for a month. It'll be like an advent calendar for your birthday."

"Never had one of those either. I know what they are though, so there's that."

My heart is heavy, "I am officially going crazy for every single holiday."

He smiles, I reach down grabbing a Strawberry covered in white chocolate feeding it to him.

I hate his parents. I hate how unloved he must have felt. I'm changing that. It's my new mission.

30

Nico

I stop in my tracks, eyeing the picture Hayley painted. It's pretty in the day, when the lights are off it gives me the creeps. It glows in the dark. The teddy bear is vibrant, it's almost blinding. If we needed a night light, we don't anymore.

My phone chimes, Cameron hasn't texted me all night, and I know it's not her presents at the door that my phone is alerting me of. I know Cameron is either at the Speakeasy, or at Willie's ten drinks in with Hayley.

I turn on my heels charging towards the door, I swing it open to bones dropping a package.

"Tick tock." His voice instantly sends a vicious chill down my spine shocking every vertebrae.

"Fuck you." I growl.

Bones ghostly skinny face smirks, before walking away.

I grab the package running to the fridge. I dump days old left overs down the sink into the garbage disposal. I quickly rip open the box, hoping to hell having a lot of food in disposal will help with this process. I don't know how else I'm supposed to get rid of this. The box has my name on it. There's no return address, at least if Cameron got it, she would be safe from the contents. I destroy everything that wasn't connected by tape. If I was about to do what I'm going to do for anyone else, I would be throwing up. There's an ear, clean cuts, just sitting here on paper. The smell is horrifying. I dump the ear, and paper in the garbage disposal, I turn the tap on and flip the switch up standing back from the counter top.

The blades are making a high pitch squeal. Then a loud noise working hard at the cartilage.

This is fucking disgusting.

Why can't my life ever be normal?

The only time my life's normal is when I'm with her, and even then, it's far from normal circumstances.

The noise finally just turns into the blades working fast, and empty. I keep the water on in an attempt to rinse it down further. Time to clean the fridge out, shove more food down, and to get that sound out of my head.

I dry my hands on a towel. That took forever. Now the smell will be covered up. I refuse to make Cami guilty in this.

I turn the corner out of the kitchen watching Cameron and Hayley nearly fall over entering the house. The bags are so heavy it's knocking them off balance. Both of them burst out in belly laughter.

There has to be a couple grand in those bags, I have no idea if Cameron's questioned how everyone has so much money or not. Those legal businesses are only able to take them so far financially. Seven of them own the speakeasy, so that's not a huge financial gain. When the FBI busted the Basilisks, they never drained their bank accounts to say thanks for helping. Everyone is still rich beyond their wildest dreams.

I heard right before Archie's mom took the fall for the killing of the Baker Cartel boss, she drained her husband's bank account and stored it away for Archie. Of course, with it being that much money, it was all flagged. They had to get normal people jobs, while they waited for life to cool down before they were able to deposit anything.

Those are just rumors. I have no idea if any of it is true.

I hate what I need to do to these people. I will fuck around her mother, and the one who set all this up, but everyone else is such a good person. I don't want to hurt them.

I can't get over how everything is getting so fucking complicated.

"I fed her alcohol." Hayley grins.

"I can see that. When are you going home?" I raise my eyebrows at her.

Cameron sucks in a breath of air, "That's rude."

I laugh, I can't help it but to notice the smile and wide eyes on Cameron's face. "Not like that. Like are you staying a while? You should."

I assumed Hayley would leave after Christmas, now we're into the new year. It would probably be good if she stayed for everything that's about to happen. Cameron won't be able to reach each other, but having Hayley on the same continent might help.

"Till February when I have to tour Asia. Then I'll go back home." Hayley drops a bag, "That's bloody heavy mate. I need another drink." She looks at me. "I'm drinking your alcohol."

She walks past me right into the kitchen, I feel like she can sniff out a sealed bottle anywhere, so I just let her go without directing her. Her squeal fills the air, I forgot her picture was delivered. Cameron drops her bag, running past me, followed by her squeals.

"Don't turn the lights off, shits terrifying." I groan.

"Archie said the same thing." Hayley says flat. Hayley explains to Cameron in deep detail about the glowing effect, from the kitchen. She's basically yelling at her.

I applaud Hayley for what she's done. Getting free of the Basilisks, taking a risk and putting herself out there. Even though she could afford to take the risk, that level of vulnerability. At the exhibit Cami was thanking Archie for taking care of her when she was painting. I don't understand any of it. Cameron was able to relate to her when she was writing her book, I was taking mental notes. If she ever writes again to check up on her, make sure she's eating, put her to bed. I don't understand how Hayley and Cameron became friends, did Hayley just look at Cameron when she was a baby and was like 'You'll be my new BFF.' The concept to me is just weird. It's also very reassuring, because I know she will fight to get Cameron free. Everyone will.

"They're going to be best friends." Hayley appears from the kitchen nudging Cameron with her elbow.

Cameron hangs her head.

I was hoping that kiss on the rooftop would communicate what I couldn't. I think I made her even more confused. I'm not trying to be hot and cold, I don't want to tell her I love her, be with her, then summon her. I can't do her dirty like that, I also can't stand walking by her, not reaching out to her. I cuddle her on the couch because it feeds my delusions of a normal life.

"Come on Nico." Cameron looks at me with shining eyes. "We need to get you on our level."

That is going to take a lot of alcohol.

31

Cameron

I'm not sure how much we drank last night, it was a lot. Hayley is on the couch groaning, I can hear her from Nico's bed. The bedside me is cold and empty, I have no idea where Nico is. I think he was here last night when I fell asleep? I honestly can't remember, I'm pretty sure he was.

I'm hungover, I feel better than what Hayley sounds like. Maybe she's at that age where alcohol just destroys her. I'm not excited to be old. I love my nights of binge drinking.

My phone buzzes.

I think I'm still drunk

I chuckle, swinging my feet off the bed. Somehow, I managed to dress myself in a sports bra, sweatpants, and a tank top before passing out. I surprise myself, because I was loaded. Between those two, I met my match, they're terrible influences. Mixing Archie in that mix is going to be an absolute nightmare, if he was here last night, I wouldn't be moving right now.

"Can you tell the sun to go back to bed?" Hayley rubs her eyes, she has makeup everywhere on her face. She looks far from comfortable sprawled out on the couch.

I burst out in laughter looking at her. She stands, almost falls over, balances herself with the arm of the couch then slowly walks to the bath-room.

I turn around to the kitchen looking at all the soda cans, two empty glass bottles of alcohol, and a few beer bottles lying on the counter. I start rinsing everything and tossing them in bags. If I don't do this now, I'm afraid I never will, the second I sit on that couch I'm going to refuse to move.

With the sound track of Hayley down the hall, I've never been happier to be nineteen and not be drugged down by hangovers.

With every can and bottle I put in recycling bags, I feel more and more at home. I'm really uneasy about how at home I feel here. I know where everything is, I don't hesitate to grab food, or a drink even though I don't pay for anything. I let Hayley just walk into the house like it was nothing, not that Nico cared, at least it didn't show. He doesn't tell me not to do anything, I keep getting more and more comfortable here. Going back to the dorms is going to be a nightmare. I don't want to share a kitchen or share bathrooms. I want to stay put.

I feel terrible having these thoughts. We got in a huge fight that ended up with Nico being in a burning building because he wanted me to stay longer. I know it was him not communicating, but damn it, I wish I knew how bad I wanted to stay that night.

If I would have tuned in to how I was feeling literally hours before, none of this would have happened. We never would have gotten in the fight, I never would have walked away, and Nico would have been safe in my arms, not battling flames.

I'm not even sure if I'm going to get a dorm again. I still haven't looked at news reports. But since they lost a shit ton of living space, I'm assuming everyone who will be getting a dorm is going to be a transplant. I am not. They'll probably expect me to move into my dad's. I love my dad, I don't want to be living with him in college. I don't think we could handle each other for another three years.

Nico's house is comfy. It's peaceful. I don't want to imagine living anywhere but here.

Plus, I get to wake up next to *that* every morning.

"Crisis averted." Hayley sits on the couch, tossing her phone on the coffee table, resting her elbow on the arm of the couch holding her head.

"Josh is being annoying. He's acting like I'm never coming back. Can you keep a secret?"

I look at her over my shoulder frozen, bracing myself. She always asks this before a bomb is dropped. It's never a good one.

"Arch is really pushing us to move here. Other than a few friends, we don't have anyone in London, and he's really been taking a liking to New York." She looks at me, watching my mouth drop. "He may or may not have already gotten the paperwork for us to move here."

My entire face lights up, before I can scream, she interrupts me.

"There's still a lot of loopholes to jump through, but because he's married to me and there's immediate family here, it's a bit easier."

I drop a can in the sink running up to her tackling her on the couch in a giant hug, of course I cry. I wouldn't be me if I didn't cry.

She laughs patting me on my back. We stay here for a while, it's uncomfortable, we don't care. Like me, Hayley's never connected with people. People always thought us having a 20 year age gap was weird, because it is. My dad just started telling people we were sisters, and honestly, I think that's why we are the way that we are. It wasn't weird that she flew me out to London on summer holidays, she came home at Christmas, she disowned my mom the second she started acting that way towards me. She's my big sister, there's no question about it.

All though, some of the looks, and the questions my father got when people realized he was only a few years older than Hayley, ended up with him rolling his eyes and walking away from the conversation. If you don't know us, then it's hard to explain to other people.

The doorbell rings obsessively. "I'll get it. You clean." Hayley sighs, like the alcohol is weighing her down hundreds of pounds.

She stands up, forcing me into a tumble on the ground. Thankfully I land on her pillow and blanket. I look up into the kitchen, there's a lot of dishes left. I push myself off the floor.

"Cam. Are you expecting mail?" Hayley stands just where I can see her from the kitchen, holding a package in front of her. It's at least three feet long. "It's kind of heavy. It was just left there."

"Nico might have ordered me something since everything burned?" I question it, "He never said anything. Open it."

"There's no return, your address isn't even on it. It's just your name. It's suspish."

I walk closer watching her rip it open. Hayley's face turns white, I swear even her brown hair is turning white. I don't think she's breathing. It looks like her eyes are about to pop out of her head, if she doesn't pass out first.

"What is it?" I ask, taking a step closer.

"Doesn't matter. I'll be back, okay?"

"No Hayley. What the fuck is it?" I pull the package from her, she shields it from me. "Let go."

"No." The scolding in her voice takes me back a step, I've never heard her talk like that to anyone before.

I try to step forward, she holds the package to her side. "Don't try to take me down, the same people who trained you, I trained with."

I grind my teeth, normally the sound would be driving me insane, right now I'm just determined. I grab onto the package pulling it towards me, she tugs it back straightening her arm, instantly I grab her arm above her elbow, quickly squeezing my thumb, and pointer finger. I watch pain from the pressure points radiate through her face. She tries to move the package closer to her body, until I squeeze harder, taking full control.

I grab it listening to her pleading with me not to look.

I do anyway. I unravel the pack, expecting her to rip it out of my hands, she doesn't. The entire top is ruffled from her trying to squeeze the box, I rip it down the side, there's something white at the top, it's like a knob? Is that bone? There's a lot of red. *What the fuck.* I rip down the entire side, dropping it, screaming. The flesh is wrinkled, there's hair on the skin, an elbow, wrist, hand, four fingers.

I cover my mouth, still screaming. I seriously don't want to be looking at it, yet I can't stop staring at it.

My phone is ringing, Hayley grabs it ignoring the call. "We need to go."

My legs want to run away, my feet are sunk into the ground. I can't move, no matter how hard I want to. Suddenly a cup of water is splashed on my face, I stop screaming, I wipe the water away with my hands. Looking at her dumbfounded.

She puts all of her belongings in her bag, "Go to the front door, get your jacket on now."

I listen, watching her disappear into the hallway.

How is she so calm? My hands are shaking, I have to remind myself to breathe, and she is perfectly calm.

"We just have to get to the school. Josh is picking us up." Hayley looks at me dead in the eyes, "We have you Cam. Just breathe."

Not a single word was said on the walk to the school, nor the ride to my fathers, if that's even where we are going. Josh saw one look on Hayley's face and sped all the way there. He had absolutely no remorse on the road, and I was numb to the fear of his road rage. If it was any other day, I would have been terrified. I sat there quietly, my hands folded on my lap trying to breathe.

My phone was ringing so much from the front seat, it eventually stopped ringing. I think she shut it off. Nico is probably terrified seeing that on the camera and hearing me losing my mind.

"Let me call him back." I whisper the same moment Josh slams on his breaks. "Please, there's cameras, I probably set them off."

"Not happening." Hayley argues.

"Wait, did he hurt you?" Josh's eyes bounce between the two of us. Until they land on me. "I swear to God if he laid a single finger on you Cameron."

"He wasn't even there." The words come out in a yell. "Give me my fucking phone Hayley."

Hayley gets out of the car, slamming the door, walking heavy foot into my dad's house. I try to unbuckle my seat belt, I'm too frustrated to push hard enough on the button. Josh follows, he comes around my side opening the car door for me. I finally get my seatbelt off, and I storm past him running after Hayley as she uses her key to get inside.

"You're not my fucking mother so stop acting like it." I yell again, I'm so angry, so confused. My hands won't stop shaking. I don't think I have it in me not to yell when I'm talking.

Dad stops downstairs wearing a tight t-shirt, and sweatpants. It's what he wears before he goes to the gym. "What the hell is going on?" he hisses, his eyes locked on Hayley.

"Something is happening. Again. She got a package at Nico's house, and someone delivered an arm."

"Again?" I ask, trying not to burst out in laughter, watching my dad's face turn rock hard. Every muscle in his body tenses.

Josh turns around, walking out of the house slamming the door so hard the decorations on the floating shelves shake.

Dad walks up to me slowly, I shake my head the entire walk to the chair in the corner, I sit hugging my knees. I ask for my phone back, again, no one responds to me. I just want to tell Nico I'm safe.

I close my eyes, all I can see is the arm. Each time I close my eyes I see it more clearly. It was a man, the mass, the hair. Girls simply don't look like that. They're talking, I don't listen. I've been asking for years, nothing. The way they act when there's a car driving behind them for a bit too long. Brittney and Spencer's love story has been mixed up so many times. Charlie's scars match Nico's. Nico's circular scar that matches everyone else's.

They haven't said anything, Hayley's reaction, the way Josh left the house, the fear or maybe it was stress that took over my father's body within an instant.

I was right, they were hiding something from me.

The door opens, I'm assuming it's Josh, so I don't look up.

"Get the hell out." Dad curses.

I look up watching Nico stand a foot away from my dad with perfect posture, his back is so straight, his arms are out to his side. He keeps flexing his left hand, it's subtle, he's trying to hide it. He hasn't acknowledged my existence. "You need to get her out of the city, far away. Now."

"What the hell does that even mean?" Hayley stands from sitting on the stairs, taking big steps closer towards Nico, blocking me from his view.

Nico doesn't flinch, it's like he saw her coming, even though she was completely out of his sight.

"I'm trying to clean up a mess I never created." He steps around Hayley to look at me, Nico's face is hard. There's still a tiny bit of expression left in it, enough for me to read him for once. His face has completely fallen, there's no hardness in his expression when he looks at me. He looks back at dad. "I'm in love with her. I should have been home to stop her from seeing that."

Before I can register Nico's words, I'm running up to him in his arms. He has me so close to his body, one arm is around my waist, the other is coming up my back, with his hand on my head, holding me as close as he can. He kisses the top of my head, I still feel his eyes shooting over me. "I'm sorry." He whispers, "I'm so fucking sorry Cami." His voice cracks.

I look up at him, searching his eyes, trying to find an answer, "What is going on?" Nico looks down at me, not dropping his hands from me, his eyes are big, his mouth is in a hard line.

Josh slams the door again, the noise making me flinch, drawing my attention to him. He's holding his jaw, "Step away from him Cameron."

I look up at Nico. I'm so confused, tears are running down my face. I want to scream.

"It's okay baby." Nico speaks softly, he wipes my tears away.

I take a step back pulling at my roots, letting my scream out. "What the hell is happening!"

Nico reaches for me again, I swat his arm away. Someone tries to touch me from behind and I let out another scream. I'm extremely overstimulated all of a sudden. "I got a fucking arm delivered, doors are being slammed, Josh is getting punched, love is being confessed, someone tell me now, or I'm leaving."

Dad says my name.

"I have a room full upstairs, start talking before I go pack."

"She needs to stay." Josh drops his hand from his face. "He's packing. He won't shoot if she's here."

32

Nico

Cameron is sitting in that chair in the corner hugging her legs, she won't look at me. I was preparing myself to tell her the truth, I didn't think that having her in the same room as me not looking at me would be this painful.

Hearing her screaming, it felt like I had bugs crawling on me. It felt like my heart was being ripped out of my body, I felt her fear. I know what it's like to suddenly have your innocents ripped from you. That's exactly what happened to her. I've forced every bit of innocents she had left right out of her.

I lean against the wall scrubbing my face with my hands. This can't be fucking real. I want to cry. *I want to cry.* That's when you know this is too real. My parents were not prepared for me to fall in love with someone I was supposed to take on a job for. They were not prepared for this.

More basilisks line up in the living room.

"This is a nasty feeling of déjà vu." Liam walks around me, looking as confused as all the newcomers feel.

Everyone's here: Erik, Cameron, Josh, Dillon, William, Spencer, Brittney, Liam, Charlie, Adam, Hayley, and Archie.

"What's going on?" Liam asks, his voice is floating around the room unsure of who to ask.

I stand facing the couch, feeling Josh shoulder checks me hard. I glare at him, he refused to let me in, so I hit him. Of course, as my arm was rising, he laid eyes on my gun. You can't keep me from Cameron, and if you try, I will lose my fucking mind. Now he knows.

Erik explains what he knows, the entire time he's talking Cameron is sinking lower and lower into her chair.

I remember the kitchen from the last time I was here. When I needed to see Cameron for comfort. I walk towards it coming straight into Erik. I match his energy, glaring at him. I know he's bigger than me, but his daughter is here, and he will not show that side of him around her. Erik steps to the side so I can talk by. I open the cupboard right next to the fridge, it's a predictable spot. I fill a glass of water from the filter in front of the fridge taking it to Cameron.

I crouch in front of her, talking low and as gentle as I can. "You're going to need this. A lot of things are going to be said." She looks at me, her brown eyes are glossed with tears, the white of her eyes are red. She's too good at crying secretly. "I love you so much. I'm sorry I never told you sooner."

"I love you." The words leave her lips, shocking the both of us.

I've heard it before, I figured with me lying from withholding a truth, having a fucking gun, it would change how she felt. I wasn't expecting to hear it, especially after what all just happened. I don't think she was expecting to say it. I lean into her, kissing her head. Even though she said it back, she recoils at my touch. It wasn't noticeable, it's enough for me to know I'm losing her.

I turn around, scanning all of their faces. Every single one of them looks like they've walked into a war. I turn back around, looking at Cameron, taking a deep breath before I speak, trying to gain enough courage. "Nemean Mafia. We originate from Italy. The Lion moved his family to LA twenty two years ago after paying every news broadcast off in America." I look at Cameron watching her eyes fill with more tears. "I'm so sorry baby." My eyes are burning. This is so uncomfortable. I blink trying to stop the tears, and I turn around standing up, "You may remember us as the McKinnon's."

Every face in the room hardens. Dillon stands up moving towards me briskly ignoring Josh, Erik, and Hayley yelling at him to stop. I grab Dillon's wrist twisting it, he completely freezes, his face written with pain. I reach my other hand into my jacket pulling my gun out, passing it to him.

"It's the only one I have on me. I just came back from my dad's, there's five bullets check the chamber. Dillon unloads it, dumping the clip out on the table, tossing the gun next to it.

"Why?" Someone speaks up.

"The Lion tells everyone that The Basilisks shed too much blood." I look over at Cameron watching her watch everyone in the room. She doesn't say anything, she shakes her head at everyone. I haven't said anything, it was enough for her to put it together.

The Basilisks fell off the face of the word, now everyone in New York looks at them like a scary story. Some people know it's real, others don't.

"I searched everyone." Cameron says in a small voice.

"The FBI wiped it all." Brittney covers her mouth. "Cam."

"Don't." She barks, she's holding the water with such a tight grip I'm worried the glass might break.

I continue, "The lion says it was bloodshed. My dad's been talking about a deal that was made ever since I've been assigned." I stop talking immediately.

"McKinnon's were messy as fuck though." William looks at me, scrubbing his beard.

"Messy worked to get on Martin's level. Once he was threatening the drug trade, dad needed a way to get in. I wasn't born, I understand it as Martin bought drugs off the Nemean, then sold it to the 'McKinnon's'. I use my fingers around the word McKinnons. I sigh, "I don't fucking know. Everything I know is just what I've been told."

"Those kids we sold it to on New Years were scared as hell." Adam speaks, holding Charlie tighter. His voice is low, I'm surprised he can even remember that.

"What's the deal?" Cameron asks me, forcing my body to face her at the sound of her voice.

"Wait. How do we know we can trust you? Or that this isn't another set up?" Brittney looks at me, the second I look at her she slides closer into Spencer. She's absolutely terrified, I can't blame her. She faked her own death to save him, all of them.

"Archie." I whisper. "That's how you know you can trust me. I'm just another one of him." I look at him pleading, I don't know why but I am. "I'm not expecting you to trust me, I'm just expecting you to believe me."

"Nico." Cameron says my name, again drawing my attention. "What was the deal?"

"You."

Her chin quivers, her hands shaking. I reach down, taking the glass away from her, setting it on the table, so she doesn't dump it on herself. "My sister is Lucia. She failed. The original plan was for me, so my training started when I was twelve. They saw you dating girls, then we got close."

Cameron is visibly numb. She's not moving, she's not even blinking. I see a blanket folded up on an otter man near the chair, I unfold it covering her up. "You were only a job for me the first night, I swear. That was it." Nothing I say can make any of this better.

"What the hell do they want with my daughter?" Erik's voice vibrates the house. He's like a pissed off Zeus.

I ignore him standing up, raising my hands to my hair. "You're really fucking quiet! Speak up." I shout. I laugh dryly once. "You guys remember that trip to London, when Cameron was what? Two months old? Lizzy refused to go, she was depressed. She needed time to not be a mother?" I speak, not directed to anyone. "So, she stayed home, so did Charlie." Every word I speak tastes like gasoline.

"I had to sell the strip club." Charlie's tone is very defensive.

"Oh perfect!" I clap my hands together once, "So you also remember getting kidnapped by my father, and instead of getting tortured for the whereabouts of Martin's unsold drug stash you made a deal? You sold my girlfriend out instead of confessing."

"He never told me anything." Charlie argues overly defensively.

"Nice try Charlie." I'm so angry, I can't look at anyone other than her. My heart rate is pounding in my ears fast. "Nemean had multiple spy's in the Basilisks. We do it everywhere. We are everywhere, so don't try to bullshit yourself out of this. Noah stayed in the hallway and heard Martin tell you after your tattoo."

Charlie's face turns white.

"He was supposed to walk around the hallway, so he could be at the back of the crowd when you arrived. He made it on stage awfully fast to pull that gun on you. Then you gave him his check, and dismissed him, calling out to everyone else who didn't believe in you and wanted to retire. I can call someone right now, that was a getaway driver for you that can verify everything I'm saying." I wasn't even born when this happened, and I know I got every detail right. I really hope this is enough for them to somewhat believe me.

"It seems brilliant to blow your cover." Archie barks.

I exhale. "I'm already dead, a cover being blown is the least of my worries. So, Charlie tell me. I'm generally curious. How did you sell yourself short because of not giving the location up."

"I couldn't go through it again!" She admits loudly, everyone turns their head to look at her in a hard expression, Adam pulls his arm back, moving his body away from her.

"I've been going through it for six years." I yell the words. I have to bite my lips together, close my eyes and take a deep breath to calm down. "The pain, the suffering. That was my training. That was what was needed to not make me feel anything. You couldn't handle it a second time, so you sell Cameron out!" My arm is widely shaking, I can't breathe. Thankfully that gun is still unloaded, and on the table.

"Nico." Cameron stands in front of me. "Those scars?" I look at her not saying a word. "What did they do?"

"It's not important." My tone is so much calmer talking to her, there's no anger, no rage. I reach out to her, brushing a stand of hair behind her ear, holding her cheek in my hand. She doesn't flinch at my touch anymore.

"Is it going to stop now?" Her eyes are wide, showing off the whites. She's so worried, and I'm so confused how she's worried about me right now. "What if I refuse? What will happen to you?"

I move my thumb against her cheek brushing the tears away, she just wanted the truth, and I'm going to give it to her. "It was reported back right away you were a girl. You are less than a year older than me. If you accept or refuse, I'm dead. This was the only reason why I was born."

Her breathing cuts off, the more I speak, tears fill her eyes even more.

"I need you to refuse. Don't do it for me. I was trying to buy you more time, and my parents turned the game, that's why I wasn't home this morning. If you refuse, they will come after every one of your cousins one by one. It will give you time to fight. Even though I know you won't stand for that." I stroke my thumb against her cheek, "I need you to think about yourself right now."

"You'll be okay Nico." Spencer says in a low voice, "Nothing will happen."

"Did Lizzy know, is that why?" Liam asks, rubbing his hands together, his voice is mumbled. Pieces of the puzzle finally look like they're coming together.

My eyes look down to Cameron watching her face lean into my hand. As much as I don't want to, I look Charlie square in the eyes. "Yes. We have a film of Charlie telling Lizzie the second she was released."

Cameron turns around, falling against me, her entire body is shaking. "You trained me. You pushed me harder than anyone to protect myself. You knew. You just wanted to look like a hero."

Charlie stands. "I didn't think anything was actually going to happen. It was so long ago. It was a complicated situation, Cameron."

Voices in the room start flooding. Cameron moves away from me, suddenly a gunshot fills the air.

33

Cameron

My ears are ringing, the guns heavy in my hands, at least it was. Now it just feels warm, and I feel absolutely nothing.

Nico steps in front of me talking, I still can't hear him, his lips are moving. He's talking with his hands, I follow his hand with my eyes, watching him take the gun out of my tight grip.

My hearing slowly comes back, everyone's voices are getting louder. I watch Nico's lips move, trying to focus on his words, "Breath Cameron."

My lungs empty on demand, I had no idea I was holding my breath. For a second, I'm light headed until I see the commotion I caused behind him.

"Get her on the fucking ground!" For a second, I thought Liam was talking about me, he wasn't.

Charlie is pale, Adam has stepped back, his hands covering his face. Spencer, and Dad are hovering over Charlie. Hayley and Josh come rushing down the stairs with a black bag.

I don't cry, I don't move, I just stand there, watching.

Dillon says something to Nico. Dillon grabs the gun, taking it downstairs.

William drags the couch, it isn't until I see the blood spattered on the cushions, tears run down my face.

"What the fuck did I do?" I grab onto Nico watching Charlie.

"Ambulance is coming." Liam barks.

"Nico." Dad looks up, "Take her to your place. I'll stop by tonight."

"No." I argue, wiping my face, "I can't. She's..." I can't even finish my sentence.

Josh pulls his eyes away from Charlie's body on the floor. "Cameron. Go. Now!" He shouts at me.

Nico grabs my hand, pulling out his phone dragging me out of the house. He's talking to someone. I can't bring myself to listen. I'm trying to understand everything that happened today, the arm, Nemean Mafia, The Basilisks. I don't know how I reached for that gun, it was like something took over me. I saw red, and my rage for Charlie was too much.

She sold me out as a newborn, I was innocent, and she gave me up. Not only that, but she lied to everyone. I lost my mother. She pretended to care about me. I'm sure all those Friday nights we spent together it could have been brought up. Somewhere along the line in nineteen fucking years it could have been brought up. We all deserved a warning at least.

I deserved a warning.

Sirens are getting closer, Nico drags me down a back alley. We're still walking, and he's still on the phone.

I'm angry at everyone. I'm angry at him. I'm angry at the lies.

I was a job to him, nothing more. *A job.*

I'm still trying to wrap my head around his sister being Lucia. We went to the bar together, she didn't know him. They never spoke like they knew each other.

Nico stops walking. We covered good ground, the closest bus stop is a few blocks away from dads house. I look at the bench, I could sit, I won't be able to sit still. My heart is hardly beating. My chest feels heavy. My entire life no one's been honest with me. If I knew about the Basilisks, I would have been careful. I love history, I dug into crime in New York. I know everything about the Basilisks. I know the FBI recruited someone that helped them partnered up with a double crossed police officer, I know they turned on themselves, I knew a new boss came in and ended everything. I knew about the Mckinnons. I know they cut off the tongue of McKinnon. Everything I shouldn't know, I know. The Basilisks were all over the place, they were messy. If I would have known the truth, I could have suspected something to be wrong. I could have protected myself mentally. I wouldn't have fought my dad so hard about him being so careful over me.

Charlie was the one to first have the idea of me to train. She knew what was coming for me. She knew that it would have been bad news to mix my anger with weight training, she did it anyway. Everyone went along with it. No one stopped to consider what might happen, because they didn't think there was any real potential threat.

The look on Adam's face, he was terrified, hurt, angry.

"Get in." Nico says in a dry voice.

I look at him, my chest moving rapidly from my breathing.

He places the back of his fingers on my face, I cringe at his touch. I'm not sure if he notices. "Baby, you're going to my place. It's okay." He opens the back door of the black SUV.

Gabe looks at me with a broken face. There's someone in the passenger, I look past them.

I push myself across the back seat, making space between me and Nico. I let myself zone out the window, worried about Charlie, trying to shove everything deep down.

We've been stuck in traffic forever. It's making me panic even more about the ambulance. I wipe my face, thankful that Nico is keeping his distance from me. "Why did Lucia take me to that bar?"

Gabe makes a weird noise. "It's the Lion's den. Everyone there is *employed* by him."

"So, you knew I was nothing but a job to Nico?" My throat feels like it's closing in. I'm going to start a huge fight, and I'm not even scared. I've already lost everything. There's no way anyone will forgive me.

"My job was to date Lucia, to fix your friendship. The Lion thought maybe we could help you get closer." He pauses to let the GPS talk. "Listen Cameron. You weren't a job to Nico, not when he saw you."

I laugh, "The break in at the dorm?"

No response.

"The fire?"

Still no response.

"You say I'm safe with you, but that's far from the truth." I gaze out my window, refusing to look over at Nico. "I wish I never met you. You destroyed my life before I even met you. I hate you."

A beeping in the front seat goes off, the same time there's a gust of wind filling up the back seat. The door slams shut. I have a feeling I'm alone back here.

Good.

We finally start moving, Gabe doesn't say a word, the passenger is dead quiet. For once, I'm not crying.

I walk into Nico's house. He's not here. I'm only here because this is where my dad expects me to be. I sit by the door, hugging my legs, resting my forehead on my knees. I want to call someone, I don't know who would answer me. Besides, I don't even think I have my phone on me.

It only took me a day to lose everyone, all the relationships I built have vanished. The switch flicked for them to leave me as fast as my mother's did.

The lock on the door buzzes, followed by the door opening and closing, I don't move. It's Nico, I don't want to look at him. He doesn't stop for me, he walks right past me. The door opens again, I hear him and Gabe talking. Gabe says something about the arm, then leaves. I'm so numb, the cold air from outside just brushes past me, not even making me shiver.

The house is dead quiet, until I hear his bedroom door slam. I can hear him talking, I think he's on the phone.

Tears run down my face, the reality of everything that's happened today, followed along with what I said to Nico hits me at once. I'm positive he can hear me crying, he doesn't come, not like he normally would.

The sun from the living room window shifts in the sky. It's getting late. The noise from the door unlocking makes me jump. I've been sitting here for hours.

Dad bends down in front of me. His eyes are red, and glossy. "Charlie died."

I cover my mouth, trying to hold in a scream. I fail, everything feels like it's closing in on me, I can't breathe. Dad wraps me up in his arms apologizing, I'm not sure what for, he won't stop apologizing.

"Daddy, I didn't mean to." I start to sob uncontrollably, trying to speak. "Oh my God."

Her family flashes through my mind, Adam, her kids. All the memories we had as a family. Everything hits me at once, turning my cries into screams.

Dad switches places with Nico, his eyes are also red and glossy. "Cami. Hey." His hand almost touches my face, I lean into sealing his touch.

I look at him, my entire face tightens, gasping for air.

"Come here." Nico picks me up off the floor, carrying me to the couch. Him and Dad are saying something to each other, to me everything sounds like white noise.

He sets me on the couch, tossing a knitted blanket over me that I always use. He kisses my head hard, letting his lips hover slightly over my skin before walking away.

Brittney leans down in front of me and passes me a coffee cup, there's a tea bag sticking out of it. I look up seeing everyone. April, Spencer, Liam, William, Dillon, Josh, Hayley, and Archie. Standing around me all looking like they've fallen into a million pieces. Someone slides my phone over the table, sliding it closer to me.

"I'm so sorry." I spit the words out like they're hot ashes.

William leans down on the other side of Brittney, he puts his hand on my knee, "This is something that happens in our life, okay?"

"We love you." Dillon chokes up his words.

Liam sits beside me at my feet, "Don't do this Cameron. We will figure it out for the kids, we have time now that we know what's happening. Just don't do this."

34

Nico

I seal a letter to Cameron in an envelope storing it under the lamp on my end table. The corner is sticking out, she'll be able to notice it. I need her to notice it. My writing wasn't pretty, I had a lot to say at once. I'm not even sure how much sense it made.

I got off the phone with my lawyer, I faxed over the signed copies of my will. I left everything to her, house, money, the few things I own here.

Even if she does hate me and what she said wasn't just from anger, it won't stop me from making sure she's taken care of. Hearing her say those words in such a strong tone, made me instantly start crying. I met her, and I felt alive for the first time in my life. Everything changed for the better. I was able to feel, I felt like I belonged somewhere. Even though I felt like I belonged was short lived, I felt it. I got to experience it. I was able to eat when I wanted, I didn't have to starve anymore, physical pain wasn't a regular occurrence, I was done with the torture. I was free. She made me free.

I'm not enough for her, and I never will be. That's just the facts, and now I'm left here alone trying to put together what comes next, hoping there is a next. There won't be. My pretending is fictional story lines. Doing what I did today was a suicide mission. I told Cameron that I might die, I will. There's no if and or butts about it. If I didn't tell the Basilisks the truth, I might have survived, now with Charlie dead, dad will know the truth. I can turn myself in and have it easier on me, or I can hide and have the pain so much worse.

It would have been easier on me if one of the Basilisks killed me like I thought they would have. They are way too forgiving.

I look down at the will, my hands are shaking, tears are running down my face. I'm not ready. I thought I was, I knew I was, living with her, feeling pure joy, laughing, I'm not ready. I'm scared.

I do belong somewhere, I belong to her.

The door for the room opens, I don't have time to cover up the mess that I am.

Brittney crouches down in front of me. Cameron's told me that she's a mother figure for her, I wish I got to experience the kind of love she has right now in the living room. Brittney takes the will from my hands, she's reading every last word.

"I thought you said there was a possibility you could live?" She looks broken, it's not because of me, it's because of the pain that will be inflicted on Cameron. Right now, I'm honestly not even sure if what happens to me will bother her much.

It dawns on me that I lost the only person who would have cared if I wasn't alive. No one will miss me. Other than Cameron no one will even remember me, and that's only if she doesn't force me out of her memories.

I'm going to disappear, and not a single person will know. I give her a half assed attempt at a broken smile, tears are still in my eyes. "I told everyone about the deal, and that she'll be with Nemean." I try to shrug it off. "I couldn't go out without trying to protect her. Can you do me a favor?"

Brittney looks at me silently.

"Can you make sure she actually reads my letter? She made it clear she hates me, and I don't want her to burn it." I look at it, bringing her eyes towards it. "I'm sorry for everything I've caused tonight."

"Did you trick me to talk about the FBI, the same time as Nemean, and the Basilisks, so she would know we have her?"

"I really hope you're still in contact with someone." I stand up off the bed, "My dad has no weakness. He's smart. My mom resorts to violence. Wear bulletproof vests. They'll take her phone, give her a tracker she can wear. They own Junction Square. Downstairs is where all the business takes place." I stop, looking at Brittney watching her eyes water, "Martin sold my parents machine guns, attack them when they won't be expecting you. I don't know where they're hidden."

I walk out of the room, stopping in the hallway leaning against the wall silently watching Cameron sitting on the couch still covered up, holding her coffee cup. "Finché non ci incontreremo di nuovo, amore" I whisper.

Hayley looks at me, her face falls. I let out a shaky breath looking at Cameron one more time before walking away.

She'll be protected. She'll be okay.

35

Cameron

Brittney called Spencer and Dad away. The rest of us are sitting here in silence. I want Nico in here, I want to be able to apologize to him. I'm angry at him, I also want to feel at peace with him. I want to be home.

"How's Adam?" I ask quietly.

"He lost his wife." April is quiet. "Cameron what happened?"

"I don't know. Secrets, lies, I didn't realize I was reaching for the gun until after I shot it. I heard what she set me up for and I snapped. I need Nico. I was such a bitch, I need to apologize." I stand. I'm acting anything but myself. I sound like a robot, I can hardly get off the couch. I see my phone sitting on the coffee table, I grab it, stuffing it into my hoodie pocket.

"Stop." Dad says, they're standing right outside the bedroom. "He's not here."

I pull out my phone walking towards them in the hall, Hayley did shut it off. I turn it on in silence waiting for it to load. Feeling everyone's eyes glued onto me.

It finally turns on to call him. It immediately goes to voice-mail. "I'm sorry. Come home please. I love you. You never deserved me treating you like that."

Brittney takes off her bracelet, "Do not take this off." She grabs my wrist, her hands are shaking so badly trying to do the small clamp Spencer is forced to take over.

Where's Nico. That's the only thing I want to ask. I've had a lot dumped on me, and I need him. I need his touch, I need to apologize. I pull out my phone calling him, again. It goes to voicemail, so I try again, and again. My heart sinks. I'm worried, I'm scared.

I don't know what I'm supposed to do. I need him to tell me what to do.

Brittney pulls out her phone, her hands are shaking, tears are soaking her face. All I can hear is Brittney and Nico talking, he sounds so hurt. My heart is shattering listening to the pain in his voice. Dad steps closer to me, wrapping his arm around me holding me as tight as he can.

"I couldn't go without trying to protect her." The tears in his voice, the way he looked at me when I was on the floor before he brought me to the couch. He covered me up, kissed my head. I cover my mouth. The second my mind understands what he's saying, my hands muffle a crying scream, I fall against the wall, my legs give out on me, dad holds me upright.

He was saying goodbye. He killed himself to keep me safe. He told Brittney how to protect me.

I'm being steadied by multiple people, I don't have the power to stand on my own, but I need to find it. I'm not going to let my family go through this again, I'm not going to let Nico die in vain. He wanted to protect me, and I want to protect everyone who's here. I'm not going to let this touch their children.

Something consumes my body, I don't know the feeling, it's like I'm suddenly possessed with confidence. My legs stand up on their own, my hands are suddenly steady. I look at my dad, before I brush his hand off of my arm. I look at this worried face, my heart breaks seeing the sudden fear in his eyes. It's like he can recognize this sudden change in me. It's like he's seen it before. He takes a step back, he nods at me.

Junction Square. Everyone who works there is employed by the Lion.

I grab my phone, calling the same number that called me on repeat the night of the fire. I don't even say anything, Gabe just says, "I'm waiting out front."

My heart sinks, my life is ending, but if there's even the slightest chance Nico can survive, he might even be with Gabe. I need to go to find out, I need to try to save him.

Hayley says my voice in a cry.

"We have you Cam." William speaks in a broken whispered voice.

"Don't go." Liam takes a step forward, his voice getting closer. "Don't pay for their fuck ups."

The room falls silent. I know what I have to do, hearing them so broken is making my decision harder, the longer I wait, the more likely Nico won't survive. If he's even alive still.

"Rooftop." Spencer looks down at me. "Whenever. We will get there."

"You guys were the Basilisks that saved each other." I look at my father with a small smile, that realization is oddly comforting. "Now, it's my turn."

I take my eyes from my dad, my face tenses up, more tears falling from my eyes. I turn around running out of Nico's house directly into the front seat of the black SUV. I needed to go before to change my mind.

I frantically look in the back seat, Nico's not here. I stare at the empty seats, waiting for him to appear. Gabe puts the vehicle into drive.

There's no music, there's no talking. The only sound is my sniffling. I have nothing with me. I don't even know if I'm going to survive after tonight. I don't know what I'm walking into. I don't know who's going to be waiting for me. I have no idea what they have on my family, or what they have on me. I'm not capable of this. I'm a college student. That's all I am.

"Is he alive?" I wipe my face, I can't cry any more tears, I've completely ran out.

Gabe sits in silence making my breathing cut off. "I don't know." He sounds defeated. "I can't get a hold of him."

"I told him I hated him." My voice is weak, I don't have any strength left in my body.

Gabe sits in silence. Nico believed me when I said it, I heard the recording. I hope there was a small amount of doubt in him that never believed me, I shot my aunt, I killed her, I found out about him, my family, my future. I couldn't hold anything in. I'm a ticking time bomb, I regret it, and I might not be able to ever tell him.

"I just left my entire family, while they're grieving. Take me back." I raise my voice, finally realizing what the hell I just did.

"I can't." Gabe's voice goes hard. "The Lion has been notified."

"Unnotify him then!"

"If Nico is alive, that would give him an even worse death."

I gaze out my window, watching the cars, and buildings pass by. My entire life changed within a day, last night was so normal.

Gabe pulls into an empty spot outside the bar. The line up to get in is huge. I don't even know what day it is anymore. I don't know what time it is, all I know is I'm absolutely exhausted. I try to focus on my breathing as Gabe gets out of the car. I raise my hand to unlock the door, it's shaking uncontrollably. My throat is dry, my eyes hurt, my head is pounding.

Gabe opens my door, I quickly ask for Advil. I watch him open the glove box grabbing a bottle, then reaching past me for an unopened bottle of water. I pop the pill, drinking the water, tipping my head back, squeezing the bottle in my palm crushing it, as the water goes down my throat. My legs kick out to step outside, I know there's no backing out, I just need to get this over with.

The bouncers see me, then without a second thought, they are moving over for me and Gabe to pass. They go on their radio pushing people out of the way to make a path, Gabe follows, I tag behind regretting every single step. If I knew he was alive, walking would be so much easier. Right now, it feels like I'm trying to breathe out a wet paper straw.

Gabe opens a door directly across from the front door, I follow him down the steep stairs, grabbing onto the railing so I don't dominos us both over. We reach the bottom, the hallway turns right, there's a door with a short wide man standing out front. He opens the door revealing a tall skinny man. He looks at me, instantly shivers shoot down my spine. He smiles, making every inch of my skin crawl.

Gabe steps out of the way, there's a man in a large leather chair, just waiting for me. I'm assuming this is the Lion, he looks nothing like Nico. They don't share any of the same features. Unlike Nico being in shape from working out, he's overweight. Nico has a full head of hair, this man has a bald spot on the top of his head. They're face shapes are different, he's sitting, and I can tell he's shorter than his son.

"Cameron. Time has come." His Italian accent is very thick, it's almost hard to understand him.

The Skinny man stands so close to me his chest brushes against my arm. "Phone." He grabs it from my hand.

I watch him walk over to the corner, grabbing something off the ground, I can't tell what it is. He drops my phone on the floor and starts wailing on it. My face crinkles up. I had pictures on that phone from Nico's birthday, he was smiling so perfectly, his eyes were sparkling, he was holding me so tightly, and now it's gone. Pictures with my family, memories that I might never get another chance are gone. My stomach sinks thinking I might not be able to see them again. Even if I got a chance to go to the rooftop, they might not know I'm there.

He just ruined the only memories I have of the people I love.

The Lion snaps, drawing my eyes back to him. "Any communication with a Basilisk is a death penalty." The way he says it, straight to the point.

My heart pulls in my chest.

"Nico found out the hard way."

Gabe slouches. "When?"

"Guys are dumping the body right now."

I almost lose my footing, I can't breathe, the air is fucking toxic. My eyes somehow manage to fill up with more tears, until I watch his dad smirk.

"Now there's no distractions."

I take a step forward the same time Gabe steps in front of me to stop myself from swinging at him. "Where do you want me to take her sir?"

"Ashley will probably be the best bet." The Lion waves his hand towards the door for us to leave. "We will have a sit down over brunch tomorrow. Make sure she dresses appropriately."

36

Cameron

I was so tired last night, I didn't sleep. I watched the sun go down, I watched the sun come up. I went to the bathroom ninety thousand times to pee. Night time anxiety apparently makes me have to pee an excessive amount. Even with me getting up a million times, I never met Ashley, she wasn't at her house this morning. I don't know who she is, or why I'm staying with her. Gabe took me to Nico's, all of the clothes were still in bags, untouched, I sent Gabe in after making him park down the block. I couldn't look at the house, let alone go into the space that I once shared with Nico. If I would have looked at the bed we shared every night, I wouldn't have come back out of the house. I changed in the back seat of the SUV, Hayley picked out all these clothes, at least I still have a small piece of her with me.

One thing I am thankful that Gabe brought out for me was a dirty hoodie of Nico's. I haven't sniffed it yet, I'm so scared to touch it and make his scent disappear. It's going to lay next to the pillow on my bed. This is going to be the closest thing I can have to bringing him back, his scent beside me at night time.

The letter Nico wrote me is sitting between my fingertips, his handwriting is on the outside, for a guy he had really nice writing. All of his last thoughts to me are in here, everything he wanted to tell me is right here. I can't bring myself to open it. I also need to know what's inside.

"What is it?" Gabe asks softly.

"I don't know." I whimper.

I can't let myself cry, I did my make up, and I'm scared that if I smug it the Lion will kill me. He allowed his son to die on his watch, his fucking son. I'm trash compared to that, he wouldn't hesitate for a second if it was me.

I have absolutely nothing left. I'm a murder, I'm broken, I can't look in the mirror because the person I used to be died with Charlie and Nico. I'm a disgrace to my family, I was a joke to Charlie when she made the deal. My mom never even fought for my life, she let it happen.

"How did you get here?" I quietly ask.

"Born into it. We all are. The only people who weren't were black-mailed from other Mafias, and Cartels, or they are brought in as test dummies to test other Mafias." Gabe turns into a hotel, waiting in the line for the valet parking.

"You mean, the McKinnon's. How many people did they kill?"

"Doesn't matter." Gabe opens his car door. "Don't remember them by their body count."

I follow. We were told to dress accordingly, both of us are in jeans, Sweaters and winter coats. In my mind I was expecting a lot fancier. Maybe that's just because of the rumors I heard.

The door of the hotel is open for us, I've been in many fancy hotels, I'm not even fazed. Shiny floor, hotel staff loading up luggage on carts, staff working the elevators, water fountain in the lobby. I follow him in a large area with tables scattered around. We walk past a buffet table, into a section with frost windows. The Skinny guy from last night closes the door behind us. I grab for my necklace taking deep breaths, trying to gain enough confidence to go through with this.

I wonder if this is why Nico bought me the necklace?

It's only me, Gabe, the skinny guy, the round guy who was guarding the door, and the Lion. We have our own private buffet section. The table is long, there's at least ten chairs on each side.

Everyone walks towards the buffet, I follow. I'm far from hungry, food on my plate will help me blend in. I haven't eaten anything in almost forty eight hours, and I don't plan to. I'm every bit fucked up, and not even food will help me feel anything right now.

I sit down with a plate full of food that will never be eaten. I wait patiently seeing what everyone else does before they eat. I'm just taking a wild guess assuming they don't say grace. I try not to look up at Nico's father, he killed my future. The one I wanted to be with, the one who I could see myself with in the suburbs. He took it away from me. He took my family away. He made it so any contact with them would get me killed, and I'm pissed.

"You will be getting a tattoo today. I recommend you eat, or you will pass out. Our tattoos are different from the level you entered in, since you were technically born into us, and as a woman you will be a lioness, just some shading. You listen, or you die. There's no rules, minus no contact with any other crime group unless it's a job. Including companies owned by that group."

I take a bit of my breakfast sausage forcing it down my throat. I've never gotten a tattoo before, and if everyone is right about tattoos, I can't do it on an empty stomach.

"You will be dropping out of school because of your closeness with a certain professor." He slides a black touch screen phone across the table. We will not track you solely because we know exactly what you do in your free time. With my son gone, and you not in school you will be going to work then back home. If you are on good behavior for a few weeks, we will let you move out of Ashley's. Miss a single call, you will be hunted down. Gabe will baby sit you to make sure you understand."

"I— I understand sir." I lock my fingers on my lap.

I don't understand. I don't understand how any of this has happened to me. I don't get how I'm in this position. I don't get how I'm suffering. I don't get how the man I love is dead. I don't get how I'm forbidden to see my dad, or my best friend, or anyone else who I love.

I eye the phone, "Can I take it?"

The lion nods, "Your number is on a label on the back."

I flip my phone over seeing a white label maker sticker with ten numbers on the back. I'm never going to remember this number. I could barely remember the number I had since I was nine. I can remember dates in history like its nothing, phone numbers I can't do. I slide it into my bag that's hanging on the back of my seat and go back to picking at my food.

I can't even help myself to imagine what Nico would think of this food. He was starting to get super critical, not in an annoying way, he just knew what he liked. If it wasn't mine or his cooking, he had an opinion. He probably had an opinion about my cooking, but he was smart enough not to speak. Not that I would do anything to him. The sausages are too greasy, the bacon isn't crispy, the eggs aren't fluffy enough. The only thing he would be happy about is the fruit.

His dad's sitting across from me, and I can't even tell him how wonderful Nico was, how he lit up a room when he walked in, how happy he made me feel. How he helped me control every bit of emotion I ever felt. How he was able to calm me down before I even started to feel anything. He knew when I needed to be alone, or when I needed a distraction. I don't know how Nico knew to do anything like that for me, because he never would have felt love in his entire life if it wasn't for me. I want to believe he felt it before he turned twelve, but I don't think he did. Now that I know his sister Lucia, she's too self centered to put any attention on him. I want to tell his father that I made him the center of my world, I was able to love him. I was able to take care of him and make sure he had every need met because as a father he failed to do so. I want to tell him that I failed to love Nico the way he deserved, that I never noticed how harsh my words were towards him. I never knew why he had such a hard time opening up to me, and why he wasn't able to communicate with me about his feelings, or what was going on in his mind. I want to tell him that I sort of understand now, maybe not completely, but I want to tell his father I'm trying to understand his son better. Even though it's too late.

But I can't.

I want to stick up for my dead boyfriend, I want him to be looking down at me with a smile on his face, I can't because he gave Brittney clear instructions knowing I would most likely hear them. He wanted me to be smart, he wanted me to be safe, if I stick up for him, I'm anything but that.

I walk into Ashley's house, taking my shoes off by the door. I rest my body against the wall, I'm so tired I don't want to move. I also know if I crawl into bed, I won't be able to stop crying. Nico's letter is in my hand, my shopping bags from his house are all on my arms, I don't have the energy to be packing them around any longer.

"I'm impressed." Gabe looks at me with a sad expression. "I don't know how you didn't shake him down."

"Nico would have lost it. Gabe. Is he really dead?" I ask, even though I know the answer. I'm almost desperate for a lie, because he cannot be dead. For once I need someone to lie to me.

Gabe looks down, not answering me.

"Babe?" A female voice calls down the hallway.

Footsteps run down the hall. I look at her black hair, her small smile, big round eyes. I know her from somewhere. The night from Junction Square races through my mind. My eyes went wide, I held her against the wall by her throat.

"There it is! I'm Ashley." She sticks her arm out in front of her waiting for me to shake it.

I don't grab her hand.

"Wow. Okay." She takes her arm back to her body, turning around walking back down the hall.

I never looked around last night. Gabe took me to my room, and I laid there in the dark. I only know where the bathroom is. I walk past the kitchen, a living room with no TV, just couches. I reach the end of the hallway, there's a huge living room. A three person couch, two chairs, a large TV hanging on the wall, and a surround system.

"If you're looking for an apology, you're not getting one." I cross my arms the best I can with the bags attached to my body.

"About that." Ashley sits on the couch hugging her legs. Gabe sits beside her, putting his arm behind her on the back of the couch.

That one simple gesture is enough to make me feel envious. They're both alive, they get to touch each other, they get to be near each other. They get to hear each other's voices. They get to be together. Me and Nico spent so much time frustrated with each other, about us not being together, we took precious time away.

"Gabe randomly broke up with me, his job with Lucia was super quiet, I heard they started dating, and I was super upset." She rubs her throat. "I could feel your grasp for a month."

I pucker my lips looking up to the roof, unable to look at their simple sign of affection. I want to throw something, I want to break whatever I can. I'm fucking shattering.

"But because of how you reacted." Her words trail off. "You will be working with me in witness interrogation."

I look at her, Gabe has pulled his hand away and is sitting on the other side of the couch purposely creating space between them.

"I'm not hurting innocent people." I shake my head. "No."

Ashley shakes her head. "It's not always hurting, it's more less threatening."

"No. I absolutely refuse."

"Cameron." Gabe sighs like he's already tired of me. "It's this or dying."

"Put a fucking bullet in my head then." I snap.

"Nico wouldn't want that." He raises his voice.

"Nico doesn't get a say, he's dead. He died." My voice shakes, my hands shake. Saying it out loud is too surreal. *It can't be true. It can't be.*

I pinch the letter between my fingers, I'm creasing the paper, just not enough to damage his last words to me.

"Cameron." Gabe says my name softly.

Ashley barks out his name. Trying to stick up for me.

"I can't do this." Tears fill my eyes falling over my eyelids, "I cry when my feet sink into the sand at the beach, sunsets make me happy, running while the sun rises brings me peace. Every single time I hold a baby, I sob." I hold the letter to my chest, tears falling down my face. "How am I supposed to interrogate someone when they watch someone they love fall into the hands of Nemean?"

Ashley looks at me completely heart broken, her chin quivers. She looks up to the roof, standing up slowly walking over to me. "I don't know. I really have no idea, but you need to find it. Nico needs you to find the strength. Lean on me. Scream at me. Your family needs you alive."

"What's your story?" I don't know where the question came from, I just blurted it out. She's as old as me and Gabe, and she seems innocent.

"My mom had a drug debt. They killed her, found me in another room and took pity on me. Whatever anger you have, I felt."

I turn around walking away into my bedroom.

I flip the light switch on, wiping my face out of frustration. I drop all the shopping bags on my floor. I take his sweater out of a bag, shoving it between my pillow and the wall. I sit on my bed staring at the envelope, twisting the necklace around my finger, I'm scared to read it. I take a few deep breaths, filling my lungs, then clearing them.

Cameron My love, I'm sorry it's come to this. I know you said you hated me. I really hope It wasn't true. Even if you did mean it, please read this. There are things I need to say, and if you did mean it, please don't think I'm trying to make you feel bad. It's just what I couldn't say when I was alive. First things first, no matter what happens, just know, my favorite food was the street Tacos we ate the very first night we hung out. If I do get killed, I contacted my lawyer the day you found out. My house, my money, everything I had is yours. I want you to be taken care of, even if I'm not there. Make it your own, hang up all of Hayley's creepy glowing art, paint the wall, set up decorations I would probably hate.

You changed my life. When I first saw you at the bar, that was the first time I ever saw you that close, and I was intrigued as hell. I kissed you, and you rejected me, it made me feel things I never thought I could feel. Then one day you kissed me, and I was on a fucking high. You never

*once gave up trying to make me smile, and when you did you felt so ac-
complished. It was adorable. Make sure you do the same for yourself. Always smile, be happy, do what makes you happy, always. Thank you for
showing me what life was supposed to be like: laughing, smiling, happy,
making plans, celebrating yourself and making it to another birthday.
It's terrifying to think that I might have lived life not knowing the kind
of joy, and freedom you brought. You made me feel human, you made
me feel vulnerable.*

*I want the world for you Cami. I want you to be happy, live life to the
fullest, work your dream job. Find a boring museum job and inspire
other history freaks. I want you to fall in love the way I loved you, get that
house in the suburbs, have a million kids. When your family gets you out
of this mess, go back to school, get your degree, work for what you want.
Nothing can or will stand in your way.*

*Even though you can't pick what you want to eat, you are a force of na-
ture, you need to remember that.*

*If you write again, I'm not going to be there to remind you to drink
water, eat, or sleep, so set alarms. Take care of yourself. I never told you,
but I read your article, I don't read, but you moved me. You are so
unique, I never deserved you.*

*When you miss me watch the shiny vampire. I'll be right there beside
you.*

*Thank you for sitting in the hospital with me, I never said that be-
cause I wanted to push you away. I wanted to fail at this task, you're not
like the rest of us. You're a genuinely good person. You brought out the
good in me, and I didn't even know it was in me.*

*If anyone ever again tells you that you are too much, be louder
Cameron. You were never too much for me, never settle for a relationship
when they can't pick up your emotions before you feel them. Be fucking
loud, feel everything you feel. You are not too much.*

*I love you. I never knew what that meant until you. I couldn't say it,
so I told you in Italian over, and over again until I got the courage to say
it in a language you could understand.*

If the odds are in my favor, if I survive this, I will come back for you. I will find you, and I will never let you go.

My lungs burn, my body is shaking, I let out a scream, tears falling down my face. I drop the letter to my feet, scared I'm going to accidentally rip it. I can't catch my breath. I'm panting, I'm shaking. The bed sinks next to me. I'm not alone, ironic because I've never been more alone.

I can't speak, I can't cry anymore. I've turned completely numb.

Gabe speaks, the only words I hear are "tattoo now."

I open my phone going to the WIFI passing it to Gabe. He takes it, typing the info in. I'm downloading every single movie. I'm going to know every word off by heart. I made him watch this as a joke, and now it's the only thing I have left of him.

I never thought I could be this numb.

37

Nico

"Where the fuck is she?" My entire body is weak, dried blood coats my hands, no matter how hard I scrub the stains won't go away.

"Oh my God." Ashley runs to the door, "What happened?"

"Where is she? Is she okay?"

I want to throw up, I had no idea it was possible to ever be this panicked about someone. I've been living in hell, and it's only been what? Thirty six hours? Not knowing where she is, who she's with, knowing nothing has been ripping me apart. Dad has been in an awfully good mood, I knew for a fact that she turned herself in.

"You can't just show up here." Gabe hisses.

My teeth clenches, blood pulsing through my veins, I'm so angry beads of sweat drip down my neck. "I will not hesitate to slit your fucking throat. Where is my girlfriend?"

"Spare bedroom. Don't wake her." Ashley speaks up, I look at her trying to give her a look of appreciation, even though I know it comes off as a death glare. She waves her hands shooing me away.

I turn the knob on the door, I know exactly where I'm going. This house is used by strangers. Ashley's a hard ass so people who need to get knocked into place come here, I've spent way too many nights in this room. I slowly press on the door suddenly thankful for knowing how wide it needs to be opened before it creaks. I slide in, almost not fitting through.

Cameron has her bags scattered everywhere. The window is open. It's so cold in here. I hear the fifth moving playing, I close my eyes trying to find comfort in her watching it. It's not bringing me comfort, it's just bringing me pain, because I know she thinks I'm dead. She's grieving me.

I stand over her, my letter is beside her, her face is drenched in tears. She's crying in her sleep, they keep pouring down her face. Her chin is shaking. She's lost everything.

I cover her up, her bicep falls, the second skin on her arm is covering a well detailed lioness tattoo. My heart feels like it's going to leap out of my body. Nemean has so many different tattoos. Each person with a certain intention has a different design. Mine has a Lion with bloody fangs, because I'm his son. The lower the level the shitter the tattoo. The people used to frame other Mafias, like the McKinnon's had a terrible outline of a tattoo. Hers has insane detail. That's only because of her killing Charlie.

The only reason I was at my parents' house that morning was because he needed to upgrade my firearm and inform me of his new plan to move down the Basilisk bloodline if Cameron never participated. He knew the delivery of the arm was coming, he knew she would run to Erik's. He knew she was with Hayley. He knew everyone would end up in one place, and he knew I would hear her screams and run towards her. Killing Charlie was a test. Now he's expecting her to be the one to kill people when disobeying the interrogations.

I cover her arm up, plugging her phone in. The second the phone registers the charger the screen lights up. Her face is showing how broken she is. She's lost everything, me, Charlie, her family, all within a few hours.

I bend over kissing her on her forehead. Trying to stop myself from crying. I let my lips hover on her chilly skin, her eyes are still closed, I hate how I can feel her pain. I hate how she's living this way. I hate how she's paying for someone else's choice.

I want to wake her, I want to tell her I'm right here.

If I do that, I'm risking her life. Instead, I walk out of the room, quietly shutting the door.

I stand in the hallway, my entire body is shaking. I'm not okay.

Ashley walks up to me guiding me to a chair. She was in school like me for the previous semester, a lot of us were. It was just to have extra eyes on Cameron, completely learn her schedule, weekend routines. It took a lot of us to figure out a very introverted person's routine. I honestly think a lot of them enjoyed school, so they only gave Cameron ten percent, at best. Not that I blame them. We all got a few months away from this. It was like a vacation.

"Her tattoo." My voice has never once been this shaky, and I just did unspeakable things to someone, yet that's not what's throwing me off. Cameron is.

Ashley and Gabe look at me until Gabe speaks. "She never even flinched. She had her head set the entire time watching a movie. It was like she wasn't even there."

"No because she's fucking numb." Ashley glares at Gabe. "When can you come back?" She looks at me with hopeful eyes.

"I don't know." I shift in my seat. "I promised her I'd come back."

Dad fired a shot on me, he was pushed out of the way seconds before the shot was fired causing the bullet to swerve. Lucia lost her mind, she was screaming at him, crying, hitting him with her open palm on his chest, she surprisingly put up a fight for me to not die. I'm only alive because she made sure I wouldn't die. He took my phone and gave me a new one. Everything Cameron could pin me on is gone.

No one asks what I've been doing. My training is now my job, disposing of the bodies is my duty. It's brutal, it's something people don't talk about. It's something I don't want to talk about.

"Can you take care of her?" I ask no one in particular.

"She basically asked us to kill her." Ashley looks at me with wide eyes.

I close my eyes, my eyelashes are becoming wet. I stand, going into her room once again.

I watch her, sliding down the wall, not taking my eyes away from her sleeping face. She moves around a lot before she finally wakes up, I'll have time to leave the room before she's awake enough to notice I'm in here.

All those nights she settled me after a nightmare, I can't even do the same for her. I wish I could. I'm risking her life just being here. Dad wants her to believe I'm dead so she can live up to her 'full potential' without distractions. Her weakness is her family, and me. He eliminates weakness'.

It's a good thing I discovered his.

Cameron moves, she reaches for a roll of toilet paper, blowing her nose, she makes the screen on her phone black before rolling over to her other side.

I hope to hell she catches me in here, because I don't know if I can keep living like this. I'd much rather be fighting for her in secret, than living everyday knowing she can't handle being alone. I want her to know she's not alone.

Wake up Cameron. I'm right here.

I want her to have something back. I want us to have each other again, even if it's dangerous.

I need to figure out how to talk to her family.

38

Cameron

Ashley knocks at the front door of a house with a hammer fist. She's knocking obsessively. She won't stop. "Well fuck you too then." She mutters.

She's walking away down the stone path back to the street. We haven't done anything, I feel like it's not done. I hope to hell it is done.

I try not to groan watching her walk around the house. I was hoping it was done. Apparently, our job isn't that easy. I follow her, trying to step over the snow. Snow is falling over into my boots, my ankles are becoming completely frozen.

Ashley stops looking up at a window. "Jump. Push it open." She points stepping back.

This window is at least three feet in the air, I'm going to have to do a muscle up to get this damn thing open. At least this time I'm jumping *into* a window, and not out of one. I take off my mittens for traction, stuffing them in my coat pocket. I bend my knees, jumping straight up, the ice cold frame makes my fingers feel like they're frostbite the second I latch onto it. I don't know how I'm supposed to do shit when I'm not even sure I can bend my fingers. I let out a loud sigh, pulling my body up, I let go with one hand grabbing onto the window forcing it up. I almost fall when I feel Ashley pushing the bottom of my shoes. She jumps, giving me an extra give. I slide the window up, throwing my body inside feeling the window fall on my back.

I will not let myself get stuck here. I lean down, my hands on the wall, I push my arms to get the rest of me inside. I land on the ground with a loud thud at the same time the window comes crashing down. My fingers are even more numb now from the instant snap of heat from the house. I stand, looking around before going to the front door to let her inside. Everything in this house has a place. Nothing looks out of place, nothing is a mess. The living room is clean, it's decorated in a modern look, the couch is a bright white. It looks like no one's sat on it before. Decorative pillows sit on the edges.

Ashley pounds on the door, I take a step, nearly slipping from the contact of the hardwood floors and snow stuck on the bottom of my soles.

I twist the lock, she barges in. "Have you heard anything?"

"I made a ruckus falling in the window. But no." I try to whisper back, even though whispering is completely pointless after my entry.

I kick my shoes together over the rug like they're red slippers taking me back home to get the rest of the snow off, so I don't almost take a tumble again. I follow Ashley through the house, we walk through the kitchen, taking a carpet staircase upstairs. Family photos are hung along the walls, there's a husband, a wife, and a daughter.

I swallow hard.

A door slams, Ashley runs towards it, kicking it in. I walk behind her looking at the damage she caused. The door has a huge dent in it, it was locked and now the door frame has a huge chunk missing from it.

I look up, watching Ashley flash her hand gun towards the wife and child, forcing the man off the ground. He stands without putting up a fight seeing where the gun is directed. My stomach drops, my hands shake, my legs are shaking. I cannot stay steady enough to stay standing. It's taking all of my mental power not to fall over, and not to break down in tears.

"Separate room!" Ashley's voice carries in a loud boom. I can't help it but to wonder how many other families she's tormented this exact same way.

He leads us down the hall, along the railing into the living room upstairs, it looks like it's a playroom. Toys are scattered everywhere, the complete opposite from the living room.

"Sit." Her voice still booms loudly.

He sits on the floor, she walks around a circle, her gun casually hanging at her side until she stops in front of him, the gun is directly in front of his face, hanging by her side. His eyes are big watching it swing back and forth in small motions as Ashley's body moves.

She squats, so her face is inches in front of him. "Your buddy who was picked up by us, you will not speak of it again."

"I wasn't there." His voice panics, shaking his head.

"We know everything about you Stephen." Ashley tips her head, like she's finding enjoyment in this. "I don't suppose your wife would like to know about your friend's debt to us?" she pauses. "Then she would realize how you spend your weekends, drugs, pros—."

He cuts her off. "What do you want?"

"Just a little secret, since you're good at keeping those. If you say anything to anyone about what you saw this morning, she will come for your entire family, and she will leave you last, just so you can watch." I think I hear a smile in her voice.

She? I'm the only other she, or human around.

Stephen's eyes go wide. "My lips are sealed." He shakes his head, "Please don't hurt them." He looks directly at me, "You'll never see me again, I swear."

Ashley bounces up on her feet, turning around. I follow her out of the house, my heart has never beat faster in my life, my hands are shaking, my throat feels like it's closing in on me,

"What the fuck!" I yell the second my door slams in Gabe's car, Ashley's door is hardly shut before Gabe drives off. "Don't be using me to threaten children." My voice raises, I feel like I'm going to puke.

"Chill." Ashley puffs out a breath of air. "It hardly ever gets that far." She looks at Gabe, "Did he not tell her at the sit down?"

Gabe shakes his head.

"Tell me what?" I speak through my teeth.

"You assassinating Charlie was his plan. You'll be the one who kills people when they decide not to listen to my threats. And before you jump down my throat, no Nico didn't know that was his plan."

"Pull the car over." I unclip my beat belt, opening the door, jumping out of the car thankful for still being in a neighborhood.

I rush over to a bush, feeling my stomach turn, I bend over, physically sick from everything. I grab snow wiping my face.

I step back in the car, buckling my seat belt, not saying a word.

I need to get to the rooftop.

39

Nico

I think it's a safe assumption to assume that Nemean has extra eyes on everyone who cares about Cameron, so I'm out of ideas on how to talk to anyone. They need to know how bad this is.

I stand on the roof of the museum looking up into the gym. I have absolutely no idea if anyone I need to speak to is in there, or if I had to climb that ladder for nothing. I don't know what floor the gym is on, I don't even know what building it is. Cameron just said it was behind us, I'm just guessing, not even sure if it's open right now.

Memory's from this rooftop flood my mind. The first time we were on here together, how she made me promise I wouldn't use this place to pick up girls, how free she was, I think about this being the center of her universe. My body takes me to the spot where the blanket was laid out. I lick my lips trying to remember the way her lips felt against mine. The way the sunset reflected off Cameron's face. I wish I never wasted so much time trying to keep her safe, I wish I kissed her more. I wish I wasn't a coward and loved her without being scared.

I never thought I would be up here alone.

"Please see me." I whisper under my breath.

I've been up here for a long time. It's cold as hell. I'm starting to give up hope. I need to go back to where I'm staying, before someone gets suspicious. I'm back to not being trusted, I'm allowed to leave once in a while, I can't make it a habit, or someone will be tailing me in no time.

I stand on the cement, feeling the sun hiding behind the clouds. The second it pops out I'm hit with a warm ray of heat, then it fades away, hidden by another cloud.

"Nico." Erick groans, before crawling from the latter on the roof.

The second his feet touch the cement he runs up to me, giving me a huge hug stealing all the air from my lungs, taking me by surprise. I hold onto him tight, I can't remember the last time any father has held me like this.

"I thought you." He pulls away, not finishing his sentence.

"Cameron's not okay." I blurt out. "Dad wants her to kill witness' who don't listen to the threats. She can't know I'm alive. If dad knows, she knows I'm alive, she's fucked." I run my glove over my neck, I didn't mean to swear in front of him, and now I feel awkward.

He brushes it off.

"Please tell me Brittney still knows people." I should really know this, other people were assigned to the Basilisks, I was assigned to Cameron. This was probably the plan to keep me in the dark.

"What's your cellphone number?" Erik asks me, pulling out his phone.

I pull my phone out flashing my number printed on the label for him to put into his phone.

"She does. She's been talking to three people we worked with. They need to know what will hurt him." He's very careful not to use the agents by name.

I hesitate. There's only one person that would weaken him if they were killed. "My sister." I shake my head, "They need to find another person. Lucia fought for me to stay alive. There has to be another way."

Erik looks at me with sympathy. "If it comes down to saving my baby girl, I don't care who it is I need to take down. Just be on the right side of this. I don't want you in the crossfire."

I look up at him, torn. I hate Lucia, but just because I hate her doesn't mean I want her dead. "Anything the FBI needs, I will tell them." I swallow hard. "They will find another way." I say, only to convince myself.

Erik looks at me even sadder now.

"What aren't you telling me?" His eyes are locked on me, Erik is standing so tall it looks like his spine is about to snap.

He slouches before talking, "If you meet them to cut a deal, you need to go into detail about everything that happened to you. You will need a polygraph for court. It was different with us, because Brittney was brought in, they watched us. But you—" He staggers off. "Just be completely upfront about everything. Don't hide anything."

"What the hell would I be hiding? I can't make up what's happened." My voice is too defensive.

I'm almost thankful for what he's gone through, it makes me feel more at ease, more understood. That's so fucked up on both our parts. He has experience with this, I know he's right, I don't think I'm ever going to be able to repeat anything that's happened to me.

"They need to know you're not going to run back to them, and report."

I shake my head, I don't know if he's asking for him or for the feds. "Not with Cameron in the position she's in. Tell them she has a lioness tattoo, detailed tattoo. If you're worried and want to throw me under the bus as collateral. Tell them I just put Tom Emerson on a medieval stretcher and tore him limb from limb. Believe me Erik. I want Cameron out before she has to do the same. If they don't cut me a deal, I'm fine with it, I deserve it."

Erick looks at me with his mouth open, his hands flinch showing a video recording on his phone.

"Good. Give them this video please, they can come after me, whatever. I'm taking my Jacket of, I'm not pulling a gun." I take my jacket off, unzip my sweater, pulling it down to reveal the lion on my bicep. "Get my tattoo."

He moves his phone closer.

"Cami's is just like this, minus the teeth. The detail gets more in-depth for their intention of going into the mafia." Erik steps away, I do my sweater and jacket up again.

"She has potential to do what I just did, but to innocent people who decided not to stay quiet about the crime they saw. Whatever you need, whatever they need, I'm going to do it."

"Thank you." Erick takes a step backwards. "When she heard the video of you and Brittney talking, I've never seen her break so fast in her entire life. It breaks my heart that I can't protect her."

"I have her. I know you don't trust me, but I need you to trust that. My dad doesn't know you know any of this. Use it to your advantage."

Erik presses a button on the side of his phone before stuffing it away, crawling over the side of the building.

Now I stay here for a while, just to make sure whoever is following him leaves.

Anything the FBI needs I will give them, even if it means I need to give them Lucia, just to weaken the Lion.

40

Cameron

I've never once been in a vehicle going this fast in my entire life. Gabe is swerving in and out of traffic so fast, I felt a huge jolt, I think we definitely side swiped someone. If the bumper is even on the vehicle, still is a mystery. It was hard, he lost control and had to steer us in the right direction again.

I'm terrified. Josh's driving was nothing compared to this.

"There was a shooting at junction Square. Hit gone wrong." Ashley looks at me, passing me a hand gun, "Take it. You might need it. We didn't realize one of the bartenders let someone go to the bathroom, they saw everything. The lion is refusing to deal with it himself, says you need to do it. I have no idea what's going on, but you need to try to talk him down."

"I cannot do that." I shake my head. "Nope."

"He's going to be watching you. I know it's hard." I almost want to laugh at Ashley for trying to pity me when I've seen her almost enjoy threatening people.

I look at her, laughing, no longer holding it in anymore. It shouldn't be humorous, but the way my life has turned out if fucking hilarious. Have a family that's the center of my entire world, find out they're all killers and liars? Hilarious. Fall in love, lose him to the same mafia who my family has a history with? Hilarious. Find out I was made into a deal? Hilarious. Being passed a black market gun? Hilarious.

No one has even tried to show me how to shoot, I realize I killed Charlie with a gun, but how do they know it wasn't a lucky shot? Yes, I've been training my entire life at Targets, but how do they know that?

Gabe slams on his breaks causing me to fly forward, the seatbelt locks slamming me back into my seat. "Cameron. Take the fucking gun and go before you kill us all."

I reach for it, my eyes watch them both get out of the car, I follow behind. I can't intimidate someone. I don't have a resting bitch face, I'm not a large person, my muscles are covered under layers. Other than being tall, I'm a small human. Gabe holds the door open for me, I follow Ashley, the gun is hanging down at my side. I'm doing nothing to hide it, just how Ashley was at the house we were at.

The Lions thick accent saying my name, pulses through my veins. I grip the handle harder, my palm is sweating. He keeps speaking, and I feel my blood pressure sky rocket. All I can think of is that I'm holding a gun, and he killed my boyfriend. He made me into a deal.

"Everyone out!" His voice radiates off the walls, not a single person hesitates.

I stand there trying to give myself a better reason than dying not to point and pull the trigger. He's taken everything from me, I have nothing left to lose.

"You guys are fucking crazy!" A man shouts, taking my thoughts away.

I look at him tipping my head, he has probably twenty, twenty-five years on my dad. He's Spanish, they stripped him down to his t-shirt and pants, I can see his tattoos, I don't bother to look at them, it'll just be another thing that weighs down on me.

The lion is staring at me, I feel his eyes burning into me.

I lean on the table with my elbows on the surface, gun pointed in the air, "What happened here?"

He spits.

The Lion clears his throat. He speaks in Italian, all I can think about is Nico. I'm expecting tears to fall down my face, instead I see that vale of red.

I raise my arm, gun level at his head, I don't speak.

The man looks at me, not saying a word.

My name is said in a thick Italian accent, my blood runs hot, my heart is beating in my ears, Italian is spoken again, Nico's face flashes before my eyes, lighting up the entire room. I really want to shoot the Lion.

My ears start ringing. I can't figure out why. I look down, I'm lowering my arm, his blood soaks me.

"Very good, that's exactly what I wanted to happen." The Lions voice is loud enough I can hear over my busted eardrums.

"Who cleans up the mess?" I ask in a calm voice, I don't even hear my own voice from the ringing.

"You have men for that. Now leave." He speaks loudly.

I turn around, the gun is still at my side, I wipe my forehead with the back of my hand, looking at thick red blood covering my hand.

"You look like *Carrie*. Don't fucking move." Gabe runs outside.

Body's pass us, I'm assuming it's the people to clean up, if I even heard the Lion correctly. I can't hear much right now.

I'm calm. I'm collected. I don't want to cry. I don't want to scream. I think I'm numb. I just need to stay this way.

Gabe passes me the towel, I wipe my face, it was originally grey. I'm a walking biohazard. "Let's go." My voice is dry.

I should have shot the Lion, not the bystander. I should have ended him like he ended Nico.

Everything I've wanted in life is gone, I need to accept that fact. If I stay like this, it'll hurt less.

I'm never going to that rooftop. I'm never watching our movie anymore. I'm never looking at his letter again.

The only way I'll survive is if I never feel anything again.

41

Nico

Cameron walks by me, she doesn't even see me. Her eyes are dark, her hand is too steady. She looks like she's already dead inside. She spoke, instantly giving me chills, she switched everything off to easy. She needs to fight this, I know she won't. Her hearts too big to let any of the other kids in her family fill her place. She won't let anyone else ever feel this way, she's going to carry all of the pain on her own, and I can't stand the thought. Not after seeing her flick her switch so easily.

I had to stop everything from reaching out to her. I wanted to scream at her, I needed her to see me.

"Nico." Bianca curses my name. "Ass over here now."

I roll my eyes, dragging my feet over to her. She pulls her long curly hair into a ponytail. I honestly have no idea how she can have it up. It's poufy as fuck. I've known her for my entire life, she's the exact same age as me. There's a lot of girls my age, I'm the only boy, and it was hell growing up.

Bianca looks at the body gagging. She's been doing this for long enough not to gag. "Jesus Christ." I growl grabbing the body bag from the bar, picking my feet off the ground to get to her so she can be far away from the blood. "Grab his feet."

I grab his arms not looking anywhere else, fully aware he was shot in the head. It's hard to ignore, his insides are everywhere. The floor is slippery. She gages again, running the other direction to run outside. Dads talking to people in the background, their voices disappear, leaving me alone with the dead guy.

I look down at him scrunching my nose. *I'm so desensitized.* I move to the side of him, bending over to zipper from his feet up. It isn't until I get to his neck, I see a black cord. My eyes widen, I panic, unzipping the bag to his hips. Pulling up his blood drenched shirt, I see a wire taped to his body. There's a black box in the pocket of his jeans. I look over my shoulder, seeing no one I rip it off of him stuffing it into my coat pocket. I roll the body bag over reaching my hand to his back pockets, feeling a wallet. It's not a wallet. It's a cover for a badge.

My heart beats in my chest looking at the name on his government ID *Carlos Rodriguez.* The badge is gold with FBI written in large royal blue writing.

Fuck. I quickly stuff the badge in my pocket zippering the bag the rest of the way.

Cameron just killed a federal agent.

All of us were taken back by the call.

Dad is a thousand steps ahead of us all.

Bianca comes back in holding her mouth, "I'm okay now."

"Are you sure?"

She snaps back at me trying to reassure me she's okay.

I'm not okay. I have no idea what he knows.

The door from the kitchen opens, I know he's coming back here. I need to be far away from my father right now. I stand pointing at the feet of the bag, Bianca listens. We pick it up and go outside.

The instant I'm outside, the cold air hits me, making me feel awake, and that's awful to feel right now.

Bianca counts to three, and on three we toss the body into the back of the van.

"Give me a second. I need air." I side step letting her walk past me. I watch the driver door shut before closing the two big doors on the back of the van. I pull out the microphone in the vans blind spots keeping my voice low. The engine turns on covering up any noise, "It's Nico.

Cameron didn't know who he was." I say it like it's an excuse, "Help her please." My voice cracks.

I never thought I would be the one to plead to the feds, here we are. The worst part is, I'm ready to cut whatever deal they need. Seeing her after tonight, they need to move faster. I'm becoming even more desperate.

I put it back in my pocket, leaving it open a crack, hoping they will be able to pick up the location we burn him at.

42

Cameron

After the night at Junction Square, I'm allowed to go home. Not really home, but Nico's. I guess it's not even Nico's anymore. It's mine. It's not mine though. This place feels haunted. I don't know why I'm allowed to be back here, and the truth is, I don't want to be back here.

This house has all the best memories, and now all the worst memories. I stop in the hallway, touching the exact same spot where I heard Nico's conversation with Brittney. I want to cry, not a single tear falls. I want to cry looking over at the couch, thinking of everyone's faces when they told me about Charlie. No tears come.

I can't even cry, and I want to. The one time I want to feel everything, I can't.

Nico's bed is going to be missing him every single night, I'm going to be alone. The future I saw with him is gone, and I can't even let myself open up to feel myself grief,

I step into the bedroom looking at the bed. Somehow, he never messed up the blankets, mine is always a disaster, all tangled up. He looks like he slept peacefully every single night. His clothes are still in the dirty hamper, everything he owned is still going to be hanging in the closet. I should be in tears right now. No wonder he was so broken when I met him. I almost feel guilty waking him up to emotions. All that did was make him feel everything he repressed. Even though he thanked me for coming into his life and showing him what it was like to be living, I made him feel *everything*.

I sit on the bed, this feels so wrong. Being here feels like I walked into a foreign country. I used to know everything here, I made myself at home way before he said it was okay, now I feel like an intruder.

I run my fingers over his side of the bed, I don't know how he was involved in all of this at twelve years old. I don't know how my family was able to do any of this. They're all so much stronger than me.

A part of me wishes I could talk to them. Now that I'm alone I could go to the rooftop and wait for someone to see me from the gym. If I do that, I'm opening myself up to feel what I did to that man tonight and actually giving me a chance to grieve my aunt's death. I want to. I can't, that's just another thing the Lion took away from me.

I stand, walking into the bathroom. Now that I unpacked both mine and Nico's tooth brushes are in the holder. We both use different toothpaste, Mines squeezed right in the middle, he pushed his up from the bottom.

I run my fingertips over his tooth paste, the old Cameron would be a weeping mess, now it doesn't affect me the way it should. I look up into the mirror, I don't do my makeup anymore. I don't even brush my hair properly. I look the same kind of. My eyes have bags under them, my hairs knotted from the shower I took at Ashley's. Mascara wasn't taken off properly from days ago, there's still a stain under my bottom lashes. I can't smile, my lips are locked into a straight line. My eyes don't shine anymore. I look older, I look dead.

I mean, I kind of am.

I grab a blanket and pillow from the spare room's closet heading straight towards the couch. Just because I can't feel anything, doesn't mean I'm ready to sleep in his bed. I'm never going to be able to sleep where he used too. Even after Nico said separate beds, I protested. I still crawled into his bed every night. If he would have tried to sleep on the couch, I would have begged him to stay. I wish I knew he was saying goodbye to me that night. I would have put up a fight for him to stay, I would have started to work on a game plan to help him. I did so many things wrong with us.

I open a streaming app, picking a cartoon, when my mind starts to wonder. *No wonder my mom started another family.*

She knew what was coming for me, she knew there was no escaping this. She knew that it was going to be hard on everyone. It can't be hard on you when you left years before.

She was smart, I just wish she told more people.

I don't even know if I'm worth saving after what I did today.

43

Nico

I can't even start to explain the amount of joy I got when my cameras sensed Cameron in the house. I let out a joy of laughter. I've been pacing back and forth worried about her, not knowing exactly where she is, then she was at home, safe.

195 Wilabay drive

I squint my eyes at the text message notification, interrupting me spying on Cameron through the cameras. I'm pretty positive it's not a job, only because Bianca isn't pounding on my door like a maniac.

I don't respond, I stand grabbing my jacket walking out of the house.

The address is in Brooklyn, it's a long ass commute. The houses are all duplexes. They're cookie cutter houses. Everything looks the same. Right down to the front doors, the lawns, brick driveways, windows all have blinds covering them. It's like there are mirrors reflecting houses making it look like there's more than there is.

195 is right in the middle of the long stretch of houses. There's not a single car parked in the driveway, or on the street. In fact, this entire space has no vehicles. Every single driveway is empty. It feels like I entered a parallel universe.

Hesitantly I walk up to the door, I'm about to knock when the door opens, someone grabs my jacket pulling me inside.

I look up completely shocked looking at Erik. "Next time, send K. Or a thumbs up, just acknowledge the damn text message."

If this is how he acts when he doesn't even like me, I couldn't imagine what being his kid would be like.

I follow Erik seeing everyone in the room. Every single Basilisk looks at me, exhaling at the same time. If I'm not mistaken, they all look relieved. Erik points to the couch, Liam pushes himself over towards Spencer making room for me.

My eyes land on Adam, he's holding a glass of alcohol looking into it. He never looked up, not until he chugs his drink, setting his cup on the ground. His eyes look sunken in from lack of sleep. He's let his facial hair grow out, he's slouching. I feel terrible, I brought the gun, I took it off of me. I'm just as responsible as Cameron.

"I'm so sorry." That's all I can say. What else am I supposed to say?

William grabs my shoulder squeezing it. "Sit." He passes me a drink. "We can go, or we can stay."

The door opens. Boxes are being brought in, the two people call them by their last names in conversation, then it dawns on me.

Agents.

They never wasted a second to get the FBI involved.

I look around at the Basilisks. They are all looking at me with soft expressions, no one is pressuring me. They're all just here for support. This is weird as fuck. It's also kind of nice. They all look like they haven't slept in days.

If I've been struggling, and I've been able to steal glances of Cameron, I can't even imagine how terrified everyone else here is.

"Holy fuck Jones, you're still dumb." Brittney pushes herself off the wall, mincing his laugh after he laughs.

"You fucking do it then." Jones throws a box on the ground. "You're the worst friend."

"Shut up." She giggles. I look over at them, she's hugging him as tight as possible. "She didn't know— I know that doesn't help. I'm sorry Carlos is gone. We can get someone else if you need it Tim."

"No." He backs away. "I thought you were just the crazy Basilisk girl before. All you want is justice. Is Nemean boy here?"

"Stay." I look up at William finally answering his question. Every single person here gives me a silent nod.

"It's going to be personal." Dillons voice is shadowed by his hand over his mouth. "Just warning you."

"Is she okay?" Hayley's voice is shaking, asking the question everyone here is thinking.

I quickly open the app on my phone, holding my phone out for her to reach over and grab it. "Physically yes."

Erik rushes behind Hayley, putting his hands on her shoulders, eyes glued to my phone.

Jones sits on the coffee table in front of where I'm sitting. He has eye bags, he looks exhausted like everyone else in the room. "We can offer you immunity, only if you are a thousand percent honest. No secrets, no beating around the bush, you need to be straight up with us."

"He'll take it." Erik speaks quickly, not looking up from his daughter on the phone screen.

"Nico. I need you to understand, you will only be the only one with immunity. Your family won't be out here with you, your friends will be gone."

"Will Cameron be out of jail? No community service, no house arrest, no warrants, no record?" I ask, locking my eyes with his, "If she won't be, you will not get anything out of me. I will be absolutely silent." There's a hand on me when I'm done speaking, I'm pretty sure Liam just squeezed my shoulder in support.

"Yes of course." Tim speaks quickly.

"I'm sorry about last night. I didn't know what else to do when I saw the wire. I panicked, then I found the badge. I— my dad must have set it up. So, he's going to know I'm here."

"Listen to me." His attention is fully brought on me. "There will be someone around you at all times hidden. Brittney can vouch, we are never spotted by anyone with The Basilisks. If there's anything out of the ordinary you will know. If anything is off around Cameron, you will know instantly."

He adds in Cameron, knowing I was going to ask. "What do you need to know?" I ask in a weak voice, I'm ready to fight. I'm already exhausted.

He explains to me that I need to remove my shirt, they need to take pictures of my back while I speak into a recorder about the stories. I grab my drink, chugging it all back, trying to explain that if I stumble over my words, or if I randomly stop talking, I'm trying, I've just never said anything out loud before.

William refills my drink, April and Britney grab my hands, getting me on my feet. I turn around, taking my shirt off resting one knee on the cushion, grabbing my cup, taking a sip before I pass it back. They're handing me alcohol. So many people in this room have lived the same type of hell.

"A few weeks ago, when the Lion— my dad noticed I was going soft, he made me do a job. This was the night everyone celebrated Cami's published article. It was a police officer, he was locked in a cage above fire, my dad showed up, they were talking about how I've gone soft. I dropped the cage, he burnt to death, I killed him. Up until recently my job was torture, but it was never the same torture I went through as my training, until that night.

The long burn on my right hand side was from the bars in the cage when I lost my balance. I was sixteen. The top of my back, and shoulders is from when I was fifteen, I was locked in a room for two weeks, started with starvation, ended with whipping.

The scars at the bottom of my neck are from a pillory. At fourteen, I was trapped for days sitting with my head and arms rubbing against the wood. All I could see was the dried blood from other people, then I started to see my blood dripping down the wood. I was small, my wrists had room to move around. I tried to escape, and it ended up making my skin raw. The indents in my back are from rocks, and, I don't know what else they used to throw at me while I was tied up, I had to go through that a lot."

I take a break, trying to breathe. I've had so much happen to me over the years I'm starting to forget about all of it. I take my glass back, taking a large sip before passing it back. I rest my forehead on the back of the couch trying to breathe. Every single person in this room knows that I was only born to seal the deal that Charlie made. Looking at any of them is going to take too much strength that I don't have. I can't even imagine the thoughts that Erik is having, having a baby probably brought so much joy to him, but it cost me everything.

I turn slightly to the right, I need to get this over with. I pick my head up speaking, "The scars on this side of my body are from an Iron maiden. It was made for people bigger than me at the time, I was able to sit at the bottom. The first time I was in it, I got poked a few times, it took a while to learn how to move fast enough. The new piece on the bottom of my back, that's from my skin graft. That's no biggie." I shrug. "You can live up to fourteen days without food. That was my normal torture, less messy. Lock me up, with water, and forget for a few days."

The camera flashes again, and again.

"I think that's all. Everything was so repetitive, it all over laps. The pain was always excruciating. They stopped it before I died every single time."

"Were there any close calls?" The woman with the camera asks.

"Honestly, I don't know. A few times the pain made me blackout."

"You can put your shirt back on. Thank you."

"Everything you endured was because of Charlie then?" I put my shirt back on, Adam is rubbing his facial hair.

"Don't put the blame on Charlie. She didn't know how it was going to play out." I reply simply trying to take some blame off of his dead wife, they all know the answer, he doesn't deserve the blame.

"So yes. Because your dad sure seems to know a thousand steps before anyone does anything. The McKinnon's were always ahead of us."

I don't respond, because he's right. He's grieving he doesn't need to know he's right.

"Your relationship with your parents was non-existent I'm assuming?" Tim grabs my attention, he's holding the recorder.

"I basically raised myself. I had to fend for myself for every meal, wake myself up for school."

"What about your sister? Was she the same?"

"No. My parents adore her."

Next, he asks me how old I was when I found out about the Nemean Mafia, I relived the rat story. Saying it out loud sounds fake. I honestly believe it never happened. If it wasn't for my dream a week's months ago, it wouldn't be feeling this real, it sounds so damn fictional. I wasn't prompted, but I'm telling him everything about everyone who's close to dad, names, nicknames, if they're married, who their kids are. I'm trying to be open, and everything is stumbling out of my mouth. After I spill all that, my mind changes on me, and suddenly, I'm telling them about the finger, ear, and arm that was delivered by the mail. The fire in the dorms, the reason why Cameron was in a boot. Everything is coming out of my mouth, and I can't stop it.

Tim closes his eyes, he mutters something quietly, he stands walking away.

My hands are shaking, I feel something wet rolling down my cheek.

"Shit Nico." Hayley's voice shakes, she hands me my phone and it's opened to a text message.

You can go home now. She chose right.

"He knows I'm here. He wouldn't send me back if he didn't." I speak quietly, panic thick in my voice.

"Was anyone following you?" Tim quickly asks, calling an agent to get to Cameron.

"Not that I know of." I shake my head.

"Go home." Tim hangs up the phone. "We will do the lie detector another day, that was a lot, for all of us. So, I imagine you are shaken past belief. We have a car that looks like a cab. It'll be the only transportation you or Cameron use unless it's a call."

"I'm not going back there. Having both of us in the same location is an easy target."

"Go home." Tim looks at me wide eyed. "Lucia will not let you die. He knows that."

I'm going home. He doesn't need to tell me twice. I stand turning around when my arm is grabbed.

I look down, Josh is looking at me with soft eyes. He slides something into my hand, "If anything feels off, if you want to talk, or if you just need anything, call me. If it's safe for you, I'll be there. Please."

I break into a small smile, my chin quivers. I don't know what the fuck this is, or why he's saying any of this but I'm going to take it. I never once in my life felt so accepted, I've never felt less judged. He hasn't brought up Cameron once, he never brought himself up, or anyone else. I nod, this feels way too good to be true, all of it.

"I need to get home to my girl." I quickly put his info in my phone, passing it back to him so there's no paper trail.

He waves me out the door.

The yellow cab is waiting outside. I hop in, he flashes me the FBI badge before the doors shut. Holy shit. I get to see her. My stomach is fluttering, my palms are sweating. I've never been this nervous in my entire life.

44

Cameron

I'm so tired. This couch isn't comfortable without me leaning on Nico. Falling asleep out here isn't the same. Sleeping in his room without him isn't going to work for me. I can't sleep on the non-existent bed in the guest room.

A part of me suddenly wants to set this house on fire because he isn't here. The other part of me wants to keep it standing to remember him. If I burn it, his memory goes with him. My memories of him will carry on, but eventually, they will fade. I know I can't live here expecting him to come back.

The silence is interrupted by the pin pad on the door, cutting the silence like a knife the lock buzzed as it unlocks. I stand against the wall, watching the door. The only person who would be able to walk in like this is my dad. As much as I don't want to see him, he's not a threat to me.

The only threat my dad is to me, is making me feel emotions again.

I blink hard, listening to the door slam. Nico is standing in front of me wearing a black puffy jacket. His body is still. I can't move, my feet are melting into the ground. My heart beats fast.

"Baby." The words leave his lips, and suddenly I can move, fast.

Our lips meet, feeling the inside of each other's mouths, I pull his jacket down his arms, pulling his shirt over his head. He pulls his oversized sweater off me, walking, pushing me into the bedroom.

We lay in bed, both panting, sweat has layered onto our skin. We don't care, my heads on his chest, his arms are wrapped around me tight.

I don't get how this is happening. He wrote me that letter, I heard his and Brittney's conversation, his dad told me he was dead. He's supposed to be dead.

I sit up, "What alcohol did we drink the first night? What did we eat? Where did we go?" This is him. I know this is my dead boyfriend. He's just not supposed to be alive. I don't get how this is happening. I have so many questions, I can't bring myself to ask any more.

"Vanilla vodka, I think? Or something like that. Chicken Tacos, museum rooftop. You said it was your happy place, the center of your universe. It's me Cami, I promise you." His hand reaches towards my cheek, I lean into his touch feeling a shock of electricity rush though my body. He rubs his thumb like wiping my tears is his reflex, no tears come.

"How?" I look at him with wide eyes. "You died. Your Dad said you died."

"He was about too, Lucia walked in. She got him to spare me. Your murder convinced him you won't get distracted. He made it so you could kill him, or the witness. You chose right."

"Districted from what?"

Nico rolls over, pulling me down on the mattress beside him, looking me directly in the eyes, "You are far from being alone. I have you. I will not let you stay in this life. I will choose you every single time."

"Can we sleep?" I watch him nod, "Can you hold me?" Nico grabs me pulling me into him tight.

I don't know what the catch is having him back, I'll take it. Whatever it is.

I let out a deep breath, nuzzling my head into his chest. "I love you. I don't hate you."

Nico kisses me on the head telling me he loves me, the words hit different this time, they sound more meaningful.

I'm going to wake up and none of this is going to be true.

"I'm not done with the questions." I whisper into the dark, his head nods slightly acknowledging me.

The sun is shining so brightly I can see it through my eyelids, if it was springtime this would be the type of morning where there would be a cold breeze coming through the window, the birds would be singing, and the sun would be breaking through at sunset lighting the sky up so many different colors. I feel the blanket bunched up around me, I have a few seconds of peace, until I remember my dream last night. Everything felt so real, I could touch him, I kissed him, I felt the way he made me climax.

"I love you." I whisper into the morning air.

"I love you more."

I jump holding the blanket at my chest covering myself up. Nico is laying down, his arm bent, his head in his hand. A smile crossed his face.

I let out a breath, staring at him blankly. I slowly smile. He's here. He's actually here. Alive. "What did you do to come back?" I watch him, I'm so happy, there's no emotion on my part. My face is cold, my body is hard. I probably look pissed. I'm so happy, I don't know how to show it.

He falls on his back, covering his face with his hands, dropping his arms on the side of his body. "I think it's what you did. After you killed that guy, Dad was in the room. You were so focused on what you did, you let me walk right by you. I have no idea why he's letting us be together. He doesn't owe me any favors."

"Should we move?" her question is instant. "He's already blown up the dorm I lived in."

"He'll just figure out where we moved."

"Let's slowly empty this house then."

"Can we please just lay here?"

I nod, cuddling up on his chest. He's doing something. His arm muscles are subtle with their movements, I'm pretty positive he's texting someone.

I feel his arms move, his head turns talking into my hair. "Do you want to see your dad?"

I can't possibly see my dad, not after what I've done. I've killed two people. This is not the person he's raised me to be. I'm not his little girl, I wish he had more kids, I wish he had a backup child like my mom has. This is not who I want him to know me by. I shake my head, he can't know me. He can't see me.

"Do you want to go to Charlie's funeral?" he asks, rubbing my arm. "We can pull the mafia move and stand at the back."

I ignore his sad attempt at a joke. I want to ask how he knows about the funeral, and I don't. I should go. Seeing her husband, and her kids weeping from what I took away from them in a split second. I changed their entire lives faster than I thought was possible. I can't see them, I can't see the pain I brought on. Seeing everyone fall apart, because of what I did. Thinking about that man's family while watching my family shatter. I would be feeling every damn emotion, then I would be feeling everything I caused. I wouldn't be able to keep my wall up, it would shatter around me.

"I— I think I hate her." I stutter. I never said it out loud before. "She knew I felt something off, I felt the lies and she still never told me. I don't want to hate her."

Nico kisses my head, he rolls over hugging me, rubbing my back with his open palm. "How ever you feel is completely valid. If you don't want to go, we won't."

"I mentally can't."

"Okay." Nico speaks fast, "So no family, no funerals. Got it. Wanna get food ordered? I need a new list, Dad destroyed my old phone. Speaking of which, grab me your phone. When you go anywhere let me know. Job, store, I need to know."

I pass him my phone, watching him flip it over putting my number in his. "I'm okay."

"No, you're not. Your words aren't you, your eyes are empty, you don't have the sparkle when you smile, I came back from the dead, and you weren't bothered. If we get called away, you need to keep me in touch." He looks at me passing me my phone. "When I promised to protect you, I meant it. I came back just like I said I would. I have you. Put down the wall please." His eyes are big, I never saw so much emotion in him before. Whatever he could be feeling right now, he's feeling it.

"You still love me after what I said?" I ask small, I want to grab his face and kiss him so passionately. "I did a lot of thinking, I was terrible to you. I treated you like shit, I was so angry because you never communicated how you felt, but I never bothered to tell you the lack of communication pissed me off."

"You went through a lot that day, you had more feelings than normal. Of course, I still do. I'm so sorry I wasn't honest from the start." His voice cracks, he shuts his eyes tight. "I was trying to find out how much you knew of the Basilisks, I was waiting for you to trust me. I'm so sorry."

"You were honest." I can hear myself talking like a robot. I repeat his statement from that way, I don't know if I'm supposed to say it's okay, or don't worry about it, because I'm completely fucked now. "You had less of a choice than I did."

Nico looks at me, pain is still written all over his face. "We both have things we need to work on, but I'm done with the pointless fighting. The words from anger have to stop."

I nod my head fast, "Whatever it takes, I swear to you. I don't know how I'm supposed to go through therapy when I'm going through this without telling them, but I will figure it out." I look at him, and my eyes are uncomfortable from the burn.

I think he notices, because his hands tangled up in my hair, and the next thing I know his lips are on mine.

My phone buzzes in his hand, "Its Ash. Get changed. She'll be here soon." His voice is sad.

My face hardens, I let go of the blanket, standing completely naked grabbing clothes.

Not a single emotion runs through my body.

The blood pumping through my veins is completely cold.

It's only been a few days, and I already hate who I've become.

I grab my phone from Nico not looking at him. My peripheral vision is completely blocked, not allowing myself to see him, not allowing myself to feel anything.

45

Nico

I open the door watching the agent on duty check the delivery driver's license, then make them take all of the food out of the bag, open it, then stack it on the under cover hood. The driver has a *what the fuck just happened* look. The agent takes the food walking it all up to the door. I ordered a lot, so she is struggling. I slip on my shoes, meeting her half way down the driveway.

"Is someone with Cameron?" I whisper.

"You don't need to check up on her." She has a sing song voice. "I'm almost offended that Brittney never gave you a full report on me. I'm the best."

I step in the house, watching her follow me in, "Just kick the snow off. Do you want some of this?"

I went so overboard with the appetizers. I'm just trying to make Cameron feel again, and I don't even know where to start. Food helped me, so maybe this is the key. She's completely lost herself, she's accepted that her life is gone. I'm almost envious, it took me months before I became numb to the pain. I felt everything, I cried, I screamed. Then one day I stopped screaming and crying as much, until it just became uncomfortable. This morning after that text, she completely shut down. She was on autopilot.

"Is there cheese bread?" I take the boxes from Agent Lee, watching her rock back and forth from her heels to her toes.

"I got two. It's Cameron's favorite." I set them on the end table, my hands are shaking. "I'm so scared she's going to come out of this once it's over and hate every single one of us."

"Hey." Agent Lee grabs my hand. "Stop. I saw firsthand how this can go. When I say it'll be okay, you need to trust me."

I don't look at her, I just grab the small box checking it, then pass it to her with a side of ranch.

"The agents are on their way back. If you feel anything out of the ordinary, I'm right outside." She turns away before I can thank her. I can't thank these agents enough.

I quickly run around the house grabbing candles, I line them up in front of the TV. I quickly make us both a strong double, I grab plates, trying to scatter the boxes around the coffee table.

My phone buzzes. I check it, it's Josh.

Hey kid. How are you holding up?

I don't know.

I promise you, you will be okay. Both of you.

Tomorrow let's go out for coffee. I'll find somewhere busy so we can blend in.

Deal

I've never had someone check in on me before. I don't know why I agreed to that.

The chime on my phone goes off for the front door camera, I set my phone down bringing our glasses to the table.

Cameron stands looking in the living room, her eyes are so dark. She looks like a ghost.

"What happened?" I try to ask in the most sensitive way, there's no way to ask.

"Just someone who saw a deal. He had kids Nico. They both had kids. I'm not made to threaten anyone, let alone children. What is this?" she raises her hand dropping it to her side.

I kneel on the couch passing her the drink, she reaches for it. The second the vodka hits her lips, she chugs half the glass back. I watch her with my eyebrows raised. We're going to need more alcohol.

"I wanted to have a night with my girlfriend. I figured you'd be hungry." I shrug after casually tossing out the G word. We spent too long not knowing what we were, and I refuse to do it again especially when she's like this. I won't even take no for an answer.

She drinks the rest of the alcohol, "Can I have another? Did you get cheese bread?"

What the fuck is with girls and cheese bread? I nod, taking her cup. I pour her drink less strong this time, I know she needs it, but I'm trying to not kill her from alcohol poisoning. I grab her water bottle from the fridge, setting it on the couch. She sat right beside my spot, at least she's still sitting in her spot. Even though it's bread crumbs, I'll take it.

"I never told Ashley you were alive. I didn't know if I was allowed too. I didn't want to just in case."

"Baby." I reach out to her, grabbing her arm. "She knows. I forced myself into your room when you were sleeping."

She looks at me, she finally has expression in her face, she's confused as fuck.

"I needed to see if you were okay. I sat there all night. I couldn't move."

Her face goes long, she looks away, setting her glass on the table right by a takeout container. *She's going to hit me.* I think to myself, bracing myself. She wouldn't be this unpredictable normally, but God damn it she's messed up mentally right now.

Cameron throws her body into mine, wrapping her arms around me. Her entire body is trembling.

Without skipping a heartbeat, I wrap my arms around her, holding her as tight as I can. "As soon as I was able to, I came to you. I wanted to wake you, but if Dad knew I saw you..." I let my voice trail off. "I was hoping you'd wake up and catch me. I didn't have it in me to make the choice for you to put you in that much danger."

"I don't care." She gasps for air, cutting me off. "I got you back." She nozzles her face in my chest, trying to get closer to me. "I'm scared that I'm going to feel everything I've done. I never had time to grieve Charlie, I killed someone else Nico. I'm scared."

I loosen my grip from her, pulling her off of my chest. I place my hand under her chin, gently forcing her to look at me. Her face is completely dry. She is feeling everything, or she wouldn't be scared. She's just not letting herself fully feel. I smile small, she's not gone. She's in there. I just have to get her back, because I will get her out of this. One thing is for sure, she can't ever know that the person she killed at Junction Square was an agent. That's not me lying to her, that's me protecting her. If she knew it would cause way more damage than good.

"I will get you out of the city, we can run if you want. We can go rent a farm house in one of the Dakotas if that's what you want. I promise you, I will make sure this is a faded memory. You know The Basilisks have you."

"No, they don't." She shakes her head, speaking softly. "How could they? Yeah, they all came here, but that doesn't mean they want me back."

Oh, she has no idea. "Plan your future. Whatever you want. Nothing's too big or too small."

"You." She looks me in the eyes, "I know it might not be possible."

"I'll make it possible." The words fall out of my mouth, all I have to do is survive the lie detector, then survive the war. I just have to make it out alive.

I lean in sealing our lips. She places her hand on my cheek, instantly sending vibrations down my back.

She pulls away, a real smile on her face. "I'm so hungry. To be continued."

***

Josh did a hell of a job finding a busy Café. This place is like a nightclub. It's also fancy, so not only do we both look out of place, no one would even consider us being here. Josh takes off his Jacket, leaning it over the back of the chair. His sweater is pulled up on his forearms. He's covered in tattoos. They all are, I've never really looked before.

"I need to know. Where's that tattoo?" I ask leaning over the table scanning his arms.

Josh flips his forearm around, the snake is slithering up his arm. "Some of us got it covered, the others didn't. It's easy to walk away from, pretending like it didn't happen is different."

"What does it feel like to be free?" I twist the cloth napkin in my hands.

"Takes a while to get used to it. I still look over my shoulder, I catch myself speeding away from cars that are following me. I can't trust anyone. I was too scared to have kids. Rightfully so."

The server stops by, we both order a cappuccino. I can't stop twisting this napkin, I might wear the seams down to nothing by the time we leave. Josh is the smallest guy out of everyone in the group, he always has the hardest facial expressions, he isn't someone you would walk up to on the street to ask for directions. It's throwing me off that he's the one here right now, he was the one that made me less nervous at Christmas. It's almost shocking in a way.

"Why are you nervous?"

"Public with you. I'm breaking so many rules, Cameron's at home. Alone."

"Sam's outside." Josh quickly speaks. "As far as the rules go, you already broke a lot, what's a few more. Are you ready for the lie detector?"

"Yes. It's intimidating."

The server comes back dropping the Coffee off. She talks to Josh, I watch them. He's treating her with the utmost respect, they're both smiling, both laughing. He might have a hard time trusting people, but I'm having a really easy time trusting him. I don't know if it's because he's connected to my girlfriend, or if it's because he's been in a mafia. He understands, or maybe it's because he watched the Basilisks fall. All I know is I'm calmer than when we got here.

I've never felt this way with an adult before. I feel, I don't know —
safe? I guess. I brought up Cameron, he reassured me, then kept talking
about me. He didn't meet up with me to ask questions about her.

She leaves the table, I look at my coffee. "Can you be there?"

"Yes." The words fall out of his mouth, he never even had time to
register my question. "I'm going to need to advocate for you. Tell me
about your childhood."

I do. Every last bit. Not the torturing, but the forgotten birthdays,
the lack of Christmas', my dog Sadie. Physical affection wasn't shown
towards me, I had to date a lot just so I could learn how to love someone.
I never graduated high school, so I have to explain how I got into
Spencer's class. I backtracked to simple things like how I had to completely fend for myself, chores, food, cleaning. If I didn't do it, it
wouldn't get done. I was a pro at using the washer and dryer by the time
I was eight, I learnt how to make my bed at six, if I couldn't microwave a
meal, I had to eat cereal. Family dinners were only for special occasions.

"Stand the fuck up." Josh puts his hands on the table sliding his chair
on the ground making an awful noise.

I listen, he powerfully pulls me into his body, squeezing me as tight
as he can. "You have yourself a really annoying, clingy family. If you and
Cameron don't work out, I will still fight for you. I think I'm the clingi-
est, so good luck with that."

I stand there with my eyes burning. I'm uncomfortable for a few reasons. He tightens his grip, and the uncomfortable feeling float away.

"Do you hear me?"

I nod.

"Good." He steps away sitting in his spot.

"I told Cameron we were going to run away to a farm house in a
Dakota to get her out of this. She came home yesterday, and I can't let
her live like this. She also wants to go to therapy, and I have no idea how
that will even work."

"Actually. That might not be a bad idea." Josh watches me. "When
everything goes down, the kids, her, the untrained, and the ones who

married into this, should leave." Josh crinkles his nose. "I'm sure for therapy, we can get a waiver signed by one of the agents explaining everything? I'll look into it."

I'm impressed by Josh's mind. "How would you guys even get everyone out of the city?"

Josh looks at me amused. "Just tell Dillon's husband he needs to get everyone ready for a slumber party. He'd hype the shit out of everyone. I'll talk to someone about it. You were gone. Do you need groceries?"

I look at him with squinted eyes.

"My niece eats like a horse, so I'm assuming that's a yes." He goes on his phone sliding it over to me, it's open to a company who will shop for me and drop it off. I open my mouth to protest, he interrupts me. "This is what it's like having an adult take care of you."

I look at him, with my eyes burning again before I look down at his phone thinking of everything we need.

46

Cameron

When Nico walked through those doors yesterday, I never felt happier. Before all this happened, I was okay when my mind wasn't busy, or when I was sitting alone in a room enjoying my own company. Now times have changed with me, as soon as I'm alone, that is when everything hits me. I was doing okay, I was somehow managing to block out my emotions, I was forcing my memories to stay hidden in my mind. Then Nico tells me he sat with me all night in my room while I slept, hoping I woke up and caught him.

Now, it's hard to try to ignore all the bad I've done in only a few days. Now, I know that people still love me despite how many people I killed. Now I know I need to face what I've done. I don't know if I'm ever going to be strong enough to face this alone. I need help, I need to figure something out to manage my thoughts. I need support.

I thought Nico was dead. There was nothing tying us together, he didn't have to come back and sit with me. He could have just pushed me off as a job. I wish I woke up when he was there. I wish I saw him. Being loved unconditionally by my family is so much different than being loved hard like the way he loves me. He could have been free, found someone else, done anything else, yet he chose to be right there with me, without me knowing it.

Now when I'm alone, I'm feeling everything I repressed. I never had my walls up for long. It was just long enough that I almost forgot about the small details. My memory takes me back, putting together bits and pieces, exactly like the nights where I drank too much. I was completely sober, and I blacked out.

I remember exactly how Charlie died, the look on her face when she saw me holding the gun. I want to go to her funeral, even though I'm forbidden from ever seeing them again. I want to try to apologize to Adam. I don't know how long funerals take to plan, I probably missed it. If that's true, I probably missed my chance to apologize to my only blood uncle for destroying his life. I got the person I love back, and he never got his love back. I get to hold Nico, and Adam is never going to be able to hold Charlie again. He has every right to never look in my direction, he has every right to turn his back on me. This is too much for me to carry on my shoulders. I'm not okay. I can't breathe when I'm alone. At least when Nico's here I'm distracted, I can pretend to be okay. Even if I'm not okay, he sees it. I don't deserve for him to comfort me when he sees me close to shattering.

I don't know how I'm going to live with myself. I don't know how I'm going to ever be able to move on with my life. Every time I look at anyone who was there, I'm going to see that look of horror on their faces. Everyone looked at me like I was a monster for snapping. The only person who was able to hide it was Nico. He spoke calm, he got the gun out of my hands, he was there. He was able to handle me. I know it's not fair to everyone else in the room, I wasn't in the position for pity, but they all heard the same thing I did. They all heard Charlie admit why she did what she did to me. I didn't even realize I had the gun, until after I shot it. My rage kicked in, I saw red, and I completely blacked out. I'm not innocent, but I also believe I deserve some benefit of the doubt. No matter how narcissistic that makes me sound.

Nico comes up from behind the couch wrapping his arms around my shoulder. "I need to run out."

"Where have you been going?" He left yesterday, and now today. He never leaves the house unless I'm with him.

"Dad needs me." He leans forward kissing my cheek.

I need a hobby, because I can't keep putting myself through this. I can't let myself fall apart whenever he shuts the front door. I refuse. I need to try to find myself again.

I grab the remote looking for any history documentary I can find. This is how I start. The girl I used to be is in me, somewhere. I think.

47

Nico

"Whatever we need to do, we need to finish it today." I shut the door behind me, "I hate lying to her."

Josh looks up at me from the back of the couch, sitting beside Tim. "I know."

I want to squeeze him. I don't know what I'm feeling. There's so much appreciation towards him. Instead, I walk up to him, placing my hand on his shoulders squeezing my hand. Just a silent thank you. I'm doing everything I can to repress me wanting to hug him.

Tim stands pointing at a chair with wooden arms. "Sit. You are going to have a monitor on to watch your breathing, one arm is going to have a blood pressure monitor. The other monitor is going to sit at your fingertips on your opposite hand, to detect the sweat from your hand. We are also recording this entire thing. More for court."

I nod, taking off my jacket, laying it on the couch walking towards the chair, I raise my arms letting him wrap a cord high on my chest, I lean forward listening to his commands feeling something being put on the back of my shirt. He opens his laptop.

Sam stands behind Tim on the computer, she watches him nod before speaking. "I'm going to answer you easy questions. Just so we can read it. Only answer yes, or no. Do you understand?"

"Yes."

"Is your name Nico D'oria?"

"Yes."

"Were you born in New York?"

"No."

"Now we will begin. Are you a Member of the Nemean Mafia?"

"Yes."

"Were you introduced when you were twelve?"

"Yes."

"Does anyone know you're here?"

"No."

"Is Cameron the reason you are here?" The questions keep coming, I keep answering yes. "Will you do anything to take down your father? Are you doing this for Cameron? If it came down to it, would you kill your family? When you walk away, are you done with crime?"

The questions were starting to blend in until they start to sound crazy, they slowly started asking about my childhood, then Sam looks at me taking a deep breath. "Are you aware we didn't know you existed?"

"No."

"Are you aware Nico D'Oria is not your real name?"

"No?" I look at Josh, he's sitting on the edge of his seat watching me.

"Have you ever heard the name Matteo Gallo?"

"No." I'm telling the truth, but I'm sweating so much I'm scared it's going to look like I'm lying.

Tim orders Sam to unhook me, and I'm terrified that means I failed. I can't read any of their faces. They are both emotionless. Josh pipes up demanding if I passed, Sam looks at him with a small smile reassuring him that it's okay.

None of this feels okay. Who the fuck is Matteo Gallo?

I get unhooked automatically cracking my fingers. I want to go home so bad. The room energy shifted the second that name was said. I pull my shirt down, rushing to sit next to Josh, getting the hell away from that wooden chair.

"Do you know this person?" Tim asks me holding a picture of a baby.

All baby's look alike. This one has tan hair, tan skin, just like every other child in Italy that have two Italian parents. I shake my head. They hold up another picture. This time there's two parents holding the baby, Tim just showed me. It's old, the color has faded, the image looks like it's at least twenty years old. I shake my head.

"What is this?" Josh asks in a demanding voice.

"Nico." Tim looks at me with wide eyes. "We searched you high and low, we found transcripts from school, and your driver's license with your name but that was it. We ran you through a database, it shows similar facial features, our IT person did it on a whim."

"Have you noticed everyone your age is a girl?" Sam asks in a quiet voice, it's almost straining to listen to her.

"There's two other boys." I argue.

"Toby couldn't have been used for the position. Violet, Sammy, their dad, they were all undercover Nemean. Gabe's dad was undercover with the Baker Cartel. Archie would have noticed him."

Josh's teeth grind, his palms wrap in a fist. I haven't told them a lot, and I actually feel bad about it. I only spilled Noah's secret.

"Many people were paid to have a baby when Lizzy was pregnant. They all found out they were having a girl around the same time. The Lion had no choice but to find a boy from a different family. You are not part of the D'oria family. You are a Gallo. Your name is Matteo Gallo."

"What?" I struggle to speak.

"From what we were able to put together, we think the D'oria's went to Italy, searching for a newborn boy that was sickly Italian roots. No one in Nemean was able to produce a boy, so they took matters into their own hands. That's when you were brought back here."

Josh sits closer to me, his body tenses as he puts his arm around me. I don't fight him off, I just sit here. I could have had a real family? I wasn't born into this? I was taken from parents who actually cared? Josh is asking questions while rubbing my arm, I'm not listening to a word he's saying, I can feel the vibrations from his chest as he speaks.

"What are the next steps?" I blurt out interrupting the conversation.

"Getting them out of town." Josh speaks directly at me. Josh has clearly spoken about this to everyone.

"Somewhere remote." Tim speaks up. "We are able to temporarily shut down the access your father has to the city cameras while everyone leaves the city."

"Farm house. With a view of a sunset. Cameron is going to need a lot of alcohol. Josh, I'm telling you that part, not them. I want to drive her there, just in case."

"Those are more than fair demands." Tim replies.

"I need to go home and get us packed then? They like to make things explode as a warning."

"Everyone needs to do that. While the cameras are down, we will get agents to move everything boxed up. Only the important things. They are going to be having to move things fast."

"Your family?" Josh questions me, squeezing my arm. "I don't think you heard, but they still hang posters. That's how they got the connection. The missing person case gets reopened every few years." He looks at me with big eyes, I think he looks hopeful?

"How do I go home pretending like this didn't happen?" I look at him with a long face, and a shaky voice.

"Just for a few days. Go pack, go tell her The Basilisks did something good for once. And that she gets to step away. I hope you're ready for a war Nico."

"I'm not ready."

Josh looks at me with a soft expression.

"But I will destroy anyone who tries to get in the way."

48

Cameron

"Wait. Back up. Did you say road trip?" I look at Nico with large eyes, I want to bounce around in excitement. "What about work?"

"I handled it." Nico looks at me with a small smile.

"Snacks!?" I say a little too loud, an entire day not worrying about getting called away? I will take it.

"I handled that too."

I jump, and shriek, my entire body pulses from my excitement. I run to the door spinning around, I want to yell at him that I love him. My legs get tangled up with a bin sitting at the door, and I nearly collide onto the ground. Nico reaches his hand out, grabbing me, pulling me back on my feet. He chuckles, pushing the bin out of the way, and opening the door for me to run through.

"Where did this car come from?" I ask looking at the shiny black car, the windows are dark. There's no way anyone can see inside of them.

"I have connections. I'm not stopping for a while. Do you have to go to the bathroom?" Nico looks at me with his eyebrows raised. I shake my head. "We need to go then. We'll stop for coffee when we leave the city." He's speaking super polite, I can't ignore the sense of urgency in his voice. "Can I have your phone?"

Cameron reaches into her back pocket, passing it to me without hesitation.

"I'll explain it in the car, both our phones need to stay here."

I say his name drawing our every letter squinting my eyes.

"I need you to trust me and go to the car."

I get in the car, without arguing. He doesn't seem like he's in the mood for me not to listen.

The inside of this car is all leather. It smells amazing, it smells brand new. It was recently detailed, there's not a single crumb anywhere. I take my coat off, feeling the seat warmer on my back through my shirt. I sink into the warmth. Nico checks a phone I've never seen before, typing a quick reply before putting the car into reverse.

Him having his license never once came up in conversation. It's honestly probably not even real. Just like our ID's. I don't know how he can even carry two on him, could you imagine going to the bar and accidentally passing someone your real driver's license that says you're under age?

"How are you feeling?" he sounds nervous. Normally when he speaks all of his attention is on me, he's driving so he's distracted, something doesn't feel right. He's not right.

"I'm feeling. And I love you. So much." Trying to ignore my emotions got too heavy. Now I cry a lot. I sit on the couch, and I sob.

A smile breaks out across his face, "It's nice seeing you coming back. I didn't even realize how much I missed overly excited Cameron."

I hate to admit, he came home the other day, and I was hyperventilating on the couch. Reality hitting me hasn't been nice, it's been fair, but not nice. I deserve every last tear I cry, and more. Nico's been here, the longer I spend with him the harder it is for me to walk out the door when Ashley calls. Thankfully, I haven't been at this for more than a week. It doesn't change the fact that the call I had last night, I felt all of it. There wasn't blind rage, there was just sadness, disgust, and regret.

Nico grabs my hand, "If you don't want to come back, we don't have to."

"Then what run from the Mafia?" I laugh nervously, feeling my happiness start to slide away.

"Yes." He replies breathlessly.

"You know I can't do that." I kiss his hand, setting it back on my lap, squeezing it, feeling his grip in return.

The car ride is silent until we finally go on the highway, when he speaks again. "I need you to listen to me. I'm dropping you off at a house, then I'm coming back."

I look at him with my mouth open.

"You are going to be with the kids, all the wife's, Theo, Max, and April. They are all under the impression Dillons husband is hosting a sleepover."

I open my mouth to interrupt him, when he squeezes my hand.

"You will have alcohol and snacks, don't worry. There will be FBI agents parked out front. We are going to end this."

I hold his hand up to my mouth kissing it again, I can't speak. Emotions are washing over me, it feels like worry is taking over everything I'm feeling.

"I spoke to Josh. He thinks the agents want to do this legally, but we aren't going to give them a chance to run anything inside a prison." He takes a deep breath. "A lot of people will die, all of us want to do this. Josh told me it's a rule, protect another Basilisks with your life."

A tear falls from my face. I saw the way Josh reacted when Nico walked in the building at Christmas. He was always watching him, I thought maybe he hated him too, until I saw how he smiled passing drink after drink. "He wasn't talking about me."

"There's more, but I need to know you understand what is happening here."

I'm quiet.

"Every single Nemean member is going to be burnt to the ground. All of our homes, and businesses will be targeted. There won't be anything left for us in New York."

"Then we leave." I belt out the words without thinking, "All of us." I love New York. Having a fresh start after everything that's happened might not be a bad thing, my dreams can become dreams in another city.

Right now, I'm only worried about what's going on in the present. "Has Josh seen Dad?"

"I did. He knew I was alive the next day. I needed to help you. I needed something. They got me into a weird neighborhood, I think it's FBI owned. I told everyone what happened to me growing up. I needed to get back to you." He sniffles his nose. "I didn't know what to do." Each word he says his grip gradually gets tighter and tighter.

"Can we get coffee?" I ask dry.

Nico nods, pulling into a parking lot in a suburban neighborhood. "Open the glove box, your new phone is there."

Before I get out, before I open the glove box, I question him about all of our things, they have every last detail figured out. Nothing is being left to a game of chance. He's been completely honest with me. It's almost surreal.

The second we hit the road again Nico spills everything that happened two days ago, with the FBI. Every last detail. I want to crawl on his lap and hold him. I've caused so much trauma, and so much agony for him without even realizing it. Hearing his stories, Hearing the way his voice shakes, hearing how my entire family sat in the room with him, it makes me proud.

I move my cup watching the ice mix the milk around. "You need to meet your real parents."

"I know." His voice is small.

Tears are already falling down my face, crying seems so wrong now, I haven't even asked yet. Asking a simple question is too painful. I wipe the tears with the back of my hands. "I've hurt you so much." Tears are falling heavily, I can't keep up. "If you can't handle what comes next, I'll forgive you if you leave me. You need to go see what it's like with them. Go live the life you deserve, go make up for lost time."

Nico parks, aggressively hitting the brakes making my seatbelt lock. "Stop Cami." He grabs both of my hands, looking at my tear filled face. "I wouldn't go through all this to leave you. If I even have a relationship with them, we can go to Italy. What comes next is us, that's it."

He unbuckles his seatbelt, leaning in to kiss me.

"I don't want you to resent me." I whimper against his lips.

He leans back, "There's not going to be any resentment. I'm in, and I hope to hell you will be too."

He's saving me. Of course, I'm in.

49

Nico

After a five hour drive, I'm finally parking the car. I hate winter driving, thankfully this is happening on a day where there's no snow falling, next to no wind, and the sun is shining. The days not nearly over, it's 10: 30 in the morning, I need to get Cameron okay with being here, she's okay for now, soon she won't be. She's going to put up a fucking fight, and I don't even blame her one bit.

She lets out a little gasp, squeezing my knee before she unbuckles her seatbelt, opening her door, and running into her father's arms at full speed nearly knocking him over.

I get out of the car, there are so many vehicles here. Everyone that could carpool did, they had to bring their families, and everyone had to come, even if they don't have kids. They needed to get out of the city away from the danger. Us shutting off the camera's was a big enough red flag, dad is probably getting everyone set up and positioned for a fight. I look past my girlfriend trying not to smile at their reunion. This house looks like a straight up barn that is drawn in children's books, instead of being bright red, it's made from brown wood. There's so much grass surrounding the house, the gravel road is blocked by trees, we couldn't even see anything other than the roof when we were driving here.

Josh comes over to me, reaching his arm over my shoulder holding me tight. Everything he's done for me, the support I have from him, him checking up on me. He's let me organize my thoughts about my birth parents out loud. He's tried to talk me through the conclusion, because of him, I decided I need to meet them, even if they don't take me for what I am, I need to know. I've sent him random questions this morning about the way here, and he will call back with an answer almost instantly. There's no hesitation when it comes to him.

A SUV pulls in, Liam jumps out of the vehicle walking directly towards us. His entire body is shaking. He lifts his hands towards his hair, that's when I notice his wedding ring isn't on. "Someone else is driving her home after, I cannot do that again."

"Not sure there will be many takers." Josh rubs my shoulder letting me free to brace Cameron for the blow that's about to come.

"Go have fun with your third marriage." Liam mutters. "I hate her. My niece, her fucking daughter Josh. This is something Martin would have done." His voice shakes. I haven't heard one person reference any of their parents. From what I know everyone here cut off their parents completely, or they died.

I run up behind Cameron wrapping my arms around her waist, feeling her sink into my body the moment I touch her.

"Top of the stairs is her room." Erik speaks up. "We only have a few minutes before we need to leave. I'll get her bags."

"Where's Hayley?" Cameron looks to her left side towards the SUV.

Both me and Erik tip our heads back. We were so damn close.

"Yeah, fuck that. Take me home." Cameron shakes her head. "I'm not going in there."

"Yes, you are." I grab her, picking her up. One arm is holding her under her knees, the other is supporting her neck. "Don't you dare try to fight this."

Anger runs through her body as she hits my chest once with a closed fist. It actually kind of hurts, and it's taking everything I have not to cringe.

"Put me down." She grumbles. "I won't make a run for it."

I roll my eyes, setting her on her feet. Grabbing her hand, pulling her inside. This house is massive. I can't even start to imagine how many bedrooms are in here. The dining room is to my right, it has a huge square table in it, hardwood floors with a rug under it. To my right is a massive living room, couches, rugs, an oversized TV, and a fireplace. I'd much rather be staying here. Straight ahead of us is a staircase, it's wide enough for multiple people to walk side by side with room. We kick off our shoes, none of them are standing nice.

"It sounds like Lizzy and Liam separated." I can't reference that woman as her mom one more time.

Cameron laughs. "Good. He should take his kids too." She looks at me with squinted eyes, "Why didn't you tell me Lizzy would be here?"

"I need you where agents will be to keep you safe. Don't be blaming us for trying to protect you. April and Brittney will have your back."

"I'm sorry." She spits the words out. "You're right." She takes a deep breath, apparently, she is really trying to not start fights anymore. "I need you to check in. I need updates. I'm going to be going crazy researching how the Basilisks did things. What I found was unsettling Nico."

We stop at the top of the staircase, that's exactly what I don't need her to be doing. I open the door for her, the room has everything she needs. Bed, dresser, blankets, pillows, and a mini fridge.

I grab her hand, sitting on the black and red checkered comforter. "Don't do that. Basilisks were messy."

Erik walks in, he drops the bags, listening to my response without saying a word, letting me continue.

"They opened fire, they blew up houses. That's what is most likely going to happen today. Innocent people never got hurt." What's the harm in telling her straight up now? I wasn't one of them, so I'm sure I'm not giving the greatest information.

"Unless you're Brittney." Erik chuckles. "K that's not funny." He sighs, bending down to face her sitting on the bed. "We will only be targeting buildings where the Lion has put his strongest people. We have to weaken him before we go after him. The FBI can deal with the rest of them, we frankly don't give a shit about the others. The ones down the chain will be lost without him."

"You guys are going to get arrested." Cameron looks at both of us.

I give her a weak smile. "I think the second the FBI signed onto this, they knew what was going to happen."

"I'll take the fall for everyone." Erik looks at her sad. "It's believable. The part I used to play, if there is an explosion..." he trails off, "You're my daughter."

"Absolutely fucking not." I blurt out.

"Shut up!" Cameron yells. "What do they want you to do?" Her voice gets lower.

"Kill him." Dillon speaks.

I look over my shoulder seeing every Basilisk standing in the doorway.

"Jack is a bomb technician. He's been in the city for a few days." Archie speaks looking at Cameron with a soft expression. "The standing Baker Cartel will not let him see the light of day again."

Cameron's eyes go wide. Baker Cartel was never brought up, nothing else was said about it. I feel terrible, more keeps getting dumped on her, and she has no possible outlet.

"We need to go." I think it's Dillon speaking.

I look at Cameron, getting lost in her brown eyes. "I love you. I will see you again, and we will all be coming back together." As tempting as it is to promise her, I know how wrong that could go.

Cameron kisses me, her lips run over mine softly, then she kisses me hard, grabbing my shirt pulling me closer. I don't pull away, I can't. I'm terrified. I've never done this before, I've never entered a building to shoot at people and run off, I've never made a bomb go off. I needed this kiss as much as she does.

She pulls away, telling everyone to stay in touch, making sure we better all be coming back. We all turn to leave when she speaks again, "I'm sorry for all this. I'm sorry for killing Charlie, I'm sorry for bringing this back. I'm sorry I destroyed everyone. I hope somewhere down the line, everyone can forgive me."

"None of this was you." Adam turns around looking at her with piercing eyes, "None of it. I'm torn between hating my wife, and missing her, that doesn't land on you."

I stand walking through the door leaning on Josh, like it's a reflex that I know he'll keep me standing when I'm too weak to do it on my own. He keeps me upright, hugging me. "Let's go. There's a blanket and pillow in the back seat for you."

I lean against the window, with my pillow covering myself up continuously reading the text from Cameron.

I can't lose you again. I managed to find one article, and I can't be okay with anyone going in those cross fires, let alone you guys. I need you to be okay Nico. I need to be loved by you, I need you to not die again.

"How does this work?" I ask, blacking out my phone. I can't respond to her, not yet.

"Have you shot a gun before?" Adam looks at me in the rearview mirror.

I tell them I have, that's the truth. I just leave out the fact that my targets were people, tied to the wall. And then when my aim was perfect, they let the targets run around the room to try to get away from me. I swallow down bile, the thoughts of that, me doing that. I'm an absolute monster, and there's no reason I should get immunity. I should be locked up. I shouldn't be dead, life in prison is worse than being dead. If someone else was in my position, I'm almost guaranteed to be someone the FBI would rather have dead.

"Grenades, guns, mail bombs." Spencer looks out his window, "Brittney is with her. She'll help her cope with this."

"How was this your everyday life?" I ask, crumbling the blanket uncomfortably.

"How did you do it every day?" Spencer looks at me. "We are just different versions of hit men. Ours was just less—"

"Traumatizing." I finished his sentence for him.

Liam turns facing me from the front seat, he looks rough. Not in a way of facial hair or sloppy clothes, he looks rough from being completely hurt and betrayed. "Josh will not let you go anywhere alone. I've never seen him so proud and more protective. It's like he's a father."

"K let's not sound so surprised." Spencer laughs.

"He taught all our kids how to use the word fuck correctly and rewarded it with cookies." Liam laughs, "Excuse me for being surprised Joshua suddenly has father intuition."

Someone feels that way towards me? I kind of want to laugh, because that can't be true. At the same time, I want to scream, laugh, and hug him. He's been there for me, that's not him being forced to be there for me, he volunteered himself.

Even still, that can't be true.

As long as I can remember no one has ever had 'father intuition' with me. Men have always pushed me down further, beat me, or mentally messed with me. I'm not someone that's meant to have parents.

"What they are trying to say." Adam sounds annoyed, "He will be extra cautious."

I'm so happy, my foot is tapping on the ground fast. I use the pillow, trying to hide my face with the blanket.

Someone might finally love me unconditionally.

50

Cameron

"I heard there's alcohol in here." Brittney busts open the door, opening suitcases, on a hunt for the alcohol gasping for air. I quickly pass her the bottle that's in my hand, from my bed, watching her twist off the top, taking a large drink.

"I just sent our husband's out there for the first time in nineteen years. I'm not okay." Brittney passes me the bottle sitting cross legged on the floor, tears instantly running down her face. "When I joined the FBI, I just wanted Spence out, and now." She pauses. "I'm sorry. I'm so sorry. I'm not blaming you. Damn it." She wipes her face standing up, clearly guilty for no reason.

I pat the bed beside me, "Stay. I don't think my boyfriends ever done this, my dad's going out there, everyone I love is going out there." I can't cry anymore. I want to stand on the roof of the house and curse at the top of my lungs. I need to hold myself together, because there's a house full of people that are oblivious to what's really going on.

"When Martin was arrested, that was Taylor's dad. He had some pretty hefty charges." She stares down looking at me, "There was 700 charges that he used for hitmen, and I personally feel like a lot went unknown. When I say they dealt with this on the regular, I'm not kidding. I know they'll all walk through the doors, but I'm fucking scared." She takes another drink from the bottle.

"Who's watching your kids?" I ask taking the bottle away from her, saving her liver.

"Some other adults who's better at adult things than me right now." She wipes her face again. "I wish I knew where this bad blood started from. I was too busy watching specific members, I never once saw anyone double cross. I wish I could have done something. I could have stopped it before this happened."

"Why is this happening so fast?"

"We spent a very long time with Martin. Long enough he retired and left the country for a bit. They're probably just learning from their mistakes. If anyone asks, you and Nico are going through it. We are watching sad movies, because that's what girls do."

I nod, grabbing my laptop while reassuring her that there was nothing she could have done. If we are going to lie to everyone, I'm going to put on a movie, it may as well be half true.

My phone vibrates, I fumble for my phone, ignoring Brittney swiping the bottle away from me,

There's a small town not far from the house you're at. There's a university. Five hour drive from the city, whoever wants to come with us can. It's not the suburbs, I don't know if I can live so close after all of this. We can talk about it. I'm not going to die Cameron, we're just starting to make plans.

I toss my phone to Brittney, "Wanna come?"

"Um yes. Then I want to go to your wedding."

I roll my eyes. Taking my phone back,

I'll go anywhere with you.

Another message comes in the second I hit send.

You are my only future. You want a million and five kids? You got it. There's a lot we need to work on. Nothing will be standing in our way. I'm going to make vows and prove how much I love you every single day.

I don't show Brittney that message, I close my eyes, biting my bottom lip.

51

Nico

"Don't touch that box mate." Jack chuckles, it almost sounds evil, "Unless you wanna go Kaboom." He smirks, it was most definitely an evil laugh.

"K dumbass." Hayley glares at him. "How do we get it from point A to B then?" she talks with her hands making point A and point B dramatic.

Jack makes a face to her. I'm taken back by how close every single person in this room is. Even in the stressful times, they're all calm when they're near each other. Everyone is holding onto the conversations so deeply. They are looking around the room, seeing each other, watching them closely like it might be the last time they see everyone here at once. They have gotten way too good at this. The fact that they're all walking into the line of fire without two decades of practice without fear, is mind blowing.

"I have a bomb suit, you cotton head." I half hold in a laugh at Jack's insult, watching other face's light up except for Hayley and Archie's.

I'm so glad we all find British slang hilarious right now.

I clear my throat. "I don't think you go up to my dad's door step lookin' like a black fucking marshmallow is going to work."

"Bomb suit is just for the way there."

Archie looks at Jack looking far from impressed. "You can't be serious Jack. No."

"Delivery clothes are much more believable. I built it. I know how to handle it. They'll pick it up and it'll get triggered. I may have put a fire work in there, so the bitch will make a pretty explosion."

"Or it'll be my sister." I mutter.

Tim speaks as the front door opens, making his entry. "We actually need you to call Lucia. Just get her out of the house. The bomb isn't for your dad, it's for your mom. We are going to try to spare your sister, if he will cooperate with us."

They're trying to break my father down hoping he'll just give in. This conversation has to be for the paperwork, because the feds were apparently dead set on my dad wanting to be dead, or so I heard.

"I'm not holding my sister hostage." I snap. "She's a terrible person, but she's also the reason I'm alive right now. I'm not sinking down to her level." All I can think about is the smile she had on her face when she saw the finger on the table, assuming it was Cameron's. The look in her face, the sound in her voice, it sends the worst kind of shiver down my back shaking me to my core.

"There's no other option." Tim looks at me. "The bombs are all threats, mail bombs don't cause enough damage. It'll just be enough to get the Lion on alert. Off the record, they also fucked with my best friends family, so he can die for all I care."

There it is.

"Yeah... minimal damage, that's it." Jack rubs the back of his neck. "On that note. Ima go change now." He sucks in air through his teeth. "Open the front door for me. I'll need a car to follow in about forty five minutes." He runs out of the living room like he's on fire.

I close my eyes, I need to get out of here. This living room is getting smaller and smaller by the second, there are way too many people here right now. I stand, walking by the wall trying to dodge the couch of people to get into the kitchen. My hands land on the counter, I bend over breathing in air. This is happening all too fast. I know what I signed up for, I now know what Nemean did to me, what they did to my birth parents, I feel everything. They're asking a lot of me right now. I just need time to feel.

Josh stands beside me, leaning against the counter, I don't look at him. I'm fucking nauseous.

I stuck in a breath of air between my teeth, "I know why I need to do this. I don't know if I have it in me."

"Just go get your sister, take her out for coffee, see if she wants to repair things, because in a few hours you will only have each other." Josh turns around facing the counter dropping his keys, "Take my car, it's the blue one out front." He opens his wallet dropping forty dollars, "Get something to eat. We can do the heavy lifting for you."

I turn my head looking up at him, I wonder if what they said on the way here is true. I quickly move, hugging him tightly, he returns the exact same amount of pressure.

"You're so short. Call me if a light bulb burns out." I don't know what I'm supposed to do here. I've never felt so much respect, I've never felt so safe with another human before. "I want to move near where the girls are, it sounds like Cameron's in, if you want too, you can come. If that's cool. Or not. Whatever." *Why does it sound like I'm asking him on a date.*

"Only if I get to watch your tall ass smash your head in a door frame." Josh is so monotone, until he breaks our hug, and he smiles. "Go get Lucia, try to keep her out until someone texts you. Let me know where you take her, we will pick you up."

I had to bribe my sister to come out in public with me. Thankfully Josh gave me the idea of food, that was the only thing that got her out of the house. I hate to say it, but it was almost tempting to leave her there. Listening to styrofoam rubbing together right beside my ear for an hour straight would have been easier than listening to her whine and bitch. I feel so bad for Gabe having to pretend to date her.

Oh my God. Gabe.

I haven't even thought about him, yeah, he was just a co-worker on this job. He went out of his way to call me to tell me about the fire, he obsessively called Cameron after the fire, he got her to the hospital. And I'm completely blind siding him. I know there's nothing I can do to help him, I never even thought about trying to give him immunity. I don't even think passing immunity around would have been possible, I gave zero attempt to try to save him.

I raised myself to look after no one, and now I'm looking after Cameron, and I'm really fucking over whelmed. Now I'm going to have to live with the guilt of him behind bars, maybe I'll get lucky and he's flying under the radar like I am. I doubt it though. *Not everyone was stolen as an infant.*

"Did dad ever get a hold of you?" She stirs her drink. *Why do girls get iced drinks in the winter?*

I shake my head, no one other than my allies have the new number to either mine or Cameron's new phone. Knowing Erik there's a tracker activated in both our phones. On the way here I was looking at the camera's at the house, and there were a lot of people stopping by. They know we skipped town, and they're pissed.

"Ballsy showing up when mom was there." She rolls her eyes. "Why am I here?"

I break off the icing of my lemon loaf, trying to come up with something quick. "It was a chance I had to take."

Police said that dad hasn't left the 'Lion's den' all day, so he wasn't a concern. Mom on the other hand, I was panicking that she would have spotted me. I crawled through Lucia's window. She was pissed, I was lucky she didn't scream.

I continue, this is a lot harder than I thought it was going to be. "I want you, me, and Cameron to fix things. I want us to actually be brother and sister."

She rolls her eyes, "Just because I saved you, doesn't mean I want anything to do with you."

"Then why did you save me?" I ask defensively, keeping my voice low from the people around us.

"My job was to make sure your birth parents don't get tips that you're alive." She belts out quietly. I'm surprised this conversation is even happening in English on her part. "Oh my God." Her eyes get wide, she covers her mouth, resting her elbows on the table, watching me with wide eyes.

I exhale a breath through my nose. I never once knew what her responsibility was as a Nemean. Maybe I should have acted surprised at her words.

Lucia twists in her chair, her hair does half a circle, she looks out the window scanning the cars, and everyone in the building, "You knew? How?" she pauses, before shaking her head slightly, "I should have known the second I saw that car." She looks at me with her jaw locked.

Her phone is on the table between us, I've been watching her closely waiting for a moment to grab it before she can without making it obvious. She reaches for her phone, I move faster, stuffing it in my jeans pocket. Trying to hold down a smirk from her predictability.

"But you didn't. You should have done your job better with Cameron. Stand." I stand, fire trucks speed by on the road.

I close my eyes, feeling my heart sink as my phone vibrates in my hand.

Liam's name appears. *Get her in the Van out back.*

"You son of a bitch!" She screams at me.

She rushes over to me pounding with close fists on my chest. Everyone in the cafe is looking at us. I'm livid, I know I can't drag her out of here or someone will think it's domestic violence and call the cops. I look around some of the looks I'm getting, people already want to call the cops. I don't blame her, not one bit. The parents she knew are dead, she doesn't know what one, or both, she just knows someone is dead. All it took for her to put the pieces together was Josh's car, and me taking her out of the house. I have to admit, I'm pretty impressed by her right now.

"Okay that's enough!" I talk loudly, my chest is getting tender as fuck. "You need to take a breath and try to calm down. I'm walking away now." Trying to stay calm with people watching me is nearly impossible. I didn't realize how many people were sitting here until she started hitting me.

I take one step to the side, she stands still in the same spot looking down, still crying. I grab her bag, holding her hand like a mother does with a child walking out of the Café. When I parked, I stayed by the alley, I knew I had to think like a Basilisk. I had to park near a back ally for a quick escape. Lucia's cries are echoing off the buildings. She's attracting so much attention, and if she hasn't already, she's going too.

I drag her behind a trash can, apologizing redundantly. She moves, but unlike me she doesn't work out, I can easily control her. I wrap my arms around her neck pressing down on her collarbone catching her. I hold her steady, picking her up cradling her body, I carry her.

The back door opens, to Liam looking at me with wide eyes, "What the fuck happened?"

I shake my head. "She put the pieces together. Is mom dead?"

"I'm sorry mate." Jake calls out from the front seat.

"I'm not. But I feel bad for her." I set Lucia down on the ground, hoping she won't be tossed around too much. "Where's everyone else?"

Liam catches duct tape, and rope mid throw in the air. He doesn't look at her before bending down to my sister, he's looking at me. "She will fuck Adam up when we go to Junction point if we don't do this, and he needs to get us out fast. Everyone is watching buildings where your dad might go, a few got raided. Nothing."

"What's the FBI doing right now?"

Adam leans back in his seat looking at both me and Liam in the rearview mirror, "Sam sent me a text saying, 'It's going to be a very long coffee break, then probably a nap'."

"Doesn't this break like every moral they have?" I ask.

"Even when they took Martin down there was a lot they never thought twice about. Maybe after a certain death tally it's just easier to let the criminals figure it out themselves." Adam responds simply. Everyone is so used to this, it's almost disturbing.

"She's sleeping like a baby. Done. Go." Liam sits down, in the middle of the seat, his arms over the back, he looks way to chill right now.

Adam hits the gas hard causing me and Liam to both nearly fall over. We both look at each other, locking eyes, buckling up the seat belts in unison.

52

Cameron

The smell of hot wings seeps through the door, my stomach instantly starts growling. Seconds later Brittney perks her head up, sniffing the air like a border collie. We both look at each other, kicking the blankets off at the same time making our way down the stairs, pretending like we haven't been snacking on the world's most unhealthy food all day. Whoever stocked my room knows me way too well. My snacks were all guilty pleasures: pretzels, liquorice, salt and vinegar chips, gummy worms.

We grab onto the stair railing taking it one at a time. I hate standing after drinking for the first time, you never realize how much you had to drink until you get up.

"Mom." Brittney's daughter passes her up the stairs giving her a giant hug.

Majority of these kids just get up for a hug from their parents then continue on with what they were doing. It physically makes my body miss what I haven't experienced. I don't care if I get a job in history, when I was younger, I wanted to be a mom. That's all I want to be. The origin has to be from having my shit mom.

Just think, not long ago I was trying to get Lizzy's husband, or soon to be ex-husband? to get her to speak to me. So much has changed since then. I've changed, my experiences changed, my life has changed. It's not that I was weak before, or maybe I was. Not letting people in, not letting myself experience life outside of a textbook. Now I'm on an entirely different playing field. There are no more lies, now there's just crippling anxiety of why no one's texted me back yet.

Maybe being through what I've gone through this last week has woken me up a bit. It's not all about my career, like I thought. It's the small things. I was looking up the town Nico was talking about. It's so small, it would be a perfect refresh. It would be the perfect place to create new dreams.

"Oh good, you didn't die up there." William's wife Julia smiles. Her smile instantly fades when she's bombarded by children on every limb. She whines, trying to shake them off.

William and Julie had the most kids. Every single kid William has he looks more and more tired. By the sixth I just expected him to be sleeping when standing up. They both love every second of it. I see how tiring it is, their house is never quiet, they're always together, and they never once stopped loving each other. All though, some of their fights you'd think they hate each other, maybe that's just from the exhaustion, but they always come back from the fights.

"Go play now!" Brittney speaks deeply, the kids all fall off of Julia, running away silently.

"Holy alcohol breath." Julia laughs waving in front of her face. She is so nice, it comes off fake. It's far from.

I heard stories of when they met. William met Julia at the gym he owns. He was absolutely terrified to make a move because she was so nice, her trying to push guys off wasn't really brushing them off, it just left everyone confused and led on. William walked away more confused than he's ever been in his life after talking to her. They saw each other at a bar downtown, and William froze seeing his gym crush looking all done up. Brittney slid next to the bar and started talking to her, they exchanged numbers, and then Brittney set them up after talking him up. According to Brittney it took forever, but if you ask Julia, she says it took no time at all.

"My fault." I whisper. I sound sad, it's not a lie. I'm so worried my stomach is tying itself up in knots, my hands are shaking, I'm holding my phone so tight I don't even know if I would feel it vibrate.

"Boy problems?" Julie looks at me with a small smile that quickly fades into a straight line.

I nod.

"I wouldn't worry about it. The way my husband talks about Nico you can tell he loves you. Guys are trash at your age."

"He talks about Nico?" This is a first.

"Everyone." She smiles small again. "After that entire fire incident, we've all been loving him. Then there's Josh."

Brittney chuckles. "Josh has a nineteen year old son. They both just don't realize it yet. Payback's a bitch."

Julia laughs, "Oh don't break up. Christmas will just be awkward."

I wave my hand in front of my chest. "Wait, what are you talking about? I knew they got decently close."

"Cam." Brittney looks at me, passing me a plate for the wings. "He's bought Nico groceries. He texted me and told me that Nico awkwardly asked him to move closer." She looks at Julia. "Don't be surprised when they get your entire family to move here. They've already got us, Erik, and Josh reeled in."

"I mean, not worrying about sending our kids to school every day would be nice." Julia ponders it. "Birds chirp here. I almost cried hearing it so clearly."

Brittney bites her lips, "And now you guys."

"Housing would be cheaper."

Brittney looks at me holding in a laugh, her entire face is light up.

I dance on the spot, it's only me wiggling my butt, but it's something to look forward to after all this. I should have known where I go, my dad goes, which means where he goes, Adam will go. I know Adam said he wasn't mad at me, I'm terrified everyone is going to hold that against me. I wouldn't even be mad if they did.

"Hey Cam." Julia takes a slice of pizza not looking at me. "Why didn't you go to Charlie's funeral?"

I close my eyes, I stop wiggling my butt, I stand perfectly still. I can't say what's going on, I can't tell them I killed her. "I couldn't do it." My eyes burn, tears try to fall.

"I'm sorry. I know you were there, you must have felt so defenseless seeing the drive by. I didn't know what to say, so I never texted, I apologize for not being there for you."

Drive by? I guess they had to come up with a cover story, I just never thought of what it *could* be.

"Don't apologize." I quickly speak. No one but me has the right to wear any guilt about the circumstances of Charlie's death, but for me. "One day I'll think of her, and that won't be the memory that comes to mind."

One day I'll think of her, and I'll see the protective side of her.

At least, I hope. I know she was protecting herself, but she absolutely destroyed lives in the process.

53

Nico

The doors of the van open, those who weren't with us pile in. Lucia is finally awake, I pull her up off the floor, setting her on a seat across from me beside Liam. Not a single seat was built when the van was made. They were all added in, they're like the long seats that sit sideways.

Hayley sits down across from Lucia, her elbows are on her knees, she's probably thinking about all those times her best friend cheated on her. They're both staring at each other. Neither one of the girls are backing down, not a single man in here is brave enough to say a word to interrupt whatever *this* is.

Hayley leans forward, putting her hand on Lucia's leg. "I'm sorry about your mum. But this is my best friend, and I will not allow her to become like us."

Lucia's body begins trembling. None of this is supposed to affect me. I was completely numb to everything just a few months ago. Watching Lucia fall part, is destroying me. I'm not supposed to feel this. I'm supposed to be numb to physical and mental pain.

Hayley sits up quickly, ripping the duct tape off Lucia's mouth, Lucia lets out a loud cry, taking deep breaths, looking at me with pleading eyes. "I won't scream, I just." She takes a deep breath, "I don't want to die."

"You won't." I grab an unopened water bottle passing it to Liam watching him pour it in her mouth.

"How could you let him go through all that?" Dillon asks in a snappy tone, "I used to hate April. I wouldn't let anyone do what they did to your brother, do to her."

"I didn't know for a while." Her voice shakes, "Every time you got starved out, I was told you ran away. You would shut down after, and I was told you were on drugs. By the time I found out, I was so guilty for not knowing. Matteo I'm sorry." Tears fall down her face.

That name feels so wrong.

"Keep crying." I whisper. "The Lion will be more on edge."

"Bro, you have as many names as Shawn has personalities." Dillon mumbles, "What the fuck is the plan?"

I close my eyes, "Are there more bombs?"

"Aye." Jack turns around, giving me a half smile. "Grenade!" He's way too excited over this.

"Pass it." I hold out my hand feeling the cold hard metal between my fingers. "Untie her legs, she's going to need to be able to run. if I scream 'move', I will wait as long as I can for you guys to clear the building."

Erik is the first to protest.

"The bar isn't open, there won't be many people. Don't bring everyone in with you." Lucia shakes her head. "I will not run, I only need one."

"I'm going in." Erick barks at me.

"No, you're not. If we don't need everyone, Cameron needs one of us to for sure get back. Neither are you, Hayley. Don't even try it." I look at her with my eyebrows raised.

"I'm in there." Josh speaks, he passes me a silencer, for my gun. Followed by a second gun.

I check the safety stacking both weapons on my lap, William reaches over on my lap taking one of the weapons, twisting the silencer on, then stacking them back where they were.

"Well, if Josh gets to go, I wanna go." Spencer sounds like he's pouting, someone in the crowd passes him a silencer.

"I got your sister. Clean up my wife's dark secrets." Liam rubs his jaw. He turns his head to Lucia, I can tell he's glaring. "If you run, I will pistol whip you with no remorse."

"Do it now." Lucia speaks quickly. "Seriously. I'm not crying, there's no mark on me. This is the most peaceful hostage situation ever. He won't believe it." She looks at me with a smile, before closing her eyes bracing herself for a hit that doesn't come.

I have no idea where this version of my sister was hiding but damn, I'm speechless. I don't trust her, as much as I want to I can't.

"I'm coming." Archie speaks, "Basilisks helped me." Just like us, Archie is handed a silencer.

I'm almost impressed after almost twenty years of none of this happening, they still know exactly what to do. They all walked away, there's the small part in them that hasn't left the Mafia, no matter how hard they tried running from it.

"Actually." Lucia pauses, "Technically Brooks was Nemean. McKinnon's weren't really a group, so you're welcome."

There's my sister. She's back.

There's a loud pop, everyone is already on high alert, causing us all to jump. Lucia groans, Hayley pulls away blood splattered on her hand. Tears run down my sister's face, swelling is happening almost immediately.

I slide the Grenade into my pocket, Adam moves the van, knowing that it's time.

54

Cameron

I stayed downstairs with the adults, it never took me long to regret my decision. I can't stop checking my phone. I thought conversation would help, I've drank way too much to remotely pay attention to the conversations. I forgot Max and Theo were here. They're staying close to Lizzy, who is completely avoiding me. Her kids looked at me confused. They have no idea who I am, I'm just the one person who drinks too much at every single family event. To them I'm going to be that drunk person they have to warn others about.

I wonder if she regrets naming me after Brittney. I think that's why we bounded so fast. In the end I completely replaced her with Brittney. Spencer is like my second dad. Whatever she was trying to do when she gave me Brittney's middle name, completely backfired on her. Call me a bitch. But I think it's comical.

April is sitting on the couch, with her legs over top of Brittney. They're watching the kids play. Shawn is setting up a spa night in the other living room with Julia, I haven't looked around that's one of the few things I pick up on of the conversation.

I sent a text to every last person that is there right now. I've gotten nothing back. Nothing. I think wanting to throw up is a reasonable feeling right now. It's probably the alcohol.

I wipe my face, trying to secretly hide my tears. April doesn't even give me thirty seconds before she's sitting beside me, using my shoulder as a pillow.

"Did you ever know why me, and Josh didn't work out?" She looks up as she speaks, watching me shake my head. "Because how you're feeling right now, is how I felt every single day. When we got married, if he never responded fast enough it was like PTSD just took over me, and my mind went on autopilot. I think part of the reason why I brought on bad blood with my brothers, and William, was the fear. Your dad was my best friend, he was a part of it less. He had a real job, he wasn't called on as much. It was less scary."

Brittney takes the open spot next to me. "It didn't matter what time it was, I sat on Spencer's bed waiting for him to come home. They always came home, Cam."

"It's not just him." I wipe my tears, choking down a tear. "My dad, my best friend, my second dad, all my uncles." My hand shakes.

April looks at her phone, "My brother's said around this time is when they will be making their move. In what seven hours? High estimate, they will be back. That's just seven hours to find out who's coming back."

"Oh April, did you hear?" Brittney slaps April's leg.

She nods her head happily, "Dillon isn't giving me a choice. Maybe my third husband will be here." She claps.

I burst out laughing. I wasn't wrong when I said everyone in this group talks to each other. If Dillon's coming, Liam's coming. Nico just created a new life for everyone without even recognizing it.

April sucks in a breath of air, pretending to be offended. "Glad to see my love life is so hilarious, it actually stops tears." She looks at me smiling, while I'm still laughing.

Seven hours.

"After seven hours, we will go outside, and scream." Brittney pushes my leg, "I need another drink, I'm slacking."

55

Nico

The van comes to a stop the second my alarms in my house go off on my phone. I pull it out, watching flames erupt through the cameras. "Let's hold off. Go back Adam."

Adam listens, not asking why.

"My house is on fire. Let's just wait for them to come back." I said that way too casually. It's hard to be surprised when I was expecting it. "Sorry you guys, if mine is..."

"We cleared them out." Adam speaks quickly.

He parks us on the second floor of an empty under construction parking garage right by the edge so we can look out. Construction signs are everywhere, it's probably not very safe. I'd say what we're about to do is even less safe. Adam and Jack pull out binoculars. Him and Jack are taking turns watching the door, it's so quiet in here. The only thing you can hear is Lucia's staggered breathing from the pain, and a phone vibrates every once in a while. Every time it vibrates, I know it's Cameron, I can't respond to her, I don't know what to say. I feel bad because I hear a phone, and no one reaches for it. We all just sit here, pretending like no one out there cares about us.

"I have to pee." Spencer breaks the quiet.

"I low key was holding it in since we got to New York." Hayley shifts her eyes. "Ima go find a corner. I didn't wanna go alone and be weird about it."

From the front seat all I can hear is, "What the fuck" from Jack and Adam bursting out in laughter.

The door opens, and a cold breeze brushes over us. I almost needed that to feel more alert. Having your adrenaline run for so long causes some major crashes physically.

Adam moves the van towards Spencer and Hayley to pick them up, we open the door, my heart starts racing. All of our houses are gone, the lives that everyone created is in literal ashes now. The Lion attacks people's houses hoping that they will be home, or if they're not home, they'll be easier to locate. This was just him saying fuck you to us.

We park on the road outside of Junction Square, I stand up, watching Lucia stand, and walk, her legs are shaking. "We need one more person. Nemean is known for double crossers. I'm not taking a chance." It's pretty clear where my faith lies, even I'm questioning my faith, and I'm completely on The Basilisks side.

I'm worried about Lucia going against her word, and there's a small piece of me that's terrified dad has gotten to another Basilisk, just to weaken us. I know none of them would go along with his threats, it's the *what if* is screaming too loudly in my mind.

Dillon stands up quickly, pushing on Williams shoulder to sit back down. They don't even think twice about volunteering to potentially lose their life, and their families. It goes way past honourable.

I jump out, gun in each hand, grenade in my pocket.

Erick comes over beside me with his fist wrapped up in a jacket, punching a hole through the glass of the door, he walks away quietly, I'm sure he's struggling to hold down whatever it is he has to say.

I pass off a gun behind me, reaching my hand in unlocking it. As soon as its opened again, someone behind me carefully nudges me with their hand quing me to take my gun back.

I walk in, the first person I see is a bartender, walking towards the main door to figure out what broke. I raise my gun, firing.

"Circle around." I whisper, nudging my head towards the other side of the bar, where the tables are.

I check behind the bar, no one's here. I watch Josh coming up behind me, he kicks down the office door finding two people in there, firing on them. Silencers don't completely cut the noise out, we will take whatever we can get right now with the Lions office being directly under us.

Lucia is completely white. I thought she's seen someone die before, the look on her face says otherwise, she's traumatized. The only thing that's making me feel better about firing on these employees is that they're still Nemean members. Like us, they have a bullseye on their back.

"Downstairs will be more. Like a lot more." I exhale, almost missing the days where my hands would shake.

"Tiny will be at the door. Bones will be inside with Dad. I don't know who else is in there." Lucia looks at Liam. "Take my rope, don't feel bad about hurting me."

"I'll be right behind you." Josh looks at me, "Don't use it, please." He's begging me.

I open the door, firing my gun emptying my clip. I stand to the side, watching the bodies fall down the stairs, while I shove the gun into the back of my sweats, Tiny comes running over, he sees Josh and grins from ear to ear. Josh fires hitting him, he's still moving towards us. Until he fires two more back to back, Tiny falls to the ground.

"Fucking Noah." Josh snarls.

Someone makes a noise in the back, like it's the first time he heard Noah was originally one of us.

I make my way down stairs, waiting for everyone to join me before opening the door.

At least thirty Nemean members are in my dad's office, they all are holding their guns looking for a fight. I swallow a lump in my throat. We are outnumbered, by a long shot.

"And my son shows up." The Lion smashes his palms on the desk.

"I brought you your daughter." I scratch my chin, making my gun noticeable. "Figured you'd wanna see her. Before, well, you know." I shrug with one shoulder.

Josh is standing directly behind me, each time he recognizes some-one I feel his body tense. I can feel the daggers from the other Basilisks eyes. I know the redhead standing off to my left is Liam and Dillon's cousin Violet, meaning their nephew Toby is in here somewhere.

"It would have been a safe assumption I'd retaliate. Then it would be a safer assumption to assume I'd kill your wife, hold your daughter hostage."

I try to keep my eyes open on dad, watching rage flick through him watching his daughter, listening to Lucia pleading. She makes a noise when Liam does something with her ropes. I bite my tongue.

"Would that be a safe assumption though?" Spencer asks out of the blue. Like it's a casual conversation.

"Well, I mean. You'd think. Abuse a child, then tangle them up with us on purpose?" Josh casually says back.

"Oh yeah, that's fair." Spencer laughs. "That was really fuckin' dumb by the way."

"What game is this? Hand her over!" Dads voice shakes the building.

I chuckle. "Did you think? No. I just wanted to give you the courtesy of seeing her again, to say your goodbyes if you will."

I look from the side of my eye, Liam has his gun shoved into Lucia's cheek, Archie is standing her up straight behind her. She's trembling, tears are pouring down her face, she's genuinely scared, and even though we aren't close, I want to protect her.

Someone raises their gun, before I can even have time to speak, I hear shot after shot pop off behind me, watching Nemean members fall. I raise my gun, shooting.

Everyone backs up, Josh is shot in the chest, my entire body goes numb. White noise rings through my mind. He falls backwards hitting the wall, I want to check on him. I'm frozen in panic.

"MOVE NOW!" I shout.

Lucia and Liam are backing out of the room, Archie is tugging on my sister, she must be fighting to stay. Spencer and Dillon reach for Josh dragging him up, until he can catch his breath.

I look around at all the guns pointed at me, there's no way I'm going to come out of this, those six need more time to get out to go home. Gabe isn't hesitant about pulling a gun on me, and I find it funny how I was carrying the guilt about him dying on my shoulders. When he is eyeing me down as nothing more but target practice.

"What's your plan for me now? Wife's dead, daughters dead. I freed Cameron against your will, you'll never find her. So don't even try." I hear the creak of the top stair, they're going to be okay.

"Grab him." Dad snarls.

Bones looks at me with a crooked smile from across the room. For the first time he looks at me I don't get shivers, there's no traumatic flashbacks, because I've already won.

I close my eyes, Cameron flashes through my mind. I'm out numbered, I can't shoot my way out of this. I also know I can't let Cameron fall apart, I know she can't lose me again. If Josh is okay, in case he does care about me, I can't hurt him by handing myself over. I want to let this all end, if this was weeks ago, I would have handed myself over no questions asked, things have changed. I have people. I never thought I would have people, now I want to fight like hell. Whatever it takes.

I reach into my pocket, taking a step back. I need to get out of here.

I take the gun out from the back of my sweats, and grab the grenade from my sweater pocket, walking out of the room backwards, tossing it as far as I can. Screams fill the basement, people are trying to escape before it hits the ground. I run up the stairs, dodging the dead bodies. I'm panicking. I'm trying to ignore the panic, I've never ran upstairs this fast before in my life. My feet land on the top step before the light follows me, followed by the explosion. I quickly shut the fire proof door, running out of the building and the van is still outside. I run to it seeing everyone standing at the back door waiting.

The second the fire proof door gives out, Junction Square is lit up in flames, I jump landing in the van, the same time the windows explode from the heat causing a large echo in the busy streets.

I crawl over to Josh, he's propped up against the wall. "Are you okay?" My eyes are burning with tears, my entire body is shaking.

He grabs me, holding me as tight as he can. "It was just the pressure from the close range shot." He catches his breath, setting me free from his grasp.

I watched everyone put on bulletproof vests, I'm wearing one, and yet I still forgot he had one on. The heat of the moment, I just forgot.

Woops.

"Are you okay?" Erik holds onto the back of the chair with every ounce of strength he has, he looks like he's about to puke.

"I'll answer that later." I whisper, anxiety, and adrenaline thick in my voice, making every word shake.

Lucia is staring into space. I grab her leg, she looks down at me. Her eyes are haunted. She was far from being innocent, today has taken away everything she had in her.

"The way you were talking." Dillons voice is quiet. "It sounded like you were just done."

"I needed time." I let out a breath, looking at Josh. "I forgot about the vest, I was losing my shit."

Josh sits up, "I am going to kick your ass." Everyone freezes from his tone. "You lost your shit because I was shot so you thought the most rational thing to do was almost blow yourself up? Are you stupid?"

I blink, he's really mad at me.

"You must be really fucking stupid. We all had two guns dumbass. Five of us, ten guns. There wasn't 170 people in there." He swats the back of my head. "I'm so mad at you."

I roll my eyes, ignore people chuckling around us.

"Josh, your car." Adam speaks.

"I'm driving. You might just think it's a good idea to drive off a bridge. Who else is coming?"

"Me! I'm not missing this." Spencer stands rubbing his hands together with a smirk on his face.

"Lucia. Come." Josh demands.

Lucia stands quickly, probably scared she's Josh's next victim.

I take my sweater off, then my vest off, looking at the ground. "I can't even begin to thank you. I know that's just right fucked up with all the bloodshed, but this was closed for you a long time ago, and not one person hesitated. I know it wasn't for me, but thanks."

"No, it was Mate." Archie looks at me with sincere eyes, "It was for you just as much for Cameron, and not one person here will deny it."

Hayley grabs my hand, "Leave before I push you out of this bloody van."

I listen, running into the same coffee shop as before ordering the car, random drinks loaded with caffeine, and snacks. I think this is the first time in my life I've ever needed comfort food, or this amount of caffeine to not have a severe crash from a drop in adrenaline.

The basilisks are destroying me.

Or fixing me.

I haven't fully decided yet.

Cameron

8 o'clock. They're still not back.

Brittney and April stand blowing on their nails. Both of them have had their eyes locked on the clock in front of them, phones on their lap. My nails have been dry long ago, I stand watching my cell phone slide off my lap, crashing onto the floor. I don't reach for it, I've been staring at the home screen waiting for a text to come through, so there's no point in checking it again. My eyes haven't moved from the spot where my text messages appear when they're incoming. I follow them out the front door, not a single one of us say a word to each other. We all know it's been seven hours, and now we are allowed to lose our shit.

Not a single text message.

Not a single word from anyone.

My feet hit the grass; the sunset is over the trees lighting up the sky. I want tears to fall down my face, wherever they are, they might not be seeing this, and that means my life is basically over. There's no way Nico got permission to let us leave the city. That means, the Lion is going to be having his way with me. That will most likely be he's just going to kill me and move onto the next kid. Killing me would be letting me off easy, and I feel like after this, there's no way he would let me off easy. My body won't let me cry. My mind is in denial.

I tried to follow the rules, I didn't want any of my cousins to be doing this. All of us were delusional thinking that we could get away with this. The Lion has apparently been outsmarting Mafia's and Cartels for decades, there's no way that I'm getting out of this life. It was just wishful thinking.

Sounds from a car travels down the dirt road, it's getting closer, I can't get my hopes up because cars have been driving down this road all day, I mean, it is the road that leads into the town. I watch it slow down to turn. My heart nearly stops beating seeing that it's grey with no tint on the windows. It's obviously not a secret FBI car that I'm assuming Nico had this morning. It's no one in my family, and I hate that it's just an undercover, and no one I'm waiting for. The undercover does a three point turn, facing the road so it's easy to leave. He gets out and begins talking to Brittney. She covers her mouth, and my heart sinks, preparing itself for the worst.

I need to walk towards her, I need to find out what's happening, the snow on the ground is making me sink. It feels like it's turning me into ice, molding me to the ground, making it impossible to move.

Adam's SUV pulls in, my heart jumps back to life watching Adam jump out. Liam, William, and Dillion are tackled by April. Dad's car pulls in, tears running down my face, I run over opening the door throwing myself at him.

"Holy shit Cameron. Didn't you get our texts?" Dad hugs me.

"What are you talking about?" I sniffle, squeezing him tighter.

Brittney comes behind me, pulling me off him so he gets out of the car. "We were in the back of the house for the last few hours. There wasn't any service." She lets out a dry laugh. "We were so stressed no one noticed."

I stand, seeing Hayley looking at me over the car, I run around, tackling her, making us both fall backwards into Archie. I want to question her about sitting in the front seat of my dad's vehicle, she's never even sat in a vehicle with him before. I want to know if they dropped whatever bad blood is between them, right now is not the time for that.

She holds me tighter, "Next time we say we have you, believe us." Her voice is so steady, so sure. I've never once heard her speak with so much compassion. And she probably just did so many unspeakable things. "Your lack of faith in us is almost insulting." She laughs lightly.

"No more next time." Dad says from over the car. "It's done."

"Where is he?" I pull away from Hayley. "Where is he!" I repeat myself, my hands shaking. "Josh. Spencer, where are they?" I back away, leaning on the car, I feel my heart rate beating in my ears, my breathings quicken. I'm scared that fear is going to make me pass out.

I can never go through this again, I don't know how Brittney did it. I understand why April and Josh' marriage failed. I can't fucking do this again. None of these people can make me do this again. I wasn't even the one behind the weapons, and I will be the one to call truce between any future Basilisks shit storm.

Another car pulls in, it's black, obviously another agent. I watch the road, listening for a car engine. Every car that pulled into this driveway is still running, making it impossible to hear for them.

"Cameron." Hayley smiles, "He's okay."

I gasp for air, I wasn't breathing, and I had no idea when I stopped breathing. I look at her, slowly. "Then where is he?" I should be grabbing my phone from inside to call him, I can't bring myself to leave this spot and miss him.

Dad calls Hayley and Archie over to the agents. I don't leave the car.

Josh's car is visible through the trees, I start running.

The car isn't even stopped, and Nico throws himself out leaving the door wide open behind him. I run faster, jumping, wrapping my legs around him, kissing him hard. Savoring every last second, we have together. He runs his hands through my hair, just as desperate to touch me as I am with him.

"What happened?" I ask pulling my lips away from him. My eyes are locked on the gold ring around his pupil.

"It doesn't matter right now. I brought someone with me." He sets me down, "I had no choice." His voice isn't sad, it's not happy, it sounds almost like he's scared of my reaction.

I stand off to the side, watching Hayley, and Brittney grab Lucia from the car holding her up right. She won't look up from the ground. From here I can see her body quivering as she cries.

"What the hell happened?" I breathe, placing my hand on his chest, forcing myself not to run over there and demand answers.

"I got her out of the house, her mom got a mail bomb. Lucia put everything together. She was suddenly on our side. I don't know what the hell happened, but she did a 180, she never even tried to fight. The fear in her when Liam held a gun to her, Cameron, I had to bring her."

I feel his eyes burning into the side of my face as I glare at her.

Lucia looks at me, her eye is swollen and black. She has the saddest expression on her face. Suddenly all of my anger is gone. She looks away from me, saying something that causes Hayley and Brittney to drop her arms, and both let out a heart filled laugh.

Nico breaths beside me, grabbing my hand on his chest informing me that they have a cover story, and telling me that the house was set on fire. I close my eyes, this is a lot to take in after today. I couldn't even imagine how the people who went into the war feel, if I'm feeling overwhelmed.

"What if your dad passed everything onto her?" I ask, nudging my head towards Lucia. Me trusting her isn't going to come easy, I think we both know it.

Nico stands in front of me, shakes his head looking me directly into my eyes. "The way she reacted seeing someone die, there's absolutely no way she was next in line. Josh and Spencer talking about that possibility on the way here. Lucia was sobbing so hard she never even tried to listen."

"What about everyone else?" I close my eyes, opening them slowly.

"FBI is making their rounds for the smaller members as we speak, worldwide. Everyone who would have been a threat is dead." His eyes turn dark, he blinks fast, washing away that emotion. "I'm sorry for what you're going to find out."

"Are you free?"

"I think so." I can't ignore the hint of uncertainty in his voice.

I reach up to touch his cheek, giving him a small but reassuring smile. "Then I don't care. As long as you do have immunity, as long as you never put me through this again. I don't care."

"D'Oria. That wasn't what we agreed on." Tim calls, making everyone turn to face him.

Nico turns around, his arm's awkwardly wrapped behind him, pulling me into his back as close as I can go. I have to take a small step to the side and look beside Nico's shoulder to see anything. I see Lucia step forward, she looks like she's about to do a full on sprint towards Tim if he tries to do anything towards her brother. Josh walks in front of Nico where he can be a wall of protection.

Tim continues opening the door of the blacked out SUV, "We hope you never see you again. Oh, by the way you're citizenship, you're no longer here illegally. Don't get in trouble again, or it's revoked."

Lucia stops moving. Nico holds me closer. The agents all get in their cars to leave, every free Basilisk, Baker Cartel, and living free Nemean member make their way into the house.

Epilogue- Nico

Lucia flicks the light switch on and falls on my bed holding her laptop. "Don't hate me."

I cover my eyes with my hand, the light is fucking bright. I think it might be five thirty in the morning, if that. I pat the mattress looking for Cameron to use as backup, when I feel the cold blanket next to me, I groan in protest.

"I've been talking to your parents, and they're on a plane right now with your siblings."

I move my hand looking at Lucia, my eyes are wide, and I'm pretty sure I'm glaring at her. I'm not one hundred percent sure. I don't even know what to say. My mind keeps asking: *What? Why? How?* I had their number, but it's safe in my mind. I have no idea how Lucia got it, or how she even found out their names. I'm not the slightest bit surprised. When Lucia wants something, she gets it. All it took was probably some internet searches of the missing infant in Italy. She has my birth name, so I'm even less surprised now.

"Also. Adam is lending you his SUV so you can pick them up from the airport." She bites her lip, "They're staying at the hotel on main Street."

"What?" my voice is quiet.

"Cameron's setting up the hotel with all your favorite snacks, and drinks." She smiles at me, "I kind of thought your relationship was just to piss dad off, but when she woke me up just to show me what she's leaving at the hotel for your parents, I was struck. I didn't even know you like football? She has a jersey there, a list of all your favorite songs and movies. She wrote them a letter, I didn't want to start the day off by crying."

I smile, letting a small laugh echo through my chest. The past few weeks we've been so concentrated on learning the small things about us, I think I somehow fell in love with her more. Somewhere along the lines from where she was rehearsing her ballet classes, and her hip hop recital from when she was a kid. Watching her knock over our new end table, smashing a lamp, and walking off like it was a part of the show. When I was a teenager I watched football, it made me seem like I was normal like everyone else at school. Now I'm going to be able to watch it under normal circumstances, how Cameron even remembered my team blows me away, I only said it once.

"What was the letter?" I ask Lucia in a quiet voice.

She taps a button on her laptop keys, she looks at me biting her lip. "Don't tell her I told you. She just said that if they don't accept you for who you were, then they don't deserve to have you for the person you're turning out to be, and that if they don't stay in your life. She's going to be there every second taking care of you, and you will be okay. Then there was something along the lines of it being impossible circumstances, and no one really understands but them and you. She hopes that they will look at you and see how perfect you really are." She scrunches her nose, "It was wrote really good, it was like a pre fuck you, but at the same time, I want you to love him, but we won't ask you to love him."

I rub my face, I think a normal person would be bothered by someone else writing something like that to parents they never met. It has to be known of what I am, who I was. By this point law officials have probably given them a very in depth description of everything that happened, for their own safety,

"Why? I wasn't even fully decided if I should contact them." I hold in a groan. Now I have absolutely no choice. "I mean, I wanted too. What if they don't like who I am."

"They know who took you, they know you were corrupted. I've never seen someone book a flight so fast in my life. I wasn't even off the phone call by the time your father shouted he had the tickets."

Lucia has a huge grin on her face, she sits up, I pull her down squeezing the absolute life out of her. The past two months, she's become a different person. I've watched her register for school for real this time, I've seen her laugh, smile, and watched her become a person I never thought I would meet. Her attitude has completely changed, she makes coffee, and breakfast before the sun even comes up, she goes to the gym, she goes to work, she's in therapy. She found an online therapist who recommended two other therapists for me and Cameron. Now there's this thing with my birth parents. I don't even recognize Lucia when I look at her. She radiates happiness.

"I know you basically have multiple families, and you're pulled in every direction, but I hope you stay. You're my only family." Her voice is muffled by my shirt, for the first time in a month I hear a touch of sadness in her voice. "I was hesitant to get a hold of them, I knew it would have been selfish. I couldn't stand the thought of you going."

I groan. Flipping her over, I roll over reaching into my nightstand. "I can't leave." I toss her a ring box.

The ring isn't huge, it's actually kind of small. I haven't even asked Cameron's dad yet, I bought it on a whim. It felt right, so I did it. I've never seen her wear jewelry other than the blue necklace I got her at Christmas, so I figured small would be the best bet. She likes to blend into a crowd, having a huge rock on her finger wouldn't let her.

Lucia kicks her feet on the bed letting out a shriek. "When!"

"I was going to do it tonight, fancy dinner at home, never mind plans have changed. I have no idea. I don't know what to do."

"Oh, it'll be a fancy dinner alright. Give me four hours."

"Don't you dare call Erik to plan dinner. I need to ask him."

She passes the box to me, "Hide that better!" She kicks her feet one more time, effortlessly getting off the bed.

"Luce." I call out, watching her turn. "They're your family too. Cameron was raised better than that, there's no bad blood. She loves you."

My sister watches me, it looks like she's about to smile before she speaks. "That's a terrible nickname."

Cameron holds my hand, both of us watching the arrival doors at the airport. It's a tiny ass airport, there's probably only a max of five plans that leave and come here every day. We are by the baggage claim, I can see the main entrance, it's maybe fifty feet from us.

"That's your dad." My girlfriend speaks quickly looking through the glass windows. "Nico, you look just like him." She strokes my hand with her thumb, she's trying to control her happiness, it sounds like if she holds it in any longer, she might implode. "If you need an escape plan, if you can't handle this, say 'platypus' it won't come up in conversation."

I exhale through my nose. "I'll be okay."

"I know. It's okay to fall apart. I'm here either way." She takes a step forward, walking up to them.

Damn this girl really loves me. She's protecting me in ways I never even thought was plausible. She's not letting me walk towards them first so I can have a few more seconds to mentally prepare for this, coming up with words is a lot harder than I expected.

They have two boys, and a girl. The tallest looks to be about sixteen, the other is close in age, and the little girl looks like she's in her early teens. It wasn't even my fault, and I feel guilty about them being terrified of having more kids. I mean, they had to be terrified right? I was taken from them and their world came crashing down. If it didn't, they wouldn't be reactivating my missing person case. I looked online, and they did so many press conferences to try to bring me back.

I think I'm going to puke.

They all walk towards me, the kids are staring at me looking up with wide eyes. My parents are holding hands, trying not to stare. "You guys must be exhausted." Cameron holds my hand, "If you're hungry we can go eat dinner."

"Mamma, ho fame." the little girl tugs on her mom's jacket.

"English please." My birth mothers accent is thick.

Looking at my sister's face. My baby picture Tim showed of me, I see those little features in her. My heart is breaking. Not only did I miss out on being raised with love, I missed out on being a big brother, I missed out on guiding them. That's enough to break my heart. I missed out on everything, I caused these parents so much pain. These kids missed out on a big brother who would have fought for them.

"We'll get you food." I smile watching her face light up when she realizes I understood. "Everything in this town is locally owned. Point at a place that looks good, and we'll go." I grab suitcases, walking towards Adam's car.

We settled on a restaurant on the corner. I don't even know what they have here. The outside had a few tables on the patio, it has wide windows. It looked welcoming. The one nice thing about living in a small town, there are no need for reservations. Nothing is ever super busy. There's no rush. Other than two tables, we are the only ones here. This is such a nice break from the wait lists in New York. Life is relaxing being here.

"I'm sorry, Lucia threw us in blind, what are your names?" Cameron asks with an apologetic voice, her shoulders are round. I grab her hand, squeezing it, silently thanking her.

"I'm Antonio, my wife is Catrina." He pauses, pointing at the little ones one by one. "Our kids are Armando, Marcello, and Rosa."

"I'm sorry." My mother covers her mouth. "I'm sorry. I thought I could do this." She closes her eyes, the oldest, Armando rubs her arm.

"No. It's okay." I try to reassure her, I can't start to deny this aching feeling in my chest. "If you need more time that's okay, we can try again tomorrow— if you want."

Cameron stands, "Let me take you to your hotel." She looks at me with a smile lighting up her face, "I'll be right back. Order me whatever." She leans down, giving me a hug, kissing my hair, hovering over me for a few extra seconds before walking away.

My mother looks at me with so many expressions I can't even make out what's on her face. She turns away, walking beside Cameron, and both are gone from my sight.

"She was hesitant." He sighs. "I needed to know." My father holds his hands in his lap.

"Lucia definitely jumped the ball on this, but I'm glad I got to at least meet you." I look at my siblings, I want to fucking cry. I wasn't expecting this to happen. I was low key expecting everyone to be excited.

"Your family— they all..." His voice trails off.

"My family is Cameron's. They're nothing less than that. Her uncle is my father. If you wanted to see if I'm okay, I'm okay. At least now I am."

"Good. Good." He nods his head.

I've never felt less connected from anyone in my entire life. It's really bothering me because I was so nervous but excited all morning. Maybe I'm not what they wanted after all, and they really did just show up to see how I'm doing now. I couldn't imagine their confusion, or frustration that they're feeling. It's easy to get angry, it's also easy to empathize.

"I'm sorry." I shake my head looking up at the roof, "If you need me to rebook your flight, just let me know."

"We aren't leaving." His words are so fast, making me look at him. "There's so much guilt, we don't know how to handle it. We turned our backs for half a second, and you were out of the stroller. We can only stay for a few days because of work. We will be back, and you will have to come see your country. You are our son, you're their brother. All we want is a card at Christmas, and monthly calls."

"But Caterina." I breathe in deeply.

"Armando means soldier, Marcello means little warrior, Rosa means courage." Marcello interrupts me, "She wanted to believe you were still alive and fighting for us, so she gave us these names to remember we had to fight for you."

"I heard the pasta's shit here." Armando scrunches his nose.

I let out a laugh between closed lips, making a vibrating nose. The conversation from Marcello just went way over his head.

"And the pizza. That's an American thing, and we still do it better." Marcello joins in, almost like he forgot he dumped all that on me.

The kids don't have nearly as thick as an accident, they're a lot easier to understand.

The server comes along, flipping her note book. "So not the pizza, or the pasta. Got it."

I chuckle, feeling the mood at the table lighten up. They want me in their life, they want to love me, this is everything I've ever wanted.

At the very least Cameron's letter shows them that she loves me no matter what, hopefully it was less blunt than the summary Lucia gave me.

I barge into Erick's house pacing back and forth. My birth family is in the hotel, I'm trying to give them space without being overbearing. Cameron is at home registering for online college. We had a long discussion a week ago, since she left New York, history isn't calling her anymore. She's switching over to English, the only thing she can see herself doing is writing or being an editor.

"My dreams changed, and that's really hard for me. I used to breathe history. Ever since I was reading about the Basilisks without knowing who they were, I have felt sick." I asked her what she thought she wanted to do, I encouraged her to switch, and we both stopped the conversation at that.

We all live on the same street just outside of the town. All of us have a few acres, our backyards are all one. Since Liam and Adam are both single dads, they were very persistent on living close to help each other. Liam used everything that happened in court to get full custody, I'm not even sure how it happened, all I know is it wasn't cheap, and Liam is understandably not losing a bit of sleep taking his kids away from Lizzie. At this point, they should just build an underground tunnel to connect their houses. Josh has the smallest house. April has her kids here in school. Spencer and Brittney have their three kids, William and Julia have their six. Dillion has Shawn and his kids. Hayley and Archie are almost moving there, they said within the next four months. They already have a house in the lineup. The only ones who refused were Max, and Theo. They figured someone needed to stay with Lizzy. And I don't think a single person argued with them. No one has spoken to any of them since we moved. Sides were picked, and it doesn't even take me by surprise that The Basilisks stuck together.

Everyone who had a business in New York is in the process of opening one here. The gym was the only thing that Nemean couldn't target because of the population in the building, Willie's, White Heart, Target's, and the Speakeasy are gone. Because it's a small town they couldn't open three bars, so they're sticking with the speakeasy, then they're opening Willies. It was a heated debate of what to open first, the only reason why speakeasy won was because of Cameron yelling at everyone that it was Charlie who started it, and all of us needed to honor her here.

This town is a clean slate for every single one of us.

My mind runs a million miles a minute. Josh, and Erik look at me with a *what the fuck* expression, they don't say a word as I walk back and forth with my hands on my hips.

I groan, pointing at Josh. "I made things awkward yesterday. I accidently called you my father, to my birth father, so sorry about those extra responsibilities that I just dumped on your lap. Here's a nineteen year old kid." I wave. I fucking wave at him.

"So, it went terrible then?" Josh crinkles his nose.

"No, he was happy someone loves me. Again, sorry."

Josh waves me off, "We just missed the diaper stage. You're my son. That's that."

"K cool." I turn around to leave. "Wait. That wasn't why I came here. I didn't even know you'd be here."

"You are a fucking mess." Erik laughs fully amused.

"I really am. I look crazy."

Erik looks at me wide eyed, nodding.

"You still scare the shit out of me, okay?" I pull the box from my pocket, taking a deep breath. "Can I marry your daughter?"

Erik moves towards me so fast, I brace myself for getting knocked out. It takes me a second to register that he's hugging me. "I couldn't think of anyone else that would be worthy enough for my daughter."

The second he says that, tears flood over my eyes, I close them tight holding onto him. All the pain I've inflicted, all the lives I've taken in such brutal ways, none of that matters here. None of that matters to them. They accept me for everything I've done.

My real birth parents are in town, the father that chose to love me is comforting me with a simple hand on my shoulder, it's become a simple thing that shows so much appreciation.

I never thought I would find love in the people who I was trained to destroy.

The Basilisks changed me for the better.

I finally feel what genuine happiness feels like because of them.

The end.